ADVANCE PRAISE

"Dehmelt does not deal in stick figures. The characters of *The Hard Way Back to Heaven* are very real, and you will laugh alongside of them, cry alongside of them, and want to bash them over the head for their repetitive stubbornness. These moving, realistic individuals are a testament to the ability of this young writer with a promising career ahead."

—Wes Peters, Author of *Between The Doors*

The Hard Way Back To Heaven

Based on a True Story

The Hard Way Back To Heaven

Karl Dehmelt

Apprentice House
Loyola University Maryland
Baltimore, Maryland

First Edition

Printed in the United States of America

Paperback ISBN: 978-1-62720-065-3
E-book ISBN: 978-1-62720-066-0

Design by Katie Krzaczek

Cover image courtesy of United States Geological Survey archive

Published by Apprentice House

Apprentice House
Loyola University Maryland
4501 N. Charles Street
Baltimore, MD 21210
410.617.5265 • 410.617.2198 (fax)
www.ApprenticeHouse.com
info@ApprenticeHouse.com

This novel is written in honor of my mother,
Patricia Lee Dehmelt,
September 30, 1961—January 11, 2011

This novel is dedicated to my friend, Shelby.
Thank you for helping me save myself.

PROLOGUE:
TUESDAY MORNING
Present Day

In the suburb of Abington, Pennsylvania, in a place called Willow Grove, a man named Harlan McGregor sits on his front porch, waiting for the world to end. He does not know by what means the end will come; sometimes those possibilities sit next to him, leaning along the sides of his wooden chair, forcing it to creak like bones. The wind occasionally tussles his silver hair. The wrinkles upon his skin touch the coarse familiarity of the wood as if shaking hands with an old friend; his boots tap to music his ears heard long ago. Even though he wears a flannel shirt, and a cross around his neck, he feels naked. Every morning at exactly six o'clock, Harlan walks outside and sits in his chair, and he does not hear a sound except for that music he can barely recall. At times, he can almost state the name of a song, but just like everything else, it flits out of his scope and eludes his grasp.

It is Tuesday.

Harlan sits in his chair, empty handed. His eyes, once vibrant and blue, still retain a glimmer of their former glory. Harlan has made friends with Father Time. Father Time lets him ignore the chiming of the bells hanging down from the sloped ceiling of the porch. Father Time gives him a cushion against the noise of the occasional passing car, gently pushing it down the street. Faces on the edge of his memory blur, the past bubbling just under the surface; a man, a woman. If not filtered by Father

Time, they would cause him unbearable pain, and he would most certainly drown.

Time allows him to look on past the simple things: the jogger, with his Labrador, who always wears the Blue-Jay jumpsuit; the bikers, their tires spinning over pavement; the distant sound of sirens whipping like bullets through the air. They all bounce off and scatter, and Harlan loses sound of them in the silence, black pebbles dropped into a pool of water so full, the bottom becomes an afterthought in the depths.

As always, Father Time passes by and greets Harlan. His fingers are long and delicate, his form cloaked by a white coat. His beard is long and mystic, and he seems to hold the secrets of the universe just behind his pearly teeth. An arcane air sits about Father Time, one of knowledge accumulated from every moment of every century now seen as the past. Harlan welcomes him wordlessly, motionlessly. Father Time always sits next to him on the porch in the mornings, and he never says a single word.

Not many people bother to pass by the houses on Harlan's street; the major highway running through the center of the area is far enough away to not disturb the residents. Shops try to draw passing cars in as they travel through: an Italian, family owned sub shop; a mechanical garage, under new ownership as of two years ago; a fancy men's apparel store. Sometimes cars stop, and other times they don't. Harlan does not look for them, he does not hear them, and he never rises from his chair.

Harlan is waiting for someone.

The path from Harlan's porch snakes to the street and the sidewalk. His yard is small, containing nothing except overgrown clusters of grass and an apple tree. It is June. The buds on the leaves are just starting to bloom into full view, and the fruit is almost ready to emerge.

Hours pass by. Those who live around Harlan rise, as they should, getting into their cars and driving away to work. Harlan worked in his younger days; he had been a mechanic long ago, retiring after 32 years in the business. Now Harlan's question is not how many years he has lived, but how many more await him.

At 8:05, someone comes walking down the sidewalk. Instead of passing by the range of Harlan's gaze, they catch his eye. As the person turns from the sidewalk and begins down the path to Harlan, Harlan's eyes seem to wake. Father Time steps off the porch to take a walk. Father Time and the figure cross each other on the path from the street to the house, and as they do, Harlan blinks. His old heart skips for a split second. He cannot make out who stands before him. He just sees a silhouette with no detail. In that moment, Harlan feels himself start to move, his mind now churning. He flexes his fingers over the angles of the wooden arms of his chair, letting the movement wash over them and give them momentary change. His relaxed lungs clench, and it feels, for one solitary remnant of Father Time's gift, that he is holding his breath for the figure walking down the path.

The figure reaches the front steps of Harlan's porch.

"Good morning, Mr. McGregor."

In an instant, Harlan's limbs, fingers, and mind sit back down on the wood of the chair, itself supported by the wood of the porch, connected to the earth and every other living person. The weight of the world rolls off his back, and he no longer baits the seconds before him. The words, whatever they were, escape him, forever remaining unsaid.

Harlan looks up at the direction of the voice, the sinews of his neck leaving rust in their path as they turn.

Before Harlan stands a teenage boy. He is of medium

build, wearing a black tee shirt. The sandy color of the boy's hair is not yet dull from age. His glasses are not yet bent by the force of time. Harlan's shoes do not compare to the boy's black sneakers. Harlan looks at the eyes behind the glass, those green eyes observing the old man sitting on his porch. The boy wears a watch upon his left hand.

Harlan clears his throat.

"Good Morning, Nathan. How are you this fine morning?"

The boy returns Harlan's smile. "I'm doing well; I've only been up for about an hour, if you couldn't tell. How are you today?"

"I'm doing fine. Just watching the world pass me by, as we used to say."

The boy does not laugh, but chuckles. "I'm glad to hear that. My parents asked me to say hello for them."

Harlan smiles again, and imitates the boy's noise.

"Tell them thank you. Is your father still enjoying his job at the station? Has he gotten any trouble lately?"

The boy's eyes break from Harlan's, looking down instead at the arms of Harlan's chair.

"There's always trouble somewhere. He's been away a bit more, with summer just starting. He hasn't had many issues that I know of, so I guess that's a good thing."

Harlan's right hand, the fingers permanently hardened from their years of use, contains two rings. One is a silver band. The other is gold, with a blue sapphire set in the center. Three rows of miniscule diamonds, with three stones set in each, adorn either side of the sapphire. Even under the awning of the porch, the sun still reflects off the gems. For each beam of light that passes Harlan by, with each taillight glinting in the sun, he still holds the rays which come from that ring on his pinkie finger.

A silence descends. Harlan sighs.

"Nathan," Harlan says.

"Yes, Mr. McGregor?" Nathan jumps a tad. He's been staring at the ring on Harlan's hand.

"Would you mind having a seat for a moment?" Harlan looks up at the boy and grins, warm and inviting as a grandfather. An empty chair sits directly to Harlan's right.

Nathan walks up the stairs, coming out of the sun, and sits down in the chair next to Harlan. Today marks his fourth visit to the property, and the first time Harlan has asked him to sit.

"Nathan, how many times have you been here to cut the grass?" Harlan asks, casting his gaze to the street. A blue Jaguar, a mid-2000s model, drives up the road, around the bend, and out of sight.

"Four, including today."

"Four." Harlan mouths the number, inspecting it like the contents of a car hood.

"Did I ever tell you about that tree there?" Harlan asks, gesturing towards the apple tree. He knows the answer.

Nathan frowns. "I don't believe so."

It's a small tree, dwarfed by the others in yards around the neighborhood. Each branch sticks out. The wood is soft, but sturdy, to bend but not break in a strong wind, even after storms. Harlan walks out and checks on that tree every morning, and the damned little brave thing never wanders off.

"A long time ago," Harlan says. "I planted that tree. It must've been at least thirty years by now. It grew from this little shrub into what it looks like today. Really, it stopped changing about fifteen years ago. I'd say that for as long as I've had that tree, it's always dropped these apples, Nathan. They are still some darn good apples if you get them at the right time." Harlan laughs, a genuine sound seemingly trapped inside of him for weeks. Nathan smiles in appeasement.

Harlan rises. The muscles that had worked for him his entire life work once more, leaving the chair. Usually, Harlan is inside again by 10 to make breakfast and clean the house. There is no use in waiting when he knows nobody will show up. As he stands, he is resolved: he and Nathan will still be standing out front, so he can continue to wait as he's outside.

Harlan walks down the steps that connect to the path cutting through the middle of the yard, carefully placing each foot up and down. His feet remember not to trip over the ground. He had done it once before, and it had hurt him a great deal, a nice fracture in his hip.

Walking over to the apple tree, Harlan suddenly feels small. He's around six feet tall when not slouching, but the apple tree is at least twice his height from base to tip. The branches reach down to shake Harlan's hand, their particular wood swaying gently in the breeze of the morning. Small budding flowers have appeared on the tree, waiting for the apples to follow. Little spheres are forming in anticipation.

Harlan reaches his right hand up to one of the branches. He plucks one of the flowers from the stick fingers, greeting it in a way he hadn't in years. It releases from the tree effortlessly, with the smallest tug separating it from the mother branch.

Nathan walks up beside him. Nathan sees a look of wonder on the old man's face. He does not see Harlan smile—truly smile—often. His mood is usually jovial, but to see the emotion of the old man's face turned into such wonderment at something so small as a tree strikes Nathan as peculiar.

Harlan turns, the small flower in hand. He holds it in front of his face.

"My grandson used to love these things. He'd pluck them off and bring them to me when he was real young. When he was able to reach them, the lowest of the low hangers, and pluck them off, you should have seen the look on his face." Harlan laughs.

"I didn't know you had a grandson." Nathan says. The old man had never talked about his personal life before.

"Yes, I do." Harlan says, letting the leaf float towards the ground as he turns back to the tree. "He's about your age. You're a senior?"

"I'm a Junior, actually. Next year will be my Senior year."

"I see. Alex just graduated high school. He lives about forty minutes away from here, in a small town." Harlan's smile dissipates, and the leaf falls to the ground on the calming pillow of gravity.

It lands on the grass gently, finally at rest.

The chimes on the porch trill.

"That was a long, long time ago." Harlan says.

Harlan hears the laughter of a boy. It starts softly, but soon echoes towards him through time, air, space, and light. It carries a name with it on the breeze: Alex. Harlan catches the thought for once, not letting it escape or slide away from him like the song. He can hear the song playing too, emitting the notes of time and the bars of a different life. They dance and pirouette around the yard, closing in just as the hypothetical ends of the world have done on the porch before for Harlan. These are benevolent, these specters. Light, love, freedom, youth; all words accompanying the sound of laughter. Harlan looks at the top of the tree, how it seems to bend willingly, not afraid to lose its original form, for change is gorgeous.

However, as the good things come, Harlan suddenly feels

a chill. It is a warm morning, but Harlan is cold. It dilutes the laughter of the boy, and a smell seems to drift from the house. Ghosts are now all around him, smiling at him, staring at him. Harlan has waited so, so long. And he will keep waiting, until it's Tuesday afternoon again.

Distinctly, Harlan hears a voice say, "May 19."

"Mr. Harlan?"

Harlan does not hear Nathan. Instead, the faces Father Time so graciously blurred sharpen in his mind's eye.

One name escapes his mouth, as the memories crash down like discordant music:

"Michael."

Part I

August 14, 2009 — May 19, 2010

1

August 14, 2009

Driving through the southern edge of Bucks County, Pennsylvania, greatness grows in secret. Majesty inhabits the fields of the area's farmers, in the faces of parents whose children graduate from the local high schools, every hope and dream nestled into opportunity. Some people claim the only way to find a great life is to leave the small towns, but the truly knowledgeable understand the value of simplicity. In one particular town, nestled into an area about 40 minutes north of Philadelphia, happiness is a rich crop, only harvestable by those with observant vision.

It is August. September has not yet awakened from its slumber to steal the children off to school again. The leaves on the trees are still as flush as emeralds. The agrarian land has weathered countless storms. There's a spirit intrinsic to the farmhouses, built into the wood and sewn into the pastures. Those who discover the soul of the land are rarely apt to stray.

History and influence have touched the area. Time brushes past people, turning their skin softer, aging their minds, and whitening their hair. It brushes past places, turning stones and scripts to particles of dust. The universe eventually reclaims all it bears. Time has turned the soil, cut down the trees, but also cultivates futures on the foundation of the years.

Route 309 runs for 134 miles through the state of Pennsylvania. It starts near Philadelphia and ends in Bowman Creek, near a town called Wilkes Barre. A town sits at a point equidistant between the two aforementioned markers. The nature of the town is a dichotomy of agrarian farms and the commercial world, referred to as a place called Quakertown. The highway runs through the town center; cars each tell their own story in every spin of their tires or blare of their horns.

Shops line the sides of the highways in clusters: a TGI Fridays, a McDonalds, the obligatory Wendy's. The Family Diner sits in the same section as the local Giant Food Store, joined by a set of connecting stairs. More people eventually gravitate to industry, creating sustainable livings. They are farmers of the land by a different method.

Off the Turnpike entrance, one comes into Quakertown via a transition. The scene changes from a National Geographic film to a sudden burst of small civilization. Frequent visitors will not mark such a change, but the residents have noticed the shifts.

From the turnpike entrance comes a 1970's red Chevy Impala. It is dark, glinting with both a classical sheen and whisky-aged beauty. The whistles of passersby appreciate its nearly pristine condition. The man behind the wheel of the car eases to the stoplight. Music drifts gently from the car radio, fusing with the notes of the world's breeze.

A translucent guitar strums; a piano plays softly. A voice cracks the air as it tries to pry itself from the speakers.

In the passenger seat of the car, a woman sits reading a book. *19 Minutes* by Jodi Picoult, the blue cover contrasting the warmness of her dress. The creases of the pages almost match the folds on her skin. A pair of modest earrings frame the sides of her face. Her eyes focus down on the text in her lap. Like the man's, her eyes look through glasses. If peoples' items could speak, the woman's possessions would attest to a life well lived.

As the car rolls to a stop in front of the light, she raises her head.

"Harlan," she asks in a voice of aged velvet.

"Yes, dear?" The man replies.

"Should we say anything once we get there?'

Harlan lets out a breath.

"There is a time and place for everything, right? I don't think it'll be constructive if we do."

The woman nods, silent. She turns back to the book in her lap. The ring on her right hand gently glides across the page.

The light turns green. The impala rumbles in delight, ready to move, a model on a catwalk of pavement.

The radio fills the conversation eagerly, a parched animal lapping from a pond.

The woman glances up from her book. She frowns, her brown eyes and eyebrows in tune.

"Is this still U2?" she asks.

"Yes, darling. *The Joshua Tree.*"

"I don't think I've heard this one before." She grins, looking at him. Even in his age, he is handsome, his complexion darkened from the sun's kiss.

Harlan returns the grin. "I think you might just have forgotten. I played it the last time we were on our way up here."

"I don't forget anything." The woman says, turning back to her book.

"I'm surprised you don't need a nametag to keep you straight some mornings." Harlan chuckles. They roll to a stop again.

"I'll build it for you myself. *Cynthia Joy McGregor*, hang it right above the bathroom door." Harlan turns to look at her now. His humor pauses, just like his heart every time he looks in her direction.

There sits his wife, peering down at the book in her lap.

Some people get sick of each other, but their thirty-six years still feels like a first date. All secrets are shared. She's looking at the page, but isn't reading a word.

Harlan reaches over and turns the music down. The traffic light is long to change.

"What's eating at you, my love?" Harlan wonders, retaining his cheeriness while his words cut like a fish through water.

Cynthia does not sigh, but her breath indicates an escaping thought.

"I'm worried about our son. And his wife. And our grandson."

Harlan nods, turning his focus back to the road.

"I am too. I don't think it's much of our business."

Minutes pass; the song finishes. Harlan reaches a hand out and adjusts the track, hitting the 'up' button four times. Track nine is his favorite. As the music starts once again, the car drifts from the commercial center and into the nucleus of town, the other half of the coin on which Quakertown is printed. One side holds the future, and the other the past. While the highway has been apt to travel, the rest of the town is not as eager to change.

Harlan guides the car to a stop, the line of vehicles in front of him at a standstill. He turns to Cynthia, as the song plays out.

Cynthia shifts her view once more from her book, her hands resting upon her place in the paragraph. Her eyes meet her husband's; a bridge across time, space, and distance. Her eyes' stir like a pool of water feeling the ripple of a fallen stone.

Next to the car is a building made of cherry red tiles flanking two different sets of doors. Proudly displayed on the building's face are the words:

Sines 5 & 10

If one were to enter the building, one might mistake the

entrance across the threshold as looking back in time at an old walk-in photograph. A soda fountain adorns a serving counter on one side of the shop, offering menus for breakfast and lunch. Only one or two individuals run the station, but the legacy of a hundred years of business in the town serves the food. History and delight season each dish.

Behind the soda fountain are lines of aisles selling toys and other various items. Plastic army men lie encased in their packaging, preparing to ship off to war. Model airplanes line the aisles, pre-assembled or in pieces. Toys of all shapes and sizes sell for a low price, which the 1950's register at the counter near the front processes easily. Children walk around in wonder—a feeling not produced by a screen, but by the spectacle of toys which fit into their hands. The amazing things one can build are the foundations of joy in life.

It's believed portions of life exist outside of time. As Harlan and Cynthia pass the shop, with the register area lined with different types of candy for sale, the spun milkshakes boasting unparalleled taste, and a smiling, bearded man dipping a shiny silver spoon into a vivacious vanilla sundae, their glance could be eternal. The love in the town adapts and evolves, because love never means to die. Such is the abundance of Quakertown.

The traffic moves again. Harlan and Cynthia break their gaze. Cynthia goes back to reading, and Harlan drives on. Time moves once more, tailgating them down the quaint street.

2

Driving further away from Quakertown, commercialism recedes as a wave from the shoreline. Shops disappear, and turn into homes. Each stone set in the earth designs itself as a childhood memory. More agriculture unfurls, with dollars nothing more than sheets of paper in the pocket of a coat. Residents prefer walking the paths. Stability is in the air as much as oxygen. The signals firing in worlds such as politics are dismissible with the click of a power button. The residents are not shortsighted; on the contrary, the most intellectual people on the face of the planet might inhabit the small borough of Coopersburg.

To a child looking from the intersection of Richlandtown Pike and Gruversville road, the world ends at the intersection of Richlandtown and Keystone Road. Home is the scope of their existence; they have no concept of stores, or of malevolent people. Where do convicted felons like to shop? Such questions aren't fit for the mind of a child. Perhaps when they grow older, the horrors of the world will arrive from the road, towards the maturing mind of a young man, via the Keystone curve. Most likely, the child will grow up, and realize how true horrors are homemade.

Alex McGregor has known one world. He's lived in the same house for all of his 13 years; he's never flown. School has been the farthest he's gone into the rest of the world, besides the Internet. If Alex had been born in 1976 instead of 1996, his atrocious handwriting would have rendered the book of his life illegible. He has some extra weight to him, and appears bright. He's a hazel haired, light blue-eyed spec on the face of the earth. His soul is far beyond his years. A tint mars his gaze, a blemish his smile does not show, and his heart refuses to nurture.

Alex sits in his living room, watching the characters bounce across the screen of his television. His father, Michael, has a great-paying job in sales. His mother, Lauren, has devoted her life to raising him. His parents often speak of their luck, but those are simply words to Alex. Alex and his generation know the sensation of owning, but lack the knowledge of earning.

When he was 11 months old, Alex had been playing on a chair in the living room. Lauren had been in the kitchen, talking on the phone to her brother, who she loved enough to see only on holidays. Alex had padded across the carpeted floor with innocent speed. The entire house had seemed expansive, with its modest red tiling gracing the outside and wooden walls covered with a white, pink-splashed paint inside. He had been racing towards a chair he wanted to climb, and with as much might as he could muster, his tiny hands had gripped the seat, and he'd stood.

Laruen checked on her son whilst she talked on the phone. Her green eyes captured the color and the vibrancy of the trees outside her home on her morning walk. She had a glow about her at that time, a resonating soul. The spiritual call it an aura. Lauren's hair, shoulder length and curly brown, had seemed to thrive on energy in its fibers; the phone pressed to her ear, her slender frame standing underneath the outline of the kitchen doorway, she watched Alex. Her heart caught every noise, and absorbed every glance.

Even in happiness, people make mistakes. Heaven may

be real, but the closest Lauren McGregor has ever felt to perfection were those minutes on that day. In her conversing with her brother, her eyes had indeed strayed from Alex, a night watchman dozing.

Jim, her brother, had sent the family a gift; it sat only a few feet away from the chair Alex climbed. It had been a set of subtle wooden blocks, meant for teaching children with their hands.

Upon his triumph of climbing the chair, Alex let his grip on the wooden seat release. As Alex fell from his standing position, he arched backwards. Alex hit the floor, whiplashing his still-developing head. The corner of a block found the child behind the right ear, its point sharply piercing the soft skin.

Lauren heard her son cry out, and had walked across the wooden floor of the kitchen. She passed the table, only slightly worried at Alex's outburst disrupting her conversation. Children cry all of the time, for they do not know the value of their tears.

Reaching the living room, Lauren's motherly inspecting of her little bundle of joy commenced:

No blood? Check.

No vomit? Check.

Tears? Yes.

Chair in close proximity? Check.

Child sitting on the floor? Yes.

Conclusion: Alex had tried climbing the chair, fallen backwards, and hit the floor unexpectedly.

Lauren comforted Alex, and his crying soon subsided. She went back to talking to Jim. Alex did not try to climb that chair again. The formerly constant babbling stopped. He still trundled around, but with a different gait. The tint in his gaze was born on that day. He doesn't remember it. Lauren and Michael have never forgotten it. The road of life can turn from a Route 309 existence into a Keystone Road existence in seconds. For the McGregors, Alex's fall would be an angular shift as unforgiving as a sinkhole in the middle of the German Autobahn's passing lane.

A couple hours later, Lauren noticed that Alex had become extremely quiet. She walked back in the living room, past the open area of the house, which holds Michael's home office, and evaluated her son once more. She saw something in her child's eyes that day, in the paleness of his skin. It was a feeling she'd felt in her own past, dancing around the edges of her existence. Then, in front of her eyes, Alex vomited.

Lauren called Michael at work. She told him of the vomiting, of the feeling gnawing at her stomach. When Death is close, he does not recognize hunches or whispers. Death has no master among people, for he can only be controlled by Father Time. Life cannot exist without an end. Michael told Lauren, from his desk, swamped with papers, that Alex probably had a slight cold. Lauren asked if she should take him to a hospital. Michael relented, deciding to trust his wife instead of fight.

The first hospital's CAT scan machine was broken. An ambulance took Lauren and Alex to Philadelphia. Alex grew paler. The radiance was dying, along with her son. No matter how fast that ambulance went, across the fading miles, it seemed as if Death sat alongside her and the medical technicians. As Alex sat there, inches away, he seemed to be drifting further and further inward. Michael was driving in to meet them from work as the ambulance galloped across both the countryside and the developments. Lauren was in shock, and still no tears came to her eyes, but her heart was fit to burst. For the rest of her life, the stretch marks on her soul from the weight of such a day have remained.

A stroke. More specifically, a subdural hematoma.

The corner of the block had punctured a vessel in Alex's brain. The blood had hungrily escaped the vein, the pressure from the fluid internally squeezing the child's precious mind. Death cackled as fate flooded the situation in red waves: Lauren had been on the phone with the sender of the blocks; Alex's vitality was killing him slowly. After the procedure, during which surgeons removed a portion of Alex's skull, drained the blood, and repaired the vessel, saving his life, Lauren and Michael were informed: if another hour had passed without intervention, Alex would have died.

Michael only saw his son post-operation. Alex's head had been bandaged, his breathing adjusted with machinery. If he made it through a couple days, he could come home, good as new, except with a scar on his head as a reminder, a roadmap for the next 13 years of his life. Michael never forgot standing in the hospital room, the lights slanted, illuminating a tragedy which grazed a family.

Michael, his striking blue eyes looking down upon his son, had whispered a promise:

"As long as you're alive, I'm going to take care of you."

In that moment, an infant of 11 months made a man of a 35-year-old child.

Alex watches the flat screen television as his grandparents pull into the driveway, the sun blinking off the polished crimson of their car's hood.

3

Michael McGregor stands on the wooden deck looking out over his front lawn, leaning against the railing, the sun beating on his head. A lit cigarette is sandwiched between his right index finger and middle finger. The smoke drifts up over his head and trails off into the sky to go and choke some member of the avian population. Michael has been smoking since the age of nine, meaning it will be 38 years come September. Michael brushes his teeth exceptionally hard, but they still yellow. He's smoked a lot recently. He smells the lovely, fresh air of the day as he takes another drag.

He stands atop everything he's ever desired. He's cast in the shadow of a house, a Palace with 13 rooms. He has a wife for whom his love is boundless, and a son who he will die to raise. The three possess loving family on all sides. They take vacations together. Gossip about the family stands nonexistent in the local community, and in all the pictures, everyone always smiles.

Michael does not consider the depth of his happiness. Not today. It's already been a week since Lauren moved back in. Thus, the beauty of his foundation shines once more, like how the cigarette casts a little light as Michael lifts it to his mouth.

Lauren. He recalls the first time they met. The two had worked in the marketing section of a small business. It had been raining. She had been walking, and Michael had offered her a ride. She'd politely declined. The following day, it rained again, and Lauren had decided to trust him. The two married a year later. The world behind Lauren's eyes had become Michael's, and their planets collided. The two bought the house together, and their child came five years later. Lauren nearly died from preeclampsia. God decided it would be the three of them and the dog, Roxy, the Corgi who is nestled against Alex's legs. One Big Happy Family, Version 2000, batteries included, white picket fence sold separately.

Lauren and Michael don't talk like that anymore. Her eyes, once misty, are muddled and tepid. Once people live together long enough, they learn how to talk without speaking. After bringing Alex home on that day long ago, no oration had been needed. After Michael's sister, Eve, had moved to California and cut ties with her family, no eulogy was delivered. Nothing has been said between Michael and Eve for seven years.

After Lauren's brother Jim committed suicide by locking himself in a garage and passing out inside his Cadillac Escalade, a whole lot had been said, but none of it made any noise.

Even if the owner keeps the packaging, nobody can guarantee, once the family set is broken, that there are instructions for placing it back together.

Jim had been a man of small sayings. He did not act in the weakness of words. Lauren has become less of herself and more like Jim since August 17, 2004. No amount of money Michael makes can fill the holes in her soul. Michael does a lot to hold their Palace up; he's Coopersburg's version of Atlas. Using emergency money to try to pay credit debt while lying to his parents about the source hadn't lightened the burden. Each dollar bill seemed to scoff at him, for as he works, it leaves his hands. The Palace is a hungry beast, and when Michael can't feed it money, it likes to eat the lining of his soul. Mortgage refinancing. A shitty septic system. Lauren and he had fallen in love with the place, and with the area, so his soul pays the price for the affection. Now, Michael considers the merits of taking a blowtorch to the red paneling, mixed with gasoline and combustibles, sending the palace up in flames like the lit end of his handheld stress managers.

The credit incident, the emotional embargos. Michael teaches his son about trust, the lies rolling off his own lips as sweet venom. He wonders at the possibility of obtaining the integrity he tells his son to value.

One time, he and Lauren argued about who was going to buy meat for a grill. Lauren compared Michael to other men, how he wasn't a traditional father with a golden retriever and a can of baked beans on ESPN. Michael yelled about her silence, and his verbal blows rooted themselves in her disconnection. Michael complained how he worked all the time, and how Lauren did nothing but stay at home and watch the child instead of parenting, and Lauren bit back and tore parts of Michael's person away with remarks regarding his past.

Lauren always starts with raindrops, and Michael knows they're the preludes to hurricanes.

Alex is the miniature mediator. Ever since the age of seven, he's engrained himself in his parents' idiocy. Michael tells him how the repeated involvement isn't normal, typically after yelling for hours on end for the 2nd time in as many months. Alex is usually the sanest one involved. He selflessly tries to make sense of their language of volume, trying to decipher words from emotional static.

Nobody in the family speaks of those arguments, except when Michael talks to Alex. Michael preaches how his points in the war are correct and Lauren's are misguided and misfired instead of misunderstood. Her medication is another detriment

to the funds of the home. His is a necessity. Alex has no
medication.

He's fine.

The landscape of the front yard hasn't changed in a decade.
The sun shines. The television breathes its nonsense, and
Alex laughs along. Michael sighs, and then coughs hard. He's
probably developing a cold, and for a second he looks at the
cigarette in his hands. He clutches it tighter and raises it to his
lips. Taking one more lengthy drag, he puts it in a bottle of
Poland Spring next to him, the water murky and brown from
the residue of the cigarettes, dead bodies in a well.

Harlan's old, beautiful car coasts into the driveway. It seems
to meet the pavement as a familiar friend, moving into the spot
next to Michael's 2001 platinum Buick LeSabre. The silver and
crimson gently play a contrast as they sit in front of the cluttered
shed, the shelter of aborted home improvement projects.
Lauren's car, a 2005 dark blue Toyota Corolla, sits diagonally to
the other cars, with direct access to the rest of the driveway.

Harlan and Cynthia emerge from the Impala, with Cynthia
leaving her book on the passenger seat and Harlan turning
the radio off. Harlan's boots carry him over the short distance
between the pavement and the main sidewalk. What could be
a garden sits next to this entryway; it's only resident is a small,
ethereal light which only works half the time at night, protected
by a short wall of stones. A large tree Lauren and Michael
planted together stands guard on the other side of the yard,
towering to the sky. The kitchen door hides behind a white fence
which lines the path to the front door, and three bushes huddle
together under three windows which peer into the kitchen of the
home. Harlan walks deliberately; Cynthia follows his footsteps
closely.

Lauren always walks separately from Alex and Michael for some reason, as if she does not want to taint their steps.

"Good afternoon," Michael greets warmly from atop the stairs. He smiles as his father draws closer.

"Good afternoon to you too," Harlan says. One clunk, two clunk, three clunks, four. Now the two stand only a couple of feet apart.

The two shake hands, and then hug. Michael feels the familiar roughness of his father's embrace bringing him closer to home.

Harlan sniffs.

"You're telling me you still haven't quit?" Harlan lets a smile crease his lips.

"I'm working on it."

"Still?"

"That's bad for your health, you know." Cynthia adds. She hugs her son while looking up at him. She's short, but her husband has allowed her to stand tall since Michael was a child.

They bask in each other's presence for a moment.

"So," Harlan says.

"How've things been with you and Lauren?"

Michael looks away, nodding. "We've been alright."

Cynthia shoots Harlan a look.

"You sure about that?" Harlan presses.

"Yeah, it's been a little awkward, but we're all here, aren't we?" Michael replies. His fingers twitch towards the pack of cigarettes.

Harlan nods, chewing the response slowly.

"Is that a good thing or a bad thing?" Harlan asks.

Michael's smile fades. "We'll wait and see."

"Have the two of you considered going to see somebody?"

"Harlan," Cynthia quips. He's acting like a bastard, once again.

"I'm sure Jack wouldn't mind the extra money." Michael opines. Lauren never joins him when he goes to see Jack.

"It's just a suggestion." Harlan says, meeting Cynthia's steeled gaze with one of titanium concern.

I'm trying to help. Harlan's eyes sparkle.

I'm scared. Cynthia blinks.

"We're just going to see how it goes for the future. We've just got to take it one day at a time, and then –"

The front door opens. The three turn. There stands Alex, a smile on his face similar to the one shared by his father and grandfather. He's already taller than his mother and inching up on his father. He's going into eighth grade, yet he could be mistaken easily for a Sophomore. Harlan knows he's a growing boy, and he'll streamline out in puberty. Acne is starting to dot his face, along with the regular facial expressions of concern which affect all middle school kids. The blue eyes shine behind his version of the McGregor glasses.

"There he is!" Harlan steps forward to shake his grandson's hand as Alex walks past the screen door.

Cynthia follows to give Alex a hug, and a big, wet kiss on the cheek.

"Hi Grandmom," Alex says, wincing slightly.

"Hello Alex. You know I'm only going to be able to do that for a couple more years, until you've got some girl doing it for me."

Michael rolls his eyes. Alex lets out a chuckle.

"You hear that, kid?" Harlan asks. "One of these days you're gonna like having that happen."

"Of course I will, Grandpa."

"Are you ready to be an eighth grader?" Cynthia is starting the process. The subconscious grandmother checklist, similar to the mother inspection checklist Lauren had used the day of Alex's accident, begins.

Kiss? Check.

Hug? Check.

Harlan chides him about girls? Check.

School? In progress.

Friends? Up next.

Talking about how his parents are messing up his life by being irresponsible, and are damaging him like a family heirloom in a fireplace?

That's Harlan's inquiry.

"I think I'm ready as I'll ever be. I've got most of my work done already."

"What did you have to do?" Harlan asks.

"Read some summer reading books."

"When I was your age, I was working, not doing reading assignments." Harlan remarks, looking at Michael.

"Really?" Michael interjects skeptically, smiling. "You were working at the age of 13?"

"Of course!" Harlan says. "I was cutting grass for an older man who lived down the street! His name was Mr. Richard Collins. Ex-military, and he paid me three dollars every time I cut his lawn."

Michael senses a story from Harlan. He interjects in the name of preventing sunburn.

"Alright, so I'll just send Alex here three miles down the street to the next house and expect him to get paid, most likely in either apples or horses, like the olden days." The nearest house is only a few feet down the road.

Harlan frowns. "He's gonna have to learn someday, Michael."

"I still haven't." Michael takes another cigarette out of his pack.

"You're telling me." Cynthia chimes.

"Hey now," Harlan says, turning to her. Cynthia laughs.

A tapping comes from the glass door, snaring their attention.

Lauren wears a shy smile on her face, her black tee shirt bearing spots from her work on the day's lunch, her jeans and bare feet comfortable on the floor of her home. Her hair descends in waves to her shoulders. Michael never understands why she makes herself look so good for his parents. A collision of emotions rocks him: there's his wife, age not having done much to her over the 42 years it has held her in its grasp. How much effort does it take to construct her smile?

"If you don't mind me interrupting, lunch is ready." Lauren says, stepping outside.

She moves past Michael, giving him just a glance out of the corner of her eye.

Cynthia embraces her.

"Hello, darling." Cynthia never fights with Lauren.

Cynthia has always been a freelance therapist, no degree or title required. She had taken a 16-year-old boy and helped turn him into the man who stands before her today. She has no biological children. Michael, and his sister Eve's, birth mother had been a woman named Janice, who loved her bottles of liquor in the basement to resolve her problems. She had passed away from heart failure on a cold October night long ago, but Harlan and Michael had both made their peace with her. Janice's words of wisdom, delivered from her occasional pulpit of sobriety, still float to Michael occasionally. The radiance and love of Cynthia's guidance has been his lighthouse on the distant shore, the smoke on the horizon in the wilderness.

Harlan hugs Lauren next, ensuring his arms do not squeeze.

Harlan knows his son can be a manipulative bastard at times, but he loves him and doesn't care for the baggage. Harlan knows his son's dreams rest in the woman he's embracing, and that she is aware of her power.

"Thank you for hosting us today, Lauren." Harlan says, the summer air in his voice.

"You're very welcome! We always love having you here." Lauren replies.

"Hey, let's not say our goodbyes, they just got here." Michael puts an arm around Lauren's shoulders. She smiles at his touch and looks to him. Alex lights up.

The moment, with Michael's arm around Lauren, Michael's parents peering at them reservedly, Alex standing to the side smiling at the boards of the porch, would be worthy of a camera. A picture should've been taken and prominently framed in a McGregor museum, as an eternal landmark in all of their lives, one where a fleeting second holds happiness.

Soon it shall be gone forever.

4

In the McGregor household, food is prepared in the kitchen, and eaten in the same room; the family does work in the dining room; the living room is in the hearth room and the hearth room is a place where chairs sit next to a wood stove and are never used. The island acts as a post for the cook to look out over their court at their expectant constituents. Turning around, one can use either the stove or the sink to prepare food. Lauren becomes upset if Michael tries too hard to change the way in which the kitchen is situated. She always prepares the house to be as if a *Home Living* magazine is coming for a photo-shoot the same day. With each cleaning session, she scrapes away the mold and mildew of her childhood. If only she could hold her emotions in a tank, perhaps under multiple layers of concrete, she might feel better with the reflection she sees in every clean glass.

The kitchen table infuriates Alex, who, when he tries to write on top of it, always finds his pencil slipping into the table's cracks. The table is a quilt of plastic and wood, with sections of squares held together by a peculiar, adhesive connective material. During his homework, Alex always pets Roxy when he should be writing and pokes the material when he should be finding the answer to an algebraic equation.

The family seat themselves around the table. Harlan and Cynthia sit on one side, with Michael at the head of the table and his back to the window. Lauren sits across from him. Alex sits in view of Harlan and Cynthia, in the middle of his parents. The family is eating sandwiches constructed from components prepared by Lauren—the finest mayonnaise, cheeses, and meats available. While eating, the talking recedes.

A bird chirps in the distance, its rhythm repeating every couple of seconds as a miniature heartbeat. A proportioned breeze of summer air floats through the window, tinged with the smell of fresh cut grass nearby. Harlan's overcoat drapes the back of his chair.

Swallowing, Michael takes a nice swig of cool milk.

"So," Michael asks, looking at his father and mother. "Have we heard anything from Eve lately?"

"Nope." Harlan responds.

Michael looks back at his sandwich quizzically, as if it's suddenly turned alien.

"Funny, she usually calls around this time of year. April, August, and December."

Cynthia and Harlan both nod mechanically.

Michael takes another bite. "I've thought about giving her a call. It's been a couple years since I've tried."

"She won't answer you, you know." Harlan says.

"I know, but I always think it's worth a shot."

"Why doesn't Aunt Eve talk to us?" Alex asks. His sandwich has fallen partially apart. A ketchup bottle stands next to his plate, a trusty companion.

"Your Aunt can be an odd person at times, Alex." Michael explains.

"Why is that?"

"She thinks that what she has out in California is better than what she could have here." Michael reasons, choosing his words like how a golfer chooses the correct club for a swing.

Alex nods, and adds more ketchup to his plate.

Roxy, the Corgi, sits and pants at Harlan's side, hoping that he will drop a piece of sandwich. The dog is lovingly expectant, a fixture at every meal.

"She'll have to come home one of these days." Harlan says. He points a finger at Alex from the side of his roll.

"You promise me something, kid. Don't move too far away from home. Your parents care too much to let you get too far away from them."

"I don't think I'd want to move far away. I love it here, with my friends, and my school."

"Friends and school are one thing. Family is another. As my own father used to say, at the end of the day, when your job and the rest of your life deserts you, the people who stay to listen to you bitch about it are the ones that really love you." Harlan playfully taps Cynthia on the shoulder.

"Watch your language, you dirty old man!" She scolds him.

"Who are you calling dirty?" The mayonnaise from his sandwich drips down his chin.

"I just wish she'd come around again. I miss her a lot of time." Michael says.

"She just doesn't understand the value of family, Michael." Cynthia replies, casting a warm look to Alex.

Lauren looks out the window, into the yard. An object prods at the wall of her mind. She can hear it tapping, like rain on the roof upstairs.

Jim Atkins.

"Well," Harlan said, taking a drink of his own. "She'll understand it after one of us is gone."

Lauren stands abruptly, the chair shooting back from the table, the rest of her sandwich now abandoned on her plate.

She walks away in a brisk step, one hand over her mouth, her footfalls padding over the floor becoming fainter and fainter. The rest of those at the table watch her leave—Harlan with his hands raised, Michael shaking his head, Alex's heart beating fast. Cynthia rises and follows her slowly, casting a glare of pure disappointment back at Harlan. Alex stands up as well, but Michael motions for him to stay. Harlan keeps his hands raised as if surrendering to an armed intruder. Michael's eyes tell his son, *sit down and let Grandma handle this.*

"What did I say?" Harlan asks Michael.

"It's been nearly five years since her brother's death." Michael picks up Lauren's half-eaten plate and moves it to the counter.

Harlan closes his eyes, muttering.

"It's alright, you didn't remember." Michael coughs.

"Didn't he …" Harlan starts. Michael's nod finishes the exchange as his hacking finally subsides.

"Yeah, carbon monoxide. She doesn't talk about it at all, but it has to be weighing on her."

Alex peers down at Roxy. The corgi never has any problems. She just needs a walk, a hug, and love, and then she'll put the family's well being ahead of her own. He pats the dog's head. The glow of the day is gone.

Lauren cries in the master bedroom. Cynthia follows her carefully. While Lauren is not her blood, her movements look to apologize for Harlan's words. She pushes through the door. Lauren sits on the bed, its maroon bedspread ruffled. Tears slowly leak down her face from her usually soft eyes, turning red as they bleed emotion. Lauren notices Cynthia as she enters, five years of her past triggered by a sentence.

"I'm sorry," Lauren manages.

Cynthia offers a compassionate smile, and then joins her on

the bed.

"No," Cynthia says. "I'm sorry. Harlan should know better."

Lauren shakes her head. "It's just, as soon as he started mentioning missing people … my brother's five year anniversary is three days away."

"I know." Cynthia takes hold of one of Lauren's hands. The older woman's wrinkled skin radiates a sense of love. Lauren holds her hand, tears starting to fall again. Her brother's face is now free from its compartment.

"I can tell you miss him a lot." Cynthia whispers.

"I do." Lauren confirms. She wipes her eyes.

"Do you ever talk to anybody about this stuff?"

"No. It's too painful."

"Well, if you ever feel the need, I'm always here."

"I know, Cynthia. I just find it so hard to believe. He was so young! He had his entire life ahead of him." Lauren starts to break again.

Cynthia pulls her close. One of Cynthia's closest friends had passed in a terrible car accident caused by a drunk driver when she had been 18, and every day, Cynthia thinks about years of opportunity lost in a few minutes of time. She's seen those older, younger, and similarly aged pass before her. Lauren needs to learn not to try and capture a container of compressed air fit to explode; if the vessel isn't strong enough, it may start to crack.

"Listen to me," Cynthia says, whispering into Lauren's ear. Lauren's breath steadies.

"He's still with you. He's always with you."

"He didn't want to be here, Cynthia." Lauren's words come out shakily, creaking like a weather vane.

"He was in so much pain. All he ever talked about was how he would be scared. He'd be sitting up late at night in the old armchair our father left him, watching something on television. He was a massive fan of baseball, and those Indians. He'd be sitting there in the middle of his house, with nobody. He never married, he never had kids. The closest he came to a son was Alex, and we saw him maybe once a year. I didn't even really call him too much. But he'd sometimes call me, saying how he was sitting in the middle of his house one minute, and the next he'd be seeing flashes, or explosions. He would always be so ashamed, Cynthia. He would be ashamed to tell his own sister about his problems, but he'd do it anyway. And then by talking to me he felt both guilt, and remorse, and he told me that there was nothing we could do for him because he was beyond all help. I'll never forget him sounding like a child, whispering to me through that receiver about how they were coming for him, with the bombs and their guns and the face of his companions blown to shreds in the back of his mind.

"And then one day I got a phone call, one I knew was coming but never wanted to answer, knowing that when I picked up the receiver I would hear those few words that nobody should ever have to hear in their entire lives: we did all we could, but it wasn't enough. My mom and dad were destroyed, Cynthia. My mom can't walk past a picture of him without crying, without seeing all the things her perfect little boy could've been, all that potential, all those memories, gone. And I think to myself, there had to be something I could've done to stop this."

Cynthia doesn't speak. She squeezes Lauren a little tighter.

Lauren sighs painfully. Shame replaces her sorrow, the frostbite after standing outside in the cold. Her curse is that she disrupts all the benefits of her life. Her family doesn't deserve such a spastic. Her brother's face floats in her mind, accompanied by a wave of guilt for her father-in-law sitting in the kitchen.

Alex peaks around the side of the door. He sees his mother embracing his grandmother, her soul a whirlpool slowing to a stop, a lulling break in the middle of a thundercloud. Alex keeps his distance, watching, close enough to help but outside the proximity of hurt. The wall shelters him from his mother's storm.

Michael views the panorama of his yard from the kitchen window: the patio holding the picnic furniture, the shed that houses unfinished jobs, the cars containing gasoline and machinery—all extensions of a Palace, which houses pain. Lauren and Michael had placed the stones of the patio amidst talk of hosting many outdoor events with family and friends, turning the home from a place on a side street to a possible nexus of celebration. Lauren had gone along with the idea. Michael never wants to be the center of attention, but he's never content being outside of the loop. He tries so hard to fit in, and always seems to be searching for something.

Michael coughs, a two breathed effort, one following the other in succession. Michael glances over to the table, and sees Harlan has moved, either to the living room or to follow Cynthia. Michael turns to the window. His coughing continues.

Michael has been hacking like an engine without enough fuel for the past four days, with the force of a probable cold or some other odd infection, such as bronchitis or maybe pneumonia. He stands at the kitchen window, the portal to the patio, and casts the residue from his cigarettes through the window fan. He always inhales the harmful part of the cigarette, no matter how much smoke he throws outside.

He coughs once more, and Michael feels the mucus eject

from his throat and into his mouth, a whitewash of plasma filling his taste buds with disgust. Jarringly, he grabs for the roll of paper towels hanging on the holder next to the sink. Michael squints a tad, the horrible taste leaving a tangy sensation, mixing with a hint of metal. The taste is familiar. As he wipes the mucus with the paper towel, he spits, and then examines the contents of the item in his hands.

The mucus has its usual white color, but with a very noticeable hue of pink, exactly like the paint of the walls in the living room. The paper towel looks as though someone's been shot over a snowy embankment, petals of their livelihood left behind on a ground of sheer white.

Harlan returns to the kitchen, his boots transitioning from carpet to floor.

"I apologized." Harlan says, looking at Michael's back. "I think everything is being sorted out. Are you alright?"

Michael stares at the tinge of pink. A chill, similar to a raindrop running down a car window, traces the skin of his spine.

"No, Dad. I don't think I am."

5
September 7, 2009

"You have a bleb." Dr. Richard Fost says, flipping a paper on his clipboard like a cue card.

"A what?" Michael says. His feet dangle a few inches above the floor. Lauren sits in the moderately comfortable chair adjacent to the examination table. Both of them have dressed casually for the occasion: Michael in his office polo and slacks, Lauren wearing a red blouse and black jeans.

"The chest x-ray results showed a very noticeable entity positioned in your right lung, near the top. Most likely, this was, and still is, the source of the bleeding in the sputum that caused you to come here today."

"Richard, you've been taking care of me for six years. Where the hell did this come from?" Michael's palms grip the thin paper of the exam table with precipitation.

"There are a few possibilities for what it could be, and also where it could have come from. The only way to positively determine an answer would be for you to undergo a procedure known as a bronchoscopy."

"What is that?" Lauren asks, her voice small. Her fingers softly trace the band of her wedding ring.

"It's a relatively minor procedure." Fost wheels to his desk, his white overcoat pressing against the hard gray of his seat. His short, black hair is tightly cropped.

"A bronchoscopy will allow us to enter your lung and physically examine the source of the bleeding. Instead of having to crack your chest open and go in there with a magnifying glass, we can stick this tube down your throat and take samples of whatever is on top of this bleb. You've had how many incidents of bleeding so far, in these past few weeks?"

"A lot." Michael says quickly.

"Right. So the fact that there is a potentially foreign body actively causing the release of blood is quite concerning, but its manageable. This bleb thing is a little pocket full of fluid that has attached itself to your lung, providing a possible entryway for foreign and malicious diseases to enter. By conducting the bronchoscopy, we'll be able to get a solid idea of what exactly may be causing this, or which, if any, possible infections may be associated with your current symptoms."

"When would I be undergoing this procedure, exactly?" Michael thinks of Alex, who had just started eighth grade not even a week ago, who falls asleep to a coughing father and crying mother.

"I'd want to have it done today, or as soon as possible." Fost says resolutely, looking between the couple.

"Today?"

"Yeah."

Michael shares a look with Lauren, her pupils aloft with fear.

"Alright, then, I guess we'd better do it." Michael pats the table in a quick beat.

"Good." Fost flips the papers on his clipboard back to their state of rest. "Let's get you over to the hospital."

———

After the initial incident of bleeding, more episodes of coughing and resulting blood had followed; Lauren had pushed him to schedule a more appropriate examination than self-diagnosis of "I'm fine" or the surgical "I probably just coughed too hard." Michael started tossing paper towels in the trash, labeling incidents as less severe by swallowing his grimaces.

At the same time, Alex dutifully went and made his parents proud by earning his grades in school. He ate the starter assignments for the year seamlessly, completing them with expedience. He recalled his review and absorbed all the new information. At the age of 13, he's already preparing for a life of compartmentalization and success in the face of stress. Such is the nature his parents have taught him through their earliest practical lessons of argument and division.

———

On the night of Michael's bronchoscopy, Lauren is the parent on duty. On a typical night, she usually tucks herself in her room with a book on mental health or uses the computer while Alex occupies himself with his electronics elsewhere in the house. Michael often pulls Alex away from the screen, ready to discuss the news of the day or potentially the activity of the music world.

As Michael's in for surgery, Lauren and Alex wait in the reception area, Alex listening to his music, and Lauren reading in the chair next to him.

Harlan and Cynthia join them, driving down after dinner. Harlan sits next to Alex, stationed like a real life version of the Lincoln Memorial. He sits examining the magazines left on the table of every hospital waiting room, thumbing through stories related to celebrities who synthesize a completely different world and ordinary people. He vests no value in their tales, yet he reads on, soaking up details to occupy his eyes. Harlan's seen the fear in his son's expression upon coughing up the blood. He can only imagine the disappointment and shock accompanying every sequential bloody paper towel, collected as mementos or tossed into the garbage.

Harlan's fingers leaf through the pages slowly, transitioning from a story on kidnapping to a story on weight loss. Society seems to be evolving in reverse, where such fickle topics as ways in which celebrities lose weight sit next to a story on how to destroy a young girl's world. The pages Harlan turn are marked with a touch of sweat. Lauren mentioned Fost speaking of a small possibility of cancer, but tragedy needs no data for a hypothesis.

Alex sits in the chair next to Harlan. The boy stares downward, his music player singing to him. Harlan and his grandson live less than an hour apart, and Harlan loves seeing him when they get together four times every year. The inches between the chairs include the opportunities never seized and the moments never spent, memories lying in wait for discovery. In only a few hours, Alex has gone from his school to the waiting room, for a parental procedure nobody in the family can correctly name. Harlan taps his grandson on the shoulder, his fingers touching the light gray fabric of Alex's hoodie.

Alex snaps out of his own mind, removing the buds. His eyes, similar to his mother's, look at Harlan reservedly.

"How're you doing, Alex?"

"I'm doing alright, just listening to my music."

"What've you been listening to?"

Alex pulls the device out of his pocket. It's a sleek gray, with an engraved trademark on the case. Alex clicks a button on the top of the device, and the screen displays an image of an album cover. A young, princely boy, with a crown upon his head, is in the motion of turning away from Alex and Harlan's intruding eyes. In red letters, the word *Train* hangs like a portrait next to the royal youth.

"It's a song called 'Drops of Jupiter', by this band named Train. It's one of my Dad's favorites."

"Train..."

Harlan attempts to reach back into the years to find a whisper of the band's sound.

"It came out in, like, 2000 or something. You might not have heard of it." Alex says softly, pressing the button to turn the screen.

Humor reaches Harlan's face.

"Are you calling me old, Alex?"

Alex grins nervously.

"Let me tell you something," Harlan shifts in his chair. "When your father was your age, maybe a couple years older, he fell in love with music. He was maybe 16 or 17, just around that age where you transition from being whiney into finding yourself. They say a 14 year old is going to be challenging, to not believe a word out of their mouths until you know they are telling the truth. You're 13, so I can trust you, right?"

Alex laughs, and puts the device in his pocket. "Sure."

"Good." Harlan continues.

"Your dad, when he got to be a little bit older, started branching out. You can't do that nowadays like we did back then. You've got your videos, or games, whatever you call them. You have music in the palm of your hand, and you can take it with you wherever you go. You have the Internet—I'm lucky if I can send an email. Your father didn't have the things you do, but he loved music all the same. Do you love music, Alex?"

"Yeah." Alex adores music; it has been his religion since he bought Ozzy Osbourne's *Black Rain* in 2007. He remembers the night he brought it home, riding with his parents, his mother shooting his father looks of concern, his father, from the driver's seat, head banging responsibly.

"Your father loves it too, as I'm sure you know. Can you believe your father was in a band at about your age?"

"Really?" Alex straightens in his chair. Alex dreams of forming a band himself, although he has no idea how to play an instrument, sing, or find band mates. He's begun to write lyrics; simple rhymes, tangible pieces of his mind and soul. He uses an orange pad of paper for his writing, no larger than the distance from the base of his wrist to the tips of fingers. His father bought him a guitar for his 13th birthday. Lyrics are his chosen method of expression; he doesn't need to develop calluses. His 7th grade English teacher told him he should consider writing as a career; lyrics are a sister to the writing his teacher mentioned to him. For all his reservation, he needs expression to survive; a songbird in an echo chamber.

"What did he play?"

"He sang. Your old father walked out there and sang!" Harlan's glasses flash in tune with his voice.

"Sometimes, he'd strut out there with a guitar draped around his shoulders. It was so natural to him. I went to see him when he played Hatboro High School in … wow, that must have been 1976, '77? I remember him walking out there, and just the way in which he sang to the crowd, it was as if he were flying."

"What happened to the band?"

"They got a female singer, actually. I guess your dad got distracted. They replaced him with some pretty redhead. She had a nice voice, too, but it wasn't the same." Harlan then remembers where exactly he's sitting, and he shakes his head as his recollection turns to disgust.

"Don't ever smoke, Alex. Just don't do it."

"I don't plan to." Alex assures him. The smell of sweetly vile smoke is a lingering constant on Alex's life.

"Can I hear that song, then?" Harlan asks, pointing to the music player.

"Sure." Alex snatches the buds from where they dangle, and hands them to his grandfather.

Harlan carefully places the buds in his ears.

"It feels like I'm contacting the mothership, kid. How do you put up with this?"

"You get used to it." Alex taps the play button.

Harlan hears the chimes of the piano first. No matter how old he gets, no matter how far he journeys from home, Harlan holds onto the music of the world. His son and grandson inherited the need for sound. Harlan closes his eyes, as the soaring voice of Pat Monahan reaches his ears. He's no longer in a waiting room, but in a chapel.

Harlan's foot taps to the beat, independent and subconsciously powered. Cynthia looks over to them, a knowing expression on her face. Her husband, the traditionalist, the lover of classic cars and mechanics, is lost in some world stemming from the palm of her grandson. Alex keeps his focus on the mp3 player, the conductor of the magic. The song speaks of a woman's journey around Jupiter.

Alex knows his father lives in his favorite songs.

One day, Alex had asked his father about his favorite musical bands; the two sat together for around three hours, discussing music, with Alex's downloading service open on the computer. Alex bought the songs his father loved, "Jupiter" included, and Alex produced a small CD for his father. The CD is a constant fixture in Michael's car. Their connection transcends whatever galaxy, whatever asteroid belt, whatever distance separates them. Harlan is sitting right in the middle of it, with his ears clogged, eyes closed, and his heart full.

The two of them barely hear the doors open from a distant world, with a visitor walking into where Cynthia, Harlan, Alex, and Lauren sit waiting, an astronaut walking on the moon.

The surgery is over.

6

September 13, 2009

Alex has attended the Freedom School District since 1ˢᵗ grade. The local community of Freedom consists of approximately 100 square miles, but only 150 students constitute a graduating class. At Freedom, bonds between students form from early ages and often strengthen over the course of time. Alex can open up one of his middle school yearbooks and honestly say he 'knows' nearly everyone on the pages. Alex considers his friends sacred, because even when his family falters, his friends remain constant.

Alex gets on the bus at the end of the day feeling familiarly tired. One of his best friends lives down the street, but rides a different route. Neighbors live next door to one another, but with more breathing room than the compression of a suburb. The high school kids are anomalies. He's read about them in the wildlife journals of gossip, observed them in their natural habitats, but only recently has encountered them face to face. They sit in the back of a bus in a cloister.

Alex is confident he will do fine in high school. Most of the time, he listens to his music and keeps his business to himself. His father warns him about the high schoolers, too—they do things that are frowned upon in the McGregor household, most often recounted to Alex as his father lights up a cigarette.

Alex stations himself near the middle of the bus, listening to his music, gazing out the window. Perhaps he will lose some of his excess weight, and become a social butterfly. Maybe his parents will fix their marital issues. Perhaps he'll fail, and the entire world on his shoulders will crash down like a space-bound submarine falling back to earth.

"Alex!"

Alex pretends not to hear. He knows, from his clinical observations, which freshman is attempting to seize his attention. The scientifically named *Kenny Locke* should only be engaged if one wishes to experience a more interesting bus ride than simple songs.

"Alex McGrugger!"

Alex laughs, and his bubble is shattered. Kenny is a connoisseur of inappropriateness, and the textbook example of his father's misplaced fear, in a convenient package of medium build. His hair is lengthier than Alex's, housed neatly under a green skater's cap.

"I know you can hear me, dammit! Take your earphones out and talk to me!"

The kids sitting nearest to Alex laugh. Alex relents and pivots around in his seat. Kenny's eyes hold a friendly combination of mischief and cordiality. For his academic shortcomings, Kenny excels in personality. Alex wasn't born with such apprehension; it's something he's learned.

In the seat across from Kenny sits a fellow freshman named Leigh Meyers. Her brown hair runs down to just below her shoulders, framing her face and accenting her electric blue eyes from any distance. She's effortlessly pretty. Alex remembers on the first day of sixth grade trying to find the bus at the back of the middle school for the first time. After debating whether to miss the bus or talk to her, he'd walked up to her and asked her if he'd found the right place. She'd smiled at him and confirmed his directions. Since then, they've talked infrequently. He doesn't consider many people friends.

Deciding to comply, he removes his buds and asks, "What do you want, Kenny?"

"Let me see your schedule!"

"What?"

Snickers come from the back of the bus. "Are you deaf or something?"

Alex already has his backpack open. "No!"

"Then let me see your schedule, dammit!"

Reaching into the pocket on his bag, Alex pulls out the folded sheet of paper listing his classes. Alex enjoys school to the point where he can completely discard everything related to his education at a moment's notice. He doesn't laugh as much as the other kids, and he doesn't mind talking to his teachers. He is conducive to interaction in a different way: quiet, benevolent, never threatening. If he has a problem, he either pushes it down or talks through a solution.

Kenny walks up and snatches the schedule from Alex, parading to the back of the bus. Alex listens as Kenny and Leigh sprout off comments about teachers and classes they've survived. Such is the role of the older students in high school: to pave the way for those yet to come without failing. Alex looks around as the two older kids soundtrack his ears. He sees Peter Morgan, the Sophomore, with his own I-Pod in at the back; Sam Edwards, the girl who lived up the street, with her mystery novel, all representatives of a mold he can potentially try to fit. He tries, and he talks, and he listens, but even after Kenny and Leigh are done with the schedule and hand it back to him, he puts his ear buds back in place and considers the miracles of modern medicine.

His father will be waiting for him when he gets home.

Rumors around his family are that his mother will have to go back to work at the New Life facility in Quakertown; Alex taps into the secret feeds of the adults. The whispers and the messages do not escape the ears of Alex. Life means not to reveal itself to people in shouts and declarations, but instead in the vitality hidden to the casual senses.

When Alex's mother is either upset or angry, he avoids talking to her. The way Leigh says hello to him sometimes makes him feel better if he's having a bad day. Kenny's jokes thin the density of the air when Alex's skies darken.

Alex feels as if the world is a big tapestry, with only a few hands painting the canvas. As the bus pulls onto his road, barreling down the steep hill past the home of the retired science teachers with their swans and the small lake, Alex feels as if the path he walks on in life is going to divert, just as his mp3 player shifts into "In the Air Tonight" by Phil Collins.

He exits the bus with the schedule the kids inspected clutched in his hand. He doesn't wave.

————

The masks are strange.

Quarantine is not a comforting word to Alex. His father is mostly restricted to the back of the house for his waking hours. When he ventures out, he has to wear a medical mask whose foreign design provides protection from airborne disease. Alex doesn't know how to say the full name of the disease they think his father has, so he just calls it TB. Anytime he tries to spell 'tuberculosis', he always puts a 'u' where the 'e' should be, just like when Michael coughs, his body puts blood mixed with mucus where there should be pure phlegm.

Lauren and Michael are losing money. The disease is forcing

Michael to operate from his dining room office with shorter hours. The routine is shattered, and among the pieces, with a Cheshire grin, sits the bloated cat known as fear. Lauren knows nobody else can see the creature. The animal must have crashed through the skylight in the middle of the hearth room, plummeting from the black shingles of the McGregor roof to the floor. She tries to keep the animal away, but the hidden nature of the disease permeating the bleb inside her husband's chest hinges on a phone call from Dr. Fost. She wears the mask and avoids looking in the mirror as much as possible. She walks around the house as if she is paddling a boat, sloshing at her ankles with the ripples from each stroke she cuts through the river of uncertainty.

Alex walks through the front door as his father, mask and all, sits at the table in the dining room, absorbed by his computer. Michael coughs as Alex sets his heavy bag down next to the chairs in the hearth room. Walking over to his father, Alex stands on the edge of the mat placed on the floor to protect the carpet from the wheels of the chairs.

"Hey, Alex." Michael stifles another cough.

"Hey, Dad. Did we hear from the doctor yet?"

"No, Dr. Fost hasn't called. I don't really expect him to until tomorrow, at least."

"It's been over a week since the bronchoscopy, right?"

"Yeah."

"Aren't you supposed to be quarantined?'

Michael wheezes a laugh.

"Yeah, I guess I am. I have to keep working, though; none of the other guys have what could be TB." Michael shifts back towards the computer.

"Why do they think it's TB?"

"Well, the symptoms, plus the cells they scraped off the part of my lung, all pretty much point one way. It could be something else; they don't have 100% certainty yet."

"I wish we could know one way or the other, that's all."

"I know, Alex. So do I. So does your mother."

Lauren shifts in from the kitchen, a soft smile on her face. Alex notices the stubs of her fingernails are jagged. She's wearing a plain tee shirt, her hair naturally tussled.

"Hi, mom."

"Hey. How was school?"

Alex's mind relaxes. He won't be gaining much more vital information from this conversation; everything seems stable.

"It was alright. Neil wanted to know if I could go to his house later, we have this science project to deal with."

"Is Mrs. Pock alright with it?"

"Yeah, as far as I know."

"And what about Mr. Pock?"

"Mom, I have no idea. He asked me at school."

Lauren places her hand on her son's shoulder, as if to steady herself.

"I don't think you should be going over there with this whole TB business going on."

"What?" Michael looks up from his laptop, accompanied by a cough.

"You might be contagious, Mike. We don't want to be going and infecting Alex's friends."

"I wouldn't be going down there with him, I'd be staying here working. We sent him to school, so I don't see why he can't go down the street."

"What if the Pocks get sick? We'd be blamed for starting a practical epidemic because we didn't listen to the quarantine order! You should be in bed." Lauren's smile has evaporated like water tossed on top of the wood stove in the hearth room.

"Lauren, you can't just keep the kid all bottled up. We can't live in fear."

The Cheshire cat, in its malignant manifestation, growls hungrily at the mention of its name. Lauren ignores it, even as it sits perched above her husband's head, using him as a pillow.

"Mike, I just think it's a bad idea."

"He needs to get his work done."

Alex's hands are sweating. "I think I can get it done without having to go down there."

Michael's voice and coughing increase in tandem. Balled up paper towels frame his workspace.

"I think he should be able to go down there and work on it. It's literally two minutes down the street."

"Mike, you're sick."

"It's nothing worse than when I dealt with that walking pneumonia back in 2003." At the end of his sentence, Michael rasps another cough. A warm substance hits the inside of his mouth.

"Tuberculosis is a big deal, Mike. This isn't some common cold you can just shove away."

Michael rises from his chair, walking across the floor to the bathroom around the corner, adjacent to Alex's room. Walking in, he removes the mask, and spits the bloody sputum into the sink. The pink tinge has deepened in color. Coughing again, he turns the small faucet on. He spits once more, and the projectile lands in the already corrupted stream of water, whisking down the bowl of the sink and into the drain. Michael dimly notes Alex's toothbrush in the corner, staring at him with the same blank expression as is on his son's face in the dining room.

The phone rings.

Michael puts the mask on and walks back into the dining room. He meets Alex's eyes for a moment, and Michael feels a stab of pain.

Lauren moves in from the kitchen, listening intently.

"Yes, Dr. Fost, this is Lauren McGregor."

Michael picks up a tissue from his desk, and he wipes the excess blood and spittle from his chin. It appears on the fabric like a miniature murder scene.

7
September 20, 2009

One of Michael McGregor's best friends had been a man named Thomas Rosenbaum. Thomas had been almost fourteen years older than Mike, but the two had been friends for over 30 years at the time of Thomas's passing. He had been soft-spoken, a man who made up for his lack of finances in the wealth of his compassion. Thomas, or Thom, as his friends knew him, had never left Willow Grove. That's where he had raised his only son, Barry, and where his wife, Nancy, had left him when she fled off the face of the planet with the tandem of a spiraling addiction to painkillers and another man named Victor. Thom raised his son as a single father into a man of quality any pair of adults would've been proud to call their own, while working two jobs, in a house he financed himself.

Michael had been married his high school sweetheart, Rachel Maria Edwards, and had gotten her pregnant when they were both 16. They ended up marrying when both of them were 20, a childless couple.

Thom was the best man at Michael's first wedding. After seven years of Rachel becoming addicted to the same vein of drugs which had stolen Thom's wife, Thom told Michael to ditch her before she wrecked Michael like a drunken teenager in a sports car. Between best friends, there is a mindset and a protection which exists far beyond the scope of logic. Six weeks following the divorce, Rachel Maria Edwards tried to sell an undercover police officer a package of the most potent cocaine in the history of Willow Grove. She became famous for creating one of the largest drug busts in the history of her county, and she fell off the face of the planet.

Michael started relying on Thom after Eve moved away. Sister Eve is a woman as strong willed as her biological mother and as benevolent as Harlan. She had caused quite an argument at their biological mother's funeral, and Michael, who had housed his biological mother and cared for her in her dying days, ejected Eve in front of all in attendance. It had taken Eve over 15 years since the woman's death to acknowledge that a part of the woman had been worth a service.

Their mom had given Eve her blonde hair and blue eyes, the angular face, medium build, and the light freckles adorning her California trimmed skin. Harlan bequeathed to her his personality, his movements, and his musical taste. Such is the reason for Eve and Michael's silence over seven years—the classic battle between their biological mother and Harlan lives on.

The argument which split Eve and Michael was over a trivial matter. Michael's heart absorbs every shot fired at him. Every communication runs a direct line to his conscience. They had screamed at each other. She had been in from California to visit, probably for either an anniversary or birthday. The words flying had been words of calamity, bringing up the alcohol, the fighting, and the darkness of a past that still lies in the house Harlan calls home. Michael never understands why Eve moved to California, and Eve never understands why Michael stayed. The apocalyptic argument hides now underneath a set of stairs somewhere in a house.

Thom had told Michael to wait, to let her come back on her own. Thom had seen the pain in his friend's face. Whenever Michael was in pain, he'd travel over to Thom's small house, and talk amidst the reruns on TV and the small air conditioner poking into the living room like a burglar through the window. Michael was convinced to follow Thom's advice, waiting for Eve to come home, rejecting the cards she sent. If she wanted a relationship with her nephew, she would have to come through him.

"Just because the two of you don't talk don't mean the two of them shouldn't." Thom would say as he lit a cigarette, the sparks bouncing off his dark skin.

"Thom, I don't get it. What is so hard about her contacting me, making this kind of stuff right?"

"People aren't put here to be understood, Mike." Thom's house had featured a brick fireplace among its five rooms. Thom would toss in the cigarette buds, brush the residue off his tan overcoat, and walk to the fridge to grab something to eat from the night before.

"Understand this much about your sister, my friend." Thom would say as he reached into the fridge. "Actually, understand it about your entire goddamn family. You McGregors have a lot of pain in this town."

"I know." Michael would look across the small path. Mike wondered what would happen if he moved his entire family across the street to live in proximity to this man, who had inspired and aided him when either his father was too busy or his sister was nowhere to be found.

"I know Eve. I've known her, you, your dad, your mom, all of them, since you were still singing those love songs in the 70's like some white version of Stevie Wonder."

Michael would smile and enjoy a laugh of freedom.

"At least you weren't blind in that way, though. Some others, like with that Rachel Edwards bitch you got hitched to, that made me second guess."

"Hey now," Mike said, bumming his cigarette on the concrete outside the door. "We all make mistakes. Some just stick with us longer than we'd like."

"Admit it," Thom replied, walking back out onto the porch, two Fillets o' Fish from the local McDonalds wrapped in his hands. "You want to talk to her."

Michael sighed. "Yeah, I guess I do, but ..."

"But what?"

"I don't know if I'm at a point where I want to do that, with the way my life is."

Thom stopped halfway through unwrapping his sandwich. "Bullshit."

"How is that bullshit?"

"Because," Thom would say, his intense eyes looking at Michael with guidance and experience, the dark complexion of his skin contrasting with the whiteness of his shirt but still falling in line with the tan jacket.

"You love your sister. You miss her to death, and you feel bad for your parents that you two can't stand in the same room without digging up things, or people, who've been dead for twenty years."

"Maybe they aren't buried that well." Mike said, lighting up.

"They're not. You know it, I know it, your dad knows it, your mom knows it, and Eve sure as hell knows it." Thom bit the sandwich. Ketchup splattered onto the ground, from the wound on the bread.

"Let me tell you something, Mike." Thom swallowed.

"Some shit you can bury, some of it you can push down, some of it you can run from. Some men run from it their entire lives, trying to go faster and faster or wait 'til it just falls away from them, as if it's gonna die. But it can't die, because it's a part of you. It's what made you who you are. So you and Eve are gonna have this conflict, this pain that comes from whatever your mama or daddy did when you were kids, whatever you left back on Wales road in 1970-whenever. Let me tell you, Mike, you can't outrun parts of yourself. You can't do it. You can jump states, jump countries, kill people, hell, you can even try to snuff that part of yourself with things like money, or sex, or drugs, or stamp collections, or even stupid shit like smoking a pack of cigs till your lungs fall out, but you will never get enough."

Thom folded the wrapper, tossing it aside.

"The only way to get true happiness in this life, the only way to do it, is through the people you love and those who love you. Look at this shithole," Thom stood up, gesturing to the house behind him.

"I don't have anything special. Yeah, I've had a job, and I've earned my money well. But I ain't no millionaire. I don't have a heaven here at the moment. But I've got a kid who I've given a good head through hard work. I have the ability to sit here and yell at you when you're acting like an asshole. I have grandkids from that same son who I spoil completely rotten, and, on top of that, I have the ability to sit down and night and know I ain't gonna go to bed with a regret for what I have done. I'm sixty, man. You're forty, forty one? Shit."

Thom walked over, and slapped Michael on the back.

"You ain't gonna be happy 'til you get Eve back in your life. That's your sister, she's the only one you got."

Mike looked up at him, taking in the words slowly, partitioning them as to not overload his senses.

"I've got you, too. You're close enough to family."

Thom grimaced in false pain.

"Mike, you're white. I'm black. Nobody would ever believe that you and I are from the same parents, especially when yours are both white as printer paper."

Mike thought for a moment.

"You know who would believe it?"

Thom sighed, standing at the threshold to the house.

"Who?"

Mike stood up, walking inside through the open door.

"Stevie fucking Wonder."

Thom laughed, a deep, hearty sound; a bass well tuned.

"Now that was just mean. You're a mean man, Mike. Maybe that's why Eve left you for California."

"Yeah, right."

Thom stopped him short of the door, and looked at him straight in the eyes.

"If you don't do it for you," Thom said. "Do it for your kid. He needs to know her."

"I know."

"Listen to me, let me tell you, as a single parent, there's one lesson I learned," Thom stood abreast of Michael, and pointed to the cautious light of the afternoon.

"To you, he may be the sun, but to those other people out there," Thom gestured to the hedges and the neighborhood.

"He's just some small little star out there in the sky, a million miles away. So you had better make him feel like he's the only son you've got, because he is. And he was given to you as a gift. You almost lost him once. He needs to have every opportunity to succeed. But I know you, Michael." Thom smiled, the wrapper from the sandwich pressed on Michael's chest.

"I know your kid, too. And I'm gonna tell you something. No matter what happens, Alex is gonna be ok. He's gonna make it."

"I'll make sure he is." Michael said, iron in his eyes.

"You'd better, or I'll haunt your ass. It don't matter if I'm alive, or dead, or in some retirement home with Alzheimer's like how my own daddy died, I'll tape a goddamn sticky note to the wall wherever it is I sleep to remind me. If I forget every other thing in the entire world besides my own family, I will remember to come and kick your ass when I wake up the next morning."

Thom developed emphysema in 2004, coupled with a crippling staph infection in 2005 that never healed. Mike remembered coming to meet him at the care facility, watching his old friend wither away from a disease no amount of heart or resolve could overcome. The very lungs with which Thom had spoken inspirational words became his downfall. For the last three months of his life, he was stuck on a ventilator. Michael had been the friend who helped him cleanse himself after using the restroom, who had aided him in dressing himself in return for every thread Thom had sewn into Michael's life.

The sound of the ventilator haunts Michael, the pulse of automatic respiration. It had taken the proudest man Michael's ever seen, the brother beyond all limits of biology, and turned him into nothing but a breath count until he passed. Only the machine remains.

Michael McGregor stares at Dr. Richard Fost.

"I'm sorry?" Michael says. Lauren sits in the same chair she used during the previous visit, flanking him. Dr. Fost reads from a chart.

"The surgery might require for you to be on a ventilator. We're talking about removing part of a lung here, Mike. It's a little more risky than the bronchoscopy."

"Well," Michael wets his lips. "At least it isn't tuberculosis.

How do you pronounce it again?"

"Mycobacterium Avium-Intracellulare infection." Fost reads the words from the assortment of paper. He holds the results of the bronchoscopy, the initial chest x-ray, and a bevy of other tests as if they are scripture.

Lauren stares at the floor, her hands folded in her lap. Occasionally, she glances up to meet either Fost or Michael's eyes. Pieces of advice flit from her mind to her teeth, bouncing off and ricocheting back down her throat.

"I'll just call it MAI, to keep things simpler." Fost continues.

"Like I said, you have two treatment options. First, we thought it was tuberculosis because the symptoms of MAI and TB are extremely similar. However, there are some major differences between them. Now, while the cells are showing a nearly flawless indication of MAI, we cannot yet rule out other diseases. The only way to be 100% certain would be to go into you lung and remove the mass. That would require the lung biopsy I mentioned earlier, and would require you, potentially, to be on a ventilator. That's the only surefire way to define your illness. The other option is a salvo of drugs that we can give you to treat this disease." Fost changes his document order like a coordinator on the sideline of a professional sports game.

"The only issues with those are that they have some detrimental side effects."

"Such as what?" Michael asks.

"Fatigue, generally. It saps the energy out of you."

"How long would I have to take these drugs?"

Fost sets the clipboard down.

"Anywhere from twelve to eighteen months."

Lauren looks up quickly. "Really?"

Fost nods.

"Yes. Again, we will continuously monitor your developments from here if you choose the medicinal route. If you choose the surgery route, which will allow us to reach a concrete conclusion, albeit at a more immediate risk, then it might be different. In the end, it is up to the two of you. Personally, I recommend the surgical option."

Lauren clicks her feet on the floor softly. "What other diseases could it be?"

Fost coughs. "There is a very, very slim chance of cancer cells being present."

Lauren freezes. She sees Michael looking at the ground. His eyes are taking the floor apart and putting it back together, tile by tile. The Cheshire cat of fear perches directly under him, grinning at her with its cold, iris-absent eyes. Fear and Hurt stare at her from that big, dumb animal.

Michael finally speaks. "I don't want to be on a ventilator."

Lauren shakes her head, and the cat is gone. "What?"

Michael's eyes are the shots of a flare gun on a distant shore. "I'm going to go the medicinal route."

Lauren digs her nails into the plastic of her chair. There's the man she fought with, loved, argued with, and made love with for 18 years. The father of her child, the man she gave herself to utterly and wholly. He's electing to deny the opportunity of surgery and instead use drugs to fight the illness. *Cancer?* The mouth of the Cheshire cat grins at her with death on its lips like a balm.

"What possibility is there that it could be cancer?" Lauren asks Fost.

"Lauren," Michael interjects, wiping his face with his hands. "It's not cancer. They'd be able to see it."

Fost selects his words carefully, a tailor mending at gunpoint.

"We cannot rule out that it might be cancer, but we're almost positive that it's MAI. If you choose the drugs, we'll monitor your treatment, if you choose the surgery, we remove the bleb, and we eventually remove part of the lung."

Michael and Lauren's eyes talk.

Why? her hazels ask.

Everything will be ok, Michael's blues reply.

"The medication, then?" Fost takes the pen from the top of his clipboard.

Michael turns to him like a soldier approaching the front of a phalanx.

"Yes."

Silence leaks into the room, a clear and odorless liquid clogging their lungs.

"Alright." Fost says, pushing his chair over to the granite desk in the corner.

"I am going to refer you to a pulmonologist named Dr. Nicholson. He runs a practice in Doylestown, and he will be able to specialize in this area past my expertise. That's not to say I'm abandoning you. I'll still be monitoring you and keeping an eye on all that goes on, but the specialists are the specialists." His keyboard clicks as Fost makes adjustments.

Lauren's skin is cold. She looks away and back to Michael, examining the coolness of his dark blue polo, the ruggedness of the facial hair he hasn't shaved in the past few days.

Fost stands. He offers his hand to Michael. The two shake.

"Best of luck, my friend."

"Thank you." Michael replies.

Thom's ventilator thumps in the silence.

The cat under the table smiles at Lauren.

Back at home in Coopersburg, Alex is fine.

8
November 2, 2009

The naming of his father's disease comes as a relief to Alex. He is the Fixer; his biggest job yet will be helping his father recover. His parents aren't fighting, so for the moment, they are Fixed. His grades are perfect, so they're Fixed. If he's broken, though, who will Fix him? His friend Zach has just come out as gay, which splintered Alex's group of amigos, due to the fact his two other friends, Louis and Neil, do not exactly approve of Zach's decision. That can be Fixed. All of it can be Fixed, he just needs enough time, just like his dad's medication. Alex Fixes things differently.

The past month has been one of doctors' visits, and other various occurrences geared towards Fixing the biggest problem Alex has ever seen: his father and his illness. Alex started feeling it; what if it can't be Fixed? What if his dad remains on drugs for the rest of his life? What if his group of friends splits up forever? What if he cannot contain this weight, and his grades start slipping?

Last Thursday, he had walked down the stairs and heard the tension in his parents' voices.

"I don't want to take the drugs all the time." Michael said. "They make me feel like shit, ok, Lauren?"

"And I'm going to work now, Mike." Lauren's been working at the New Life facility in Quakertown, an assisted living center. Michael is now only able to go into the office a couple of days per week. Nobody wanted to make dinner.

"We have a child to feed, Lauren." Michael said, barely noticing Alex standing on the stairs.

"I know that."

Silence again leaked through the crevices from the outside.

"Why don't you just get surgery, Mike?"

"I've told you, Lauren. I've been on these drugs for over a month. We're starting to see progress in the right direction. I don't need to risk myself on that ventilator. Thom's son is now grown up, and his kids don't have a grandfather. We don't need to take unnecessary risks like that. Yes, the drugs suck, yes, we have to work more, but we'll buckle down and get through it!" Michael chucked the remote he had been holding down on the couch.

"What if its cancer, Mike?" Lauren asked.

"Oh for Christ's sake." Mike said, rolling his eyes. His bare feet hit the floor, making a soft pad on the carpet.

"I don't want to see us end up being wrong, Mike. We should opt for the surgery, Call Dr. Fost and Dr. Nicholson, and just be done with it! We don't need to do this for 6 months."

"First of all, it's my body, not yours, so it isn't 'our' decision. Secondly, it might not even take six months, Lauren." Michael said. He had been eating a bowl of soup. Dinner was supposed to be for the entire family.

"And what if it takes the 18?" Lauren asked.

"Then it takes the 18, Lauren. It takes the 18, and we deal with it."

"Why won't you use the ventilator?"

Mike sighed and put the spoon down. Drops of soup splatter his desk.

"Are you trying to start a fight, Lauren?"

"No, I want to make sure you're safe."

"I saw my best friend lose his pride on one of those ventilators. I saw him waste away, from being a much stronger man than I am, to being nothing at all. You know exactly how it feels to lose somebody like that, Lauren. I don't ask you to go out and buy a fucking Escalade and drive it if your car broke down, because I know that's what your brother killed himself with."

Alex grew cold.

Lauren flinches.

"Now, see? That's what it feels like if I were to go on that ventilator. I might get on that, never get off of it, and then our kid gets to grow up without a fucking father." Michael stands up, pushing his tray aside. Lauren tracked him as he walked over to the television.

Michael throws up his hands.

"What the fuck do you want me to say?"

"I just want what is best for all of us." Lauren managed, the concern going out of her voice. Tears formed at the base of her eyes.

"So do I, so let's stop talking about this ventilator bullshit."

"But you might not even have to go on the ventilator!"

"And if I do, then I might die."

"Where are you getting that?"

"You know exactly where I'm getting that."

Alex thought about jumping in, but instead, he turned around and went to his room. Usually, he would have been directly in the thick of it, a net over which tennis balls of curse words and thoughts would sail. Some occasionally shoot towards his ears. His father's usually docile and polite tone shifts and becomes riddled with harsh words, changing from intellectual into the street vernacular.

On one occurrence, Alex had heard his father toss touchy words such as 'separation' and 'divorce' into the conversation. What did they mean? To Alex, they meant his entire world as he knew it would be prepared and shot as if propelled by a giant pool cue into some other dimension.

Lauren's parents had stayed together; they lived in a small home in Bethlehem up until Alex's grandfather's death back in 2005. Michael had told him how Lauren's father had tried to commit suicide when Lauren had been 11 or 12. Death had chosen not to take him, and instead took Alex's Uncle Jim thirty years later. Death's potential victim this time is his parents' marriage. With the way in which those two argued, Alex wondered if part of them wasn't somehow already dead, masquerading to keep him happy like a puppet on the strings of God. Alex feels older than his 13 years.

As he walked into his room, closing the door behind him, he heard the words from the walls seep through the wood. His father's sick. Mom's working again. There was still no dinner on the table, and it was almost 7:30. For some reason, the Fixer was down, so hopefully the entire fabric would hold together for a night.

Alex looked around the room, which had held him for nearly as long as he could remember. When he had been a child, he had slept in a room further down the hallway in a crib; now he felt almost like an infant again. Sitting on his bed, with a blanket draped of powdery blue, Alex questioned the viability of his potential repairs. His father had always told him how Alex is going to change history. No more division among the family, nothing but wholeness and stability.

Alex heard him cursing again from the living room. The drugs. The pain. The blood Alex had seen him trying to hide.

God needs to upgrade to FIOS or something before the Fixer loses his edge.

Alex walked over to the desk and picked up one of the little notebooks. Alex's father had written music when he was younger, so when Alex told him of his interest, Michael showed boundless encouragement. Alex hasn't shared these songs with anybody, with their pages starting to crumple slightly due to use. Alex's handwriting is famously terrible. He hears the adults carry on from the other room. If there's anything he keeps, if all else fails, it will always be writing.

And so Alex McGregor writes, never letting any of them see those words.

He's fine.

9
March 20, 2010

Six months have come, and six months have passed for the McGregors.

Each morning, Michael is no longer able to easily go to work. He has to get up and take three pills. He coughs up red blood, and sends red pills down in its place. The whiteness of mucus gave way to the snow of Winter, which now melts into Spring. Energy is a precious commodity for Michael. As the drugs heal Michael's lung, they harm his spirit.

Michael wakes up in the morning and looks at the curtains blocking his view of the street. They allow sunlight inside, but he can't see the trees in the middle of the yard or the lush of the blooming flowers. The same maroon blanket has covered this bed for the past ten years. From his vantage point, whenever he wakes, ready to take the three pills waiting for him, it does not seem as if he's reaching a solution. The cure waits just around the corner, Dr. Nicholson promises. Dr. Fost's sentiments towards recovery are the same phrases reworded, with determination towards correcting the illness resting in the methods prescribed. The three pills make their home on a small wooden table next to his bed. He feels as though he's a doll in a dollhouse, invisible fingers controlling his operation.

The first pill is called the Past. When Michael swallows the Past, it tastes like the smell of alcohol; it does not carry a remedy for relieving pain, but a placebo. As he swallows the Past, it reminds him of the aspects of life that have delivered him to his situation. A freeze frame of his sister swaying in the winds of the far west lands. His mother's tombstone, lurking in some cemetery reached by directions he can't recall. Past is best absorbed with a shot of Pity, so he drinks those waters down as a chaser. His mother had loved alcohol; his father loved his kids. His stepmother can't save him now. The Past goes down his throat, threatening to lodge in residence and restrict his airways. Thom's ventilator sputters on from the edges of his eyes, clogged with the still sleeping tears nestling behind their lids.

The second pill is jagged and pointed. Its name is Pain. It's the feeling that occasionally comes with the cough from the lung containing the bleb, the spot where the enemy roots in his system. The fire which turns the memories of his wedding day into embers instead of roses, clumped up with returning shadows of distrust and cursing. The look in Alex's eyes when Michael asks him about his day, knowing it's about to get worse. For the past six months, this little pill has become part of the daily routine.

Cynthia used to say, "If you're living, you've got problems." Being alive in and of itself is now a problem. The little pill takes a slippery slide down Michael's gullet, joining the Past to line his stomach.

Finally, the last pill is a misanthrope of medicine. It is uncomfortable, and Michael can barely seem to squeeze it between his fingers enough to reach his tongue. Its complexion is hairy, disgusting to the senses. It is alien, different, and vile. Its name is Fear. Fear joins Pain and the Past as the drugs Michael consumes every morning, and it can fall out of his mouth at any moment, no matter how many shots of Pity or Pride he uses to drown the pill.

What if the lung bursts?

What if he gets divorced?

What if this takes 18 months?

What if this is hurting Alex?

What if he never gets better?

Michael tries to swallow, but the pill skirts around the entrance to his throat, refusing to take the plunge.

What if it's cancer?

What if the surgery is the only route to take?

What if Lauren needs me?

What if I'm a terrible father?

What if I'm turning into my mother?

The pill sticks in the refuge of his mouth. It is the moment of trepidation when, each time he swallows his prescriptions, the feeling of routine breeds malevolence. Instead of healing, it feeds numbness, boredom, and loneliness.

Michael checks the small calendar on the fridge in the kitchen after he shuffles out of the bedroom. Instead of a month at the top of the calendar, four letters stare back at him.

LOST

He writes down the medicinal names in small, timid script. Each block on the calendar is not a number, but instead the symbol for infinity. Michael tries to turn the pages to see a different month, but the days only repeat. Six months of pages have turned. Another opportunity lost, another memory abandoned, another moment murdered.

His fingers trace the stenciled words on the boxes of days: Lauren's therapy appointments, Alex's extracurricular activities. The accomplishments leave a slight residue of lead on his fingers. His own sessions with Jack Hammond hide under the long, complicated names of the medications.

He and Lauren had found each other, and now neither

of them can locate themselves. A union once so beautiful, so brilliant, now relies on two people as distant as strangers. They no longer fight for each other, but for who the pictures on the walls house in their frames.

On his way back to the bedroom, Michael examines the photographs, with the pills in his stomach, the infection in his lungs, and the scarred tissue of his heart. He cries. He sobs for Lauren's reclusion, for the hours of clockwork arguments that have only increased in frequency. These tears can't pay for their debts.

Alex lives through every stupid fight, listens to every curse and every silence more offensive than words; even he cannot elicit the dormant glow of the people in the pictures.

The future had been the light shining through the curtains next to Michael's bed, dancing on the family's eyes. The curtains had been the years to come, promising happiness, love, joy, and peace. Michael's face in the picture, of solely he and his new wife, speaks: the light was something beautiful, and the sun would bring them daily miracles. Sometimes, Michael walks back into the bedroom, and he opens up those white curtains to see what it looks like outside on a given day, to see the source of the light, to receive the greatness promised to him.

He opens the window, and the cruel arsonists of disease, medicine, and Father Time have set his world ablaze.

Lauren's at work, Alex is at school.

He is alone. So is his wife.

Michael recently found one of Alex's lyric pads, seeing the unruly handwriting partitioned into beautifully pained phrases. Michael expresses his pain through Jack Hammond; Alex expresses his through writing. Michael has taken risks before. He had taken a risk with his first wife. He had another relationship in his late twenties, which failed. Lauren was supposed to be his adult relationship, his salvation. Now she's turning into the past tense. A majestic structure doesn't rest upon a shifting foundation. The wedding picture will be nothing but kindling stored in a drawer.

Michael grabs the golden framed picture from the wall, gazing down at he and his wife, her white dress accenting her features with threads of hope and youth, her eyes looking into the camera at a future glowing with auspicial essences of wedding vows.

Michael walks over to the bathroom adjoining his and Lauren's room. A mirror hangs over the sink. Michael stares. His eyes have hollowed since his picture taking days. He has seen the fire, the source of the light poking through the curtains every morning; this man has felt the heat burn his skin, seen the hurt inherited in the eyes of his only son. They've taught Alex how to be broken.

The frame of his life has been crippled and torn from a pristine condition. Michael sees in the reflection every single aspiration he could have realized, every second he could have spent, flushed down his throat as if swallowed by a sinkhole.

Michael rockets the picture down onto the floor of the bathroom. It strikes tile in-between the two blue carpets adorning the crisp white floor. The glass pane shatters and the back of the frame ejects, the black plastic free from the touch of the hypothetical and tossed into reality.

Michael bends down, turning over the projectile. There they remain, smiling, the bits of the glass panel lying protectively over the photograph. The picture is fine, but any observer can tell the frame is shattered, the edges are bent, and the faces are fading.

Somewhere, a ventilator hums.

10
May 19, 2010

May 19, 2010, started as any other day for Alex.

School is ending for the year; high school seems to lurk around the corner of every hallway. Another straight A year in the books, and the grades are above average, too. Everything will smoothly transition into high school. It's less than a month until middle school graduation, something Alex is looking forward to with all the joy he can muster underneath the blanket of sleep. He does not check his calendar today. Alex does not mark down that May 19, 2010, is special. He does not think to hold onto every hello he gets today, whether it be from Leigh on the bus or from Lou in homeroom or Neil in Geometry or Mrs. Cronkite in English. He desires only for his father to heal.

In a way, God grants his wish today.

At the end of the school day, Alex gets off the bus. He doesn't have a lot of homework, just final projects to complete. It's Wednesday. "Hump day," as Harlan would say. Alex likes talking to Harlan; he imagines the man as an older version of himself.

Why not an older version of Dad?

Harlan doesn't have to take pills; Harlan isn't on medication. Grandma isn't called a whore by Grandpa, or a motherfucker by Grandpa, and Grandma doesn't work a job because Grandpa can't work because it's a marathon for him to walk in the morning. Grandma's brother didn't commit suicide. Grandpa had never threatened to divorce Grandma over the fact Grandma didn't want to sell the house back in 2003, and then Grandpa has most certainly never had a breakdown when he discovered Grandma was using emergency money to pay credit card debt. They do not need Fixing.

Grandma and Grandpa tell each other they love each other.

Up until May 19, 2010, Alex is Fixed. Nothing, no matter what happens, will change the fact Alex is fine. He is certifiably fine, as far as his friends can tell, as far as his teachers can tell, as far as President Obama can tell, and as far as God himself can tell. Alex is the one who was going to come out unquestionably, undeniably fine. His father always reminds him how he is being raised differently than his parents, and how he is going to break some 'cycle' of warped childhood experiences by simply being less fucked up than his ancestors.

There will be no happy memories from May 19th.

Michael worked from home today, doing his best to keep up with paperwork and transactions. He greets Alex when Alex comes home, with the same corrupted air of sickness. Alex says hello to his father and sets his bag down on the empty chair. One day, the drugs will be gone. Mom and Dad will stop fighting. The dream promised to him will come to fruition, and everything will be fine. He lies awake at night and imagines such a future, painting a picture with mental watercolors.

When Mom walks in the door at 6:43, everything is fine.

The dinner call comes at 7:19: spaghetti and meatballs, made by Mom; the food's great. The absolute silence at the dinner table is peaceful. The way Roxy hides in her house is peachy, peachier than the peaches used in the small salads Dad used to make with dinner. More floor space under the table.

When Alex goes to his computer to talk to friends online at around 7:33, all is calm.

When he puts his earphones on at the computer, and listens to Green Day's *American Idiot*, it's fine. He's going to see Green Day in August. All three of them are. They bought the tickets in April. That's fine, that's Fixed, that's just absolutely *dandy*.

When Dad walks into the kitchen at 8:23 with a trash bag full of papers, while Mom sits at the table, and Dad dumps them all over the island and whips the bag to the floor, everything is still fine.

Two opposing forces have been gathering across an open field for months, with everything Alex holds dear spread out in the distance between them; their boots are strapped, their guns loaded, their gazes metallic. They both fight for the same cause, which sits only attainable via eradication. Silence hangs in the air with anticipation, breaking gravity, forgetting any future, ready to make history.

They need the Fixer.

"Where did you put it?" Michael asks. His voice drips with agitation. The past month, he's been incubating in the nurturing atmosphere of silence. Sleeping alone at night, he's used the space to charge his anger. Their eyes lock across the kitchen.

"Put what?" Lauren's voice is like a shield. She puts her book down on the table, where it flutters peacefully to rest.

"The letter from Nicholson. The report from my doctor." Michael gestures to the cluster of papers that now dot the kitchen counter, bodies taking cover in the wide-open space.

"I didn't put all those papers in there, Mike." Lauren says.

"Fuck you." Michael hisses.

Lauren stares.

"You were cleaning off the island earlier today." Lauren feels it coming. 19 years.

"Yeah, because you had covered it with so much shit I

couldn't even see the countertop. This house is a mess."

"I'm sorry, I've been working too much to clean it."

"Working too much?" Michael's tone rises.

The battalions shift in their ranks; the soldiers peer across the field. The letters tremble with resonating fear.

"I'm sorry that I have to take these pills, Lauren. I'm sorry that I can't just work the day away anymore, only to come home and deal with another pile of shit left everywhere just to piss me off." Michael casts some of the papers onto the floor. They skate across the wood of the kitchen, trying to run.

Alex's headphones are off.

"Now, where did you put it?"

"Put what?"

"WHERE DID YOU PUT THE LETTER FROM NICHOLSON?"

Alex's heart skips familiarly.

The soldiers' grips tighten on their rifles. Their breaths are as frigid as the loneliness felt in a room where the most important person in a life is now an obstacle.

Dr. Nicholson had sent Michael a report earlier in the week. Michael had placed the letter next to his bed, and forgotten.

The bitch is hiding it from him, another trick.

"This is the exact same thing you did to me back in 2003."

Atop a hill overlooking the field, Alex can see the waiting armies.

He kept a running tally in his head, waiting to see which years they're traveling back to during each argument. 2003, as Alex likes to call it, finds explicit use in situations prone to escalation.

"Here we are, back in 2003 again." Lauren stands, her chair displacing itself across the wood.

"All you want to do is talk about how I can't forget my past, how I can't let go of whatever you never listen to. And here you are, Mike, it's May 19, 2010, and you can't stop talking about some stupid night back in 2003. Who is the one living in the past, Mike? Who is the one who screams at their wife after their wife just went out and helped pay the bills her husband is too sick to work for, after taking care of and watching over her husband and our child? Am I 'mentally unsound' now, Mike? Am I? Or are you just trying to paint me like that to make it seem as if the money you're spending on some goddamn shrink is worth the effort spent to earn it?"

The two stand very close to each other, almost equidistant to their spacing in the wedding photo.

The armies walk forward, muscles tense, waiting for the silent command none will officially hear, but shall unanimously obey.

"I see the money we pay for your therapy is doing a lot of good, Lauren." Michael steps away. He walks into the living room. Alex watches them from the background.

"And so what if it isn't?" Lauren's voice sounds distant to Alex.

"Then I guess we're just wasting our time, aren't we?" Michael grips the love seat in the living room.

The soldiers on one side of the gap imitate the intensity.

"Is that what you call this?" Lauren feels her voice cracking. "A waste of time? Is that all I am to you?"

Michael laughs, a sound born out of pure anger, a mulatto child of rage and happiness.

"Don't insult me like that." Michael says, leaning on the couch. "Don't you try to say that you're a waste of time to me after all I've done for you. After every night I listened to you say the things you wanted to say to Jim, or -"

"Alex," Lauren interjects. "Go to your room."

Alex has been spotted by a soldier who is down on the field, his position compromised. The solider motions for him to leave, to flee.

Alex stands still. Michael's voice presses to life once more.

"Or about how much guilt you've got over what you didn't do, about how you want to live in some past world that you locked inside your own head until right at this very moment? Don't you *dare* say that I wasted my time with you, when all you've shown me is how worthless you think I am."

Lauren feels it; she's going to cry in front of her son, once again. Michael pushes through the current of her emotions, his voice pointed to kill.

"Did you think I was a waste when I decided not to pursue a sales job in Connecticut in order to move in with you? Did you think that I considered you a waste when I helped you open up to somebody? How about when I told your mother, when I did what you should have done, about how much she had hurt you and continues to destroy you to this very second? Or how about, was I a waste, Lauren, when I made the decision to refuse a promotion to keep us in this god forsaken shithole of a house, this fucking garbage house that has swallowed over 300,000 dollars of our money, and then see you *fuck me over when you used my savings money to pay for the debt on your credit card?*"

Michael is suddenly very close. The bleb on his lung reverberates with the screams. Sweat beads his pale face, his expression a snarling mask of barbs and sinews of muscle.

The soldiers have pointed their guns. They follow orders in unison across the field, their speared heads primed, their ammunition locked.

"We talked about that! I told you, we would have been able to afford an apartment! Maybe not a house, but an apartment!" Lauren's words emerge muffled, as they resonate from beneath the beautiful eyes Michael proclaimed he would always protect and never abandon.

"Or how about when you lied to your mother about that same debt?" Michael snickers, his self-loathing and projected viscosity spinning in each syllable.

"Was I a waste, then? I think you only wanted my money."

"You know that isn't true!"

"And now, that I'm just about worthless, now that the going is tough, you're ready to leave. Oh yes, I heard you talking to your mom the other night, about how much you wanted to leave me here, leave me here with your child when you know I'm sick. They said until death do us part, Lauren. I guess death only counts if the person decides to lock themselves inside a fucking Cadillac instead of just pulling the fucking trigger like a real man."

Lauren's words are empty, her tears falling full down her face. The black Cheshire cat known as Fear is as large as the entire living room.

The soldiers have clashed before in skirmishes. They've only been preludes to a real war.

Now Michael moves. He walks over to the closet and grabs his coat, the same sleek black jacket Lauren had bought him in 2006 as a birthday gift. The keys come off the fake gold plate on the kiosk near the front foyer, jingling in delight.

The Fixer springs into action. He's used to jumping in front of bullets.

"Dad, don't leave." Alex says, his voice calm and confident, the calamity a maze to navigate.

"No, I'm leaving. I'll go and stay with my Dad. I can't do this anymore. I can't do it to you, I can't do it to myself. I'm too sick."

"You shouldn't be going out there if you're sick, Dad. Mom should go instead."

Alex stops.

He has seen his father cry, but has never seen his father sob.

The shakes of his shoulders are from a realm beyond noise and larger than the volume of water, past a point of drowning. It comes from his father's very soul, out through the lungs that had, only a few months ago, spat up blood; they now spit up a darker kind of substance. It's the lifeblood of a marriage, of a union, of a once majestic testament built with care and love.

The soldiers switch their safeties off, and take their aim.

"I'll go." Lauren says.

She walks past Alex and Michael, in the direction of the bedroom.

As of 8:47, everything is still fine. They're all still in the house. Everything will be ok. At 8:58, when she re-emerges with a trash bag full of clothes, everything is still completely normal.

At 9:04, as Lauren uses the phone in the kitchen and Michael sits on the couch, Alex standing only a few feet behind him, everything is still fine.

Then, Lauren tries to take the small clock sitting on the wooden table next to the couch.

"Don't touch my father's clock." Michael says.

"It's ours."

"Don't touch my father's god damn clock."

Written in gold on a plaque beneath the clock face are the embroidered words *Michael + Lauren*.

Open fire.

The soldiers' projectiles stream across the field at 10 million miles per hour, ripping memories, futures, hopes, dreams, and wedding vows apart as they reach their targets.

Michael stands in front of Lauren, who tries to sidestep him. He blocks her. She changes direction, switching sides, but Michael cuts her off. He reaches for the clock, which Lauren is holding onto so forcefully, her knuckles are white like the drapes in their bedroom.

Alex watches his parents grapple, tears streaming down his Mother's face. She tries to whip the clock away, but Michael only intensifies his grasp. Their fingers bounce off metal, the hands still ticking away the seconds, the slivers of innocence left in the day.

"Stop," Alex says.

Bodies of the combatants fly everywhere, and for a moment, Alex wishes he were watching some cinematic war sequence take place instead of parts of his life ricocheting into outer space at the velocity of evaporating love. Instead, he comes back down the mountain and is standing in his living room, watching the two people he cares about the most destroy each other.

Now Lauren is hitting him. Her blows deflect off his fatigued shoulders, every single impact landing as a faraway drop of a bomb.

"*Stop.*" Alex takes a step.

Lauren wrenches the clock free. Michael raises a hand, drawing back like the taut bow of an archer.

"FUCKING STOP IT."

They cease.

Michael and Lauren McGregor stand across from each other, the voice of their son echoing. Lauren cries. Michael pants, drenched in a blanket of sweat. Lauren's hands cradle the clock, blood from her broken fingernails running over the face. Her palms are battered and red. Carnage litters the floor around the family, and Alex's own crying escape him, despite how long he's suppressed them.

"Keep your clock, Michael. You can have it all." Lauren's anger is gone; her voice is as desolate as a crater.

She chucks the clock at Michael and exits the living room. Michael catches the clock, and the glass protecting the two turning hands shatters on his jacket.

Lauren stops, giving Alex a hug, whose own tears now dot the redness of the shirt he wore to school earlier in the day.

Lauren says,

"It's going to be alright."

Alex nods. "I love you, mom."

Lauren grabs the keys off the side of the wall, and she walks towards the front door. Alex hears it open, hears the screen door follow with a resounding clang, and can just make out the echoes of his mother's light shoes on the wooden porch and stairs. He hears the engine to her car start in the driveway. A couple minutes later, the wheels spin across the pavement and trail down the road.

Michael sits in the middle of the living room floor, sobbing. Each tear hits the floor from both father and son, and Alex staggers around the couch to join Michael on the ground. He feels his father's arm wrap around his shoulders. It is 9:24. He has school tomorrow.

The small clock is on the floor, in a mix of tears, blood, glass, and history.

It was a wedding gift from Harlan to the family. The panel with his mother and father's name together has popped out, sitting discarded under the love seat. Alex had only ever seen those two hands stop when the battery needed replacing; they could've gone around forever. Each second and minute would tick into the past on each passing day, another gigantic possibility held by innocent hands.

The hands are still.

Part II

May 20, 2010 — September 23, 2010

11
May 20, 2010

At the corner of his office, in the small building just outside Quakertown, Jack Hammond stands firmly on the ground, his feet adorned in modest dress shoes, his brown pants arching up to just above his waist. His mind, the tool with which he has made his living for the past twenty-seven years, is most certainly not on the ground with the rest of his body for two reasons. Firstly, it resides inside his skull, behind a pair of woodsy eyes colored with knowledge, placed on top of a pair of shoulders built by years of work, covered with a sweater of taciturn blue.

Secondly, Mr. Hammond's mind is off the ground because it sits between the last session and the next, the transition occurring with each stroke of his pen. For his client, who has just departed the office, their next session will be the following Thursday at approximately 4:30 PM. Until then, the paper shall rest on file in the cabinet next to the window overlooking the bustling highway from a safe distance.

Rising from the desk, his watch beeping a moment later, he pushes his chair into place and walks to the door leading to the hallway. Opening it, he ensures the door stops before hitting the small fan sitting in the corner. It hums audibly, blocking out excess sound, and trapping whatever spoken words in the room to a specific audience.

Hammond's shoes are slightly wet from the break he took before writing the notes. The floor is made of wood, much like the building itself, but is different. Instead of being wild as a tree, the boards of the floor are paved and domestic.

Hammond easily could have been a Priest as his ancestry dictated. Instead, he deviated from the divine path in favor of helping those who are on the hard way back to heaven. He dares not concern himself with the happenings that transpire after clients leave his office. Such is one of the first things his father told him upon learning of his son's career choice:

"You can't fix them, Jack, but you can help them fix themselves. You can't expect to be a miracle worker; there's only one person who succeeds in that line of work, and you aren't Him."

Hammond turns the corner, running a hand across his short beard. It hasn't decided whether it wants to be gray or stay brown, sitting in the middle of its fourth decade. Casting a glance across the lobby, he finds the man he searches for perched in one of the chairs against the window.

The man is wearing a homely jacket, dotted with kisses from the rain starting to fall outside; there is something markedly different about him today. A young man, aged about 13 or 14, sits in the neighboring chair; his earphones, playing music, block out the world in the same way a moon eclipses a star. His glance casts down at the space between his feet as if he's never seen a floor before. Hammond has seen the same look on the faces of adults, children, teenagers, and in the mirror that hangs on his desk in his office.

Michael emerges from his chair, meeting Hammond halfway across the lobby. Their handshake is firm, but also familiar. When a person's job consists of listening to emotions and the innermost thoughts of others, a gray area melds; the highest echelon of medicine cannot numb the bonds of the human spirit. Such is a practice no computer or android shall ever replace, for there is no anatomy for human emotions as concrete as a skeleton or a system. Emotions can be mapped and planned out, decoded and classified, but the same song which causes a man of sixty years to cry might seem as just a passing breath of air to a woman of 23. Genuineness cannot be manufactured.

"Hello, sir." Hammond's voice is naturally optimistic, weathered and perfected.

"Good afternoon, Jack." Michael replies, his voice as red and raw as the circles under his eyes.

Hammond examines Michael's irises. Michael has screamed in his presence, Michael has been angry, Michael has cried. Hammond's never seen this particular shade.

"How are you today? You seem tired." Hammond releases his grip.

"You could say that. I didn't get a lot of sleep last night, unfortunately." Michael lets a weak smile out of his mouth.

"Did something happen?" Hammond's mental pen skates across the pallet of his mind, tracing words and patterns.

"Yeah, Lauren moved out, actually."

"Really?" Hammond sounds surprised, but a skilled listener can decipher the notes of his voice like a chord progression in a song.

"We had a massive argument, and she went to live with her Mom over in Bethlehem. I haven't spoken to her since, but she must've come back to the house after I went to take Alex to school."

Certain items, such as a golden clock, were missing when Michael returned home from driving Alex to school earlier in the morning.

Hammond nods. "Is that who you've brought with you today?"

"Yes it is, as a matter of fact. I've wanted to bring him before, but I guess the incident yesterday was the last straw."

"Wonderful, so now I'm a last resort to you?" Hammond claps Michael on the shoulder.

"You know better." Michael filters his laugh through the strainer of his teeth.

Alex notices the two men speaking, and removes his headphones. The way he sits echoes his father's posture. Michael motions, and he walks over to the two men stoically.

"Alex, this is Mr. Jack Hammond. He's going to be your therapist."

"Nice to meet you, Alex." Hammond shakes the boy's outstretched hand. He notices a respectful grip. Standing next to each other, the lineage is noticeable, both in the appearances of their eyes and their resonating pain.

"Nice to meet you, too." Alex replies.

"How old are you?"

"14."

"His birthday was back in February." Michael adds in, an expert on the subject.

"Oh, a Pisces?" Hammond returns his hand to his side. "You like to write, Alex?"

"Sometimes." Alex doesn't mention the lyrics which sit in the front seat of the car only a few feet outside. His father had read them today, and his father beamed at the depth of his 14 year old. Michael said they're better than any of his own work, and Alex swelled with pride, sans vanity.

"I used to write songs when I was younger, you know." Hammond says, turning to Michael. "I never was in a rock band, though. What did you tell me you were?"

"The white Stevie Wonder." Michael's laugh is a genuine

splash of easiness. Lauren's face fades from the forefront of his thoughts.

"What?" Alex is incredulous. "How is that even possible? You're not even blind."

Hammond chuckles. "There's more than one way for a person to be blind, Alex."

"Oh God, you even *sound* like my Dad." Alex rolls his eyes.

Silence—the alleviating, not the suffocating kind—pervades the group of men. Hammond checks his watch, and sees that four minutes of their scheduled time has evaporated. Part of his job rests in being able to enable such moments, with no compensation required. If he could, he would offer his services free of charge, but he has a family to feed. Therefore, as he suggests for the session to begin, Hammond knows the real work in his profession values a currency separate from payment. As he closes the door, he looks at the handwritten letters dotting the bulletin board on his desk. While Hammond never promises miracles, he still believes they exist; if he didn't hold such a belief, he would've quit long ago.

———

Harlan McGregor drives as carefully as he acts in life. While the action is cautious, his way of carrying himself is unique. His car coasts over the black pavement under the fading sunlight, the hotness of the material radiating from his tires as they roll toward their destination. Harlan lets each second play over a memory in his mind from a distant past. Turning the wheel of the dark cherry car ever so slightly, he moves around a turn in the road like a seasoned veteran. Darkness has almost fully replaced the day, with the last glimpses of the setting sun falling behind the horizon of the sky. He'd gotten off the highway only a few moments prior, returning to the streets of his neighborhood. These roads now aren't just pavement to roll over; they are each small sections of a life.

Many aren't driving tonight, he sees. Most are either parked at home or performing tasks more important than traveling. Harlan has already accomplished his important tasks for the day, and now, these unimportant, paramount subconscious thoughts line the journey leading him to home.

"Lauren moved out last night, Dad."

Harlan thinks of the stupid games the kids Alex's age play, wasting their time inside instead of leaving their homes and embracing the air that runs shorter in his lungs every day. His thoughts conflict to paint a tapestry of neither ignorance nor overt compassion, but instead a combination of expansive and ranging reflection meant to act as background music for his eyes on the road. He had learned in early adulthood how to prioritize the important aspects of life, and no thoughtful distractions of any kind shall force him over the yellow lines into oncoming traffic.

"She broke your clock, Dad. I don't think she's coming back."

He has never found solace in religious indoctrination. He has lived as a moral man on his own, to aid those in need.

"Alex was really upset."

No matter how fast Harlan pilots his old car, or no matter how in shape he stays, his race will eventually conclude. Some do more laps around the track than others, some go faster and crash, some keep going and going until they run out of fuel, and some are never able to compete. Most aren't as lucky as Harlan McGregor, and Harlan McGregor's life makes him aware of the defining truth of such a statement every single day he gets out of bed, which is always better than the alternative.

Does his son understand the equity of life? Or does Lauren? Are they teaching the right kind of value to Alex?

"It was like the time we tried to sell the house in 2003, only worse."

Their stupid house has lost the couple so much over the years, after amateurish money management and idiotic renovations. When a couple falls in love, every aspect of life is bloated due to potential. One of the biggest crimes in life is the death of actualization. In the case of his son and his wife, they had taken potential to mean perennial success no matter the situation; they were proven wrong due to their financial decision-making, their endless arguments, and with each dumb decision championed as gospel.

Harlan is only a couple minutes away from home. He passes the auto shop, where both he and his vehicles have enjoyed splendid service. A small Italian eatery resides in the building across the street. Cynthia always loves going there. They make splendid grinders, cold sandwiches warmed to both enhance flavor and the dining experience.

Michael and Lauren will sort it out, they just need some time.

Depending on the person asked, people can sense great feelings of intuition, and can even possess the gift of foresight. Harlan McGregor is no psychic. He has no idea that the owners of the Italian place will be moving in three years, and the grinders will eventually stop turning.

He also has no idea, as he pulls up to the house where his children were raised, why the lights of an ambulance dance across his windshield, bouncing and weaving from their source in his driveway across his aging face.

One word blinks across the fabric of his mind:

Cynthia?

There she is, wheeling out of the house on a ghostly white stretcher. He sees the form in the headlights, slowly rolling forward, her face hidden by the pale blue uniforms of the surrounding medical technicians.

Harlan parks the car, opens the door, and jumps outside. The skin underneath his flannel shirt is instantly arctic. The very essence of his life rolls down his walkway, the paralysis breaking from his body and falling off as sheets of ice.

As he works his way towards the clump of people, he reads only one word in the eyes of the woman who is his entire heart and soul:

"Help."

12

June 3, 2010

Two weeks after Lauren McGregor moved out of the house
at 1333 Gruversville Road, Harlan McGregor became the newest
tenant of the Palace. An agreement was made on a summer night
in 1994 that if Harlan or Cynthia were ever hospitalized, the
other would move in with Michael. Cynthia's hospital is only
20 minutes away from Michael's home. The only alternative
location with sufficient equipment to cover the extent of her
injuries is all the way in Abington. Harlan packed a suitcase of
essential items carefully, and left his home—filled with furniture
and the hibernating pieces of his married life—empty.

He pulls into the driveway of the Palace the same way
he arrived back in 2009. Instead of a smile on his face—he
still holds a cigarette in his hand—Michael bears the look of
a painting whose print is being washed out by rough hands,
scraping the layers of beauty off in strips.

Harlan and his suitcase trundle up the solid stone of the
sidewalk like two old business partners walking to a conference.
Harlan feels as if he's captain of a ship looking out to a shoreline
blinded by the sun, making the illusion of his vessel drifting
closer, but he can't be sure if they're in motion or if the waves
of time are just kissing the bottom of the dark and effervescent
ocean floor.

Michael steps off the porch.

"Let me get that, Dad."

Harlan, who usually likes carrying his own weight, allows

Michael to handle the luggage. Another suitcase waits patiently in the car. Michael helps the suitcase to the top of the porch and then returns to his father's side.

"Any word from Lauren yet?" Harlan asks as the two walk towards the house. A curious rabbit observes them from the other side of the driveway, its tiny nose wrinkling as it smells the smoke from Michael's cigarette.

"Nope." Michael spits. The rabbit, seeing the motion, decides to abdicate through the bushes on the side of the field. Michael watches it dash away, something else running from him that he cannot chase.

Harlan stops and looks at his son.

"Did you tell her your mother had a stroke?"

"Of course. But she's too worried about herself." Michael smiles maliciously, the smoke emanating from his lips, the stick in his hand, and the smoldering wreckage of his union.

"Lauren believes that she's been abused for the past nineteen years, Dad. This is after all the bullshit she pulled with the money, all of the ways she's manipulated me while I've been sick, all the little things that have been biting at me for the past months, after she didn't go to counseling and then blamed me for it all. She's real good at blaming, Dad."

"But I don't understand. Your mother is in the hospital for God knows how long, we have no idea what's going on with her, except that the stroke was bad enough that she can't string a sentence together. Your sister is on her way from California, by the way."

"I know, I talked to her yesterday."

Harlan walks back to the trunk of the Impala, grasping the cool handle of the other suitcase. He lifts it out of the back and places it on the ground.

"Your mother had been telling her about your illness. She was going to come out anyway to try and help, Mike."

"I know, she told me the same thing. Did you tell her I'm getting better?"

"I told her what the Dr. Fost told us." Harlan heaves the suitcase as if he's transporting a body, starting towards the porch. "The infected area, the radius spreading out from that bleb, is starting to decrease with the medication."

"But it still isn't going anywhere." Michael closes the trunk, tossing his cigarette to the ground and stomping down, imagining it's Lauren's foot.

"I don't know what to say, Mike. I thought for sure she would've come back."

"I thought a lot of things, Dad. I thought I knew a lot of things. I also never imagined a lot of things, and I've stayed awake realizing how wrong I was. I never thought my kid would need therapy, I never thought my wife would turn out to be such a selfish bitch, and I never thought that my mom would have a stroke at nearly the exact same time as my marriage fell apart."

Michael sits on the step which transitions the driveway to the sidewalk, his head bowed. Harlan sighs and moves towards him. If someone had been looking at a distance, they might have mistaken Harlan and Michael for Michael and Alex on the night of the 19, since a father's protective arm around a son doesn't depend on age. The demands of life cling to Michael like an anchor on a vessel, and the pills he takes every morning are becoming harder and harder to swallow.

How long can he go before choking?

———

At the same time as Michael and Harlan sit on the porch,

Lauren McGregor works in silence at the New Life facility in Quakertown. The job doesn't pay as well as Michael's, but after her husband's illness, she'd reluctantly pieced herself together enough to work again.

The thoughts encircle her, carnivores catching a scent of blood around a wounded animal: the way she'd tossed the clock at him, the way he cursed at her, yelled, and blocked her. How she'd hugged her son as she walked out the door. She hasn't seen him since the night of the 19th, and part of her doesn't wish to fix such a situation. He's siding with his father, as always. The kid is borderline corrupted thanks to the shit Michael's feeding him, about how it's all *her* fault, and how *she's* the one who can't deal with *her* problems. She's dealt with her problems all her life, being beaten and broken on innumerable occasions; Michael's only pristine due to his ability to leech onto others to carry him through the future.

Lauren had moved on. She had taken those early days and put them into boxes, separating and carving space out of her mind like vaults in a bank. Such is the evaluation her therapist, a woman named Geraldine Worth who works out of the same office as Hammond, hypothesized. She'd survived by applying herself to the small jobs. Those aspirations Lauren had developed during her teenage years were great; she had originally wanted to move somewhere out west, to blaze a trail. She and her sister in law are almost cousins in their aspirations; Lauren loves to paint, and she envisions worlds upon worlds unfolding on her canvas. Eve has never been an artist, but Eve had been creative enough to be rid of Michael's shit and cut him out of her life. She, Lauren, never should've married him, especially not when his problems

(her problems)

aren't fixed.

They bought the beautiful, disgustingly picturesque house on the corner of the two country roads, which had cost them over $150,000, and then plunged their credit into willing oblivion. Lauren remembered her hands shaking, filing bankruptcy back in two-thousand-what-ever, and the horror on her husband's face when their perfection died. Michael's never been strong with money, so of course studious Lauren was the one to take the blame, even when Michael worked the job with better pay. As Lauren's fingers work over the keyboard, her barriers crack in perfect sequence with the strokes of the keys.

Next to her high-heeled feet, plaintive black skirt, and modest shirt drawn out from the wrinkled bag of clothes, is the Cheshire cat known as Fear. It's mass is increasing, and its gluttony is tangible. It no longer feeds on the meat of potential events; the divorce is imminent. From every sign Michael sends, every argument she has with either him or Alex signals the end of the world. Instead of listening to her common sense, or her mother, she had simply stuck in the fight. Now the kid is living with Michael, hearing a bunch of things about how Lauren is nothing short of the spawn of the devil, and now she talks to the kid as if he's Michael every time they talk. Instead of taking the advice of everybody who had seen the problems, instead of listening to the course she should have taken for herself, the stupid, imaginary, idealistically horrid lie called love had stolen her, and now threatens to crush her under the weight of her husband's collapsing world.

Oh, and she loves him.

She loves him more than anybody she's ever met. She'd trusted those secrets behind her walls to his hands, the ones her mother told her to store away for life. The keyboard under her fingers is now dotted with moisture. Nobody ever values tears; they're either produced in silence or overspent. After she trusts him with her scars, he still calls her emotionally absent, still calls her a whore, and still knows exactly how to hammer those soft spots only his touch has known. He manipulates and moves her just as she had done with the stupid checking account. It's a chess game, but instead of playing for victory, with each piece taken and pawn moved, irreplaceable objects are forever lost.

Alex. She and Michael are both going to burn in hell for the thievery of his childhood. All his happy memories shall be viewed in the future through tainted telescopes. Thanks to their mindless fighting, lack of listening to advice, their eyes blinded by the cruel heist of love, the light at the end of the tunnel was nothing but a freight train. She'd thought he'd get better; his disease would be cured, she would quit her job, and then the counseling would let them stop talking about things from 2003 and things from 2004 and Jim killing himself with the gas from an exhaust pipe and coming home from school every day wondering if her mother had finally done it and-

Lauren stops typing. The tears coast down her cheeks, the cat at her feet lapping hungrily, catching the drops like a puddle in an empty parking lot.

One of her coworkers, a young girl named Tiffany, pokes her head into Lauren's office, a concerned look on her face. There the mother, whose family used to smile from the stations on her desk, is having the cross around her neck portraying peace, hope, and faith being splattered by salty rain. Lauren tells her she's alright. From the rumors Tiff hears, she and her husband are divorcing.

Lauren will set the barriers in her mind back up, a license-readiness evaluator replacing cones after a failed attempt, and she

will push the ugly thoughts, every single goddamn
Cadillac escalades have a great output of carbon monoxide
memory and argument and fight, back in the same silent,
numb suppression.

The Cheshire cat rests, well fed.

In two weeks, Alex McGregor will graduate from 8th grade.
His principal informed him he will be graduating ranked 7th in
his class, along with honors for his achievements in the history
department. He owns a near perfect GPA, unblemished by the
residue of the debris falling near him by the fools he finds at
home. Even with those accolades, when he exits the bus at the
end of the day, he knows no awards can mend the aspects of life
that are not measurable by material.

Walking inside, Roxy greets him. Her hair is aging, but
she bounds over to him at every possible opportunity, her eyes
delighted to see her boy returned. As Alex bends down to pet the
dog's soft fur, he sees his dad moving in the kitchen. He notices
the phone is off its receiver.

He sees two suitcases sitting side by side on the couch.
Grandpa Harlan is joining the Palace. Alex figures Harlan is
probably down at the hospital with Grandma Cynthia, just as
he's been nearly constantly over the past couple days. Setting his
bag down on one of the eternally empty chairs in front of the
wood stove, Alex peers into the kitchen, hungry for anything but
food.

The phone clicks. Michael finishes the conversation as soon
as Alex's feet meet the wood of the kitchen floor. It may have
been coincidental, but the phone rocketing to the ground in the
next instant, akin to a meteorite crashing from the atmosphere,

is undeniably deliberate.

Alex freezes. The sickness inside his father is much more than just a bleb or infection traceable by machines.

Michael lights a cigarette and steps over near the kitchen window. The 16-year-old blades still spin, taking the smoke from Michael's lungs and pumping it out into the realm of the trees next to the house for small animals to choke on instead.

Alex sees his father's shoulders moving up and down, mountains in an earthquake unhinged from the soil.

Carefully, as if he's a bomb detector in a desert, Alex navigates around the now-occupied doghouse.

"Dad?"

His father's breathing stabilizes.

"Hi Alex."

"Are you alright?"

"No, I'm not."

"Is it Grandmom?"

"No."

"Mom?"

"Yep."

Michael bums the cigarette in the nearly full ashtray. The small bits of residue bounce over the edges as the newest resident takes its place.

"She's still not coming home, is she?"

"No, she isn't, Alex."

Michael's next sentence consists of words Alex had only heard in the far off corners of impossibility, sneaking out of the bulwark of his bad dreams.

"We might be moving, kid."

"What?" Alex's stomach drops.

"We might be moving to Willow Grove."

"Why?"

"Because, Alex, I'm sick. I'm not supposed to be doing all of this. I've been taking care of the house, taking care of work, taking you places, performing all sorts of tasks. I'm in constant motion. I'm supposed to be resting. Your mom was here to pick up the slack, so it worked, but now that she's gone I can feel it. I'm dying."

Michael plucks another cigarette out of the pack.

Alex's tongue is sore from constant biting.

"So we'd be moving in with Grandpa Harlan?"

"Yep."

Alex's words rise to the brim of speech—damaging words.

"I don't want to do that, Dad."

"Neither do I, especially with the stuff that's gone on with Grandma. But we have to. It feels like if I stay here, I'm going to die, Alex."

Alex allows his father's words to hang in the air momentarily.

"But all of my friends are here. If we move to Willow Grove, we'll be over an hour away."

"You've lived here all your life, so it might be good for things to change. I think we both need a new start, to be honest." Michael's unsteady hand places the cigarette alongside the other recently deceased stubs.

"If your Mom hadn't left, if she'd come back to help take care of you—and this place—then maybe we'd be able to stay. But your mom isn't coming back, not for me, not for you, not for grandma. She's only interested in herself."

Alex can't identify the end goals of his life anymore. With that said, the one stance he believes, with 100% certainty, is that he does not wish to move in with Grandpa Harlan in Willow Grove.

"Well," Alex says, noting his father's shaking hands.

"If you have to move to Willow Grove to save yourself, then you should."

Michael's hands become still.

"So you wouldn't be coming with me, then?" Michael says, turning to his son. Suddenly, Alex sees Michael's emotion shift from sadness to anger, a flame overcoming his eyes as if triggered by a switch.

"You'd rather move in with your Mom?"

"No," Alex says, his voice infused with the echoes of concern.

Michael moves away, stalking across the kitchen and into the living room with newfound speed.

"We can go over to your mom's place right now, and you can have her. I'll fucking go to Willow Grove myself, we'll just tell Grandpa Harlan that's what we're doing." Michael yells from the living room, arrows designed for Lauren now piercing the neutrality of his son.

"Let's go, get your shit. We'll be in Bethlehem in 20 minutes!"

"No, Dad!" Alex screams back. He sees the room blurring, his heart rate increasing.

"You're just like your mother, you know that?" Michael's voice is now wild. In the child before him, half of his own heritage, half of his wife's, he smells treason. The little shit is turning out to be just *like* the ungrateful bitch that left him here to die.

"You know that isn't true Dad, I'm sorry for what I said!" Alex apologizes.

"She left you here, Alex. She left you here with a father who she knew was going to have trouble taking care of you, who she knew relied on her for support and for working and for a whole bunch of other things she didn't want to do! And now you're saying you'd rather stay with *her*?"

"No, I just don't want to leave my friends!"

"You selfish little bastard! You're just like her, only thinking about yourself while the rest of us can get fucked! Do you understand how easy it would've been for me to leave, for me to just walk out of here and leave her here with you? Remember those times I listened to what you thought, after all those fights, all those nights we spent screaming at each other, and now you're saying you'd rather live with *her* instead of me?"

"Dad, stop yelling at me. You know that's not what I meant."

"Ok, *Lauren*, I'll stop yelling."

"My name isn't Lauren. I'm not mom, no matter how much you want me to be!"

Michael pauses, the anger spiking in his irises.

"You want me to be mom so you can have an excuse just to shit all over me like this after I come home from school, after you toss the phone onto the floor, just so you don't have to pay attention to the stupid shit you do, or the things you say, and how *they* affect other people. Any you call *me* the selfish one?"

"You goddamn brat." Michael says, walking over to Alex's desk. He picks up Alex's phone, which had been minding its own business, but now is an active weapon in the volley of words.

"What are you doing with my phone?"

"It's not yours, I pay for this."

"What?"

"I spend my money, money I could easily use to do a bunch of other shit, going out with my friends, to let you have this. If you're going to be a mommy's boy, then you can have her pay for it, just like how she paid for everything else, right? Mommy's the saint, Mommy can't do anything wrong, it's all just *dad*. Dad's sick, right? Dad can't do enough, Dad can just get shit on and ignored and just pushed aside, right, *Alex*? You say you're not Lauren, but you act exactly like her! The words coming out of your mouth are the same ones I hear from her. 'Stop yelling, Mike.' Well then, how about you think about someone other than yourself for a change! 'It's not my fault.' Well then, whose fault is it, *Alex*? You said you want me to move to Willow Grove? Fine, I will!"

"I don't want anybody to move anywhere, I want mom to come home!"

Alex's hysteria is palpable, his eyes too stunned to dare to cry.

"Well, how about you tell her that after she comes here and gets you. I'm calling my Dad, then I'm calling my fucking sister, you can stay here." Michael puts Alex's phone in his pocket.

"No, I need my phone!"

"Why?" Michael asks, a synthesis of a laugh and a cry.

"I have lyrics on it!"

"There you go again!" Michael slams the couch with a closed fist. "Only thinking about yourself. Well let me tell you what, *Lauren*, you can have your phone, you can have this house, you can have your fucking mother, I'm done."

Michael tosses the phone back on the cushions, amazingly intact despite the impact.

"Go ahead, call her."

Michael walks over to a rung where his keys hang on the wall, in tune with the pillaging like a head on a stake outside a burial ground.

"Dad," Alex whimpers, as his father reaches the door.

"I'm sorry. I love you."

Michael wheels around, a look of rage in his eyes unlike anything Alex has witnessed. The man usually so complacent, so reserved, so warm, has turned into an imposter.

"Your mom loves me too."

Michael opens the door, and in two steps, is walking down the porch.

Alex flounders for his phone, grabbing it from the couch. In disbelief, he finds his mother's number, the woman with whom he has spoken four times over the past two weeks, resulting in nothing but arguments that render only desolation. His mother is the absence, and his father is supposed to be the force that filled the void.

As he punches the number in, he hears the door open again. Surprised, hurt, and alone, Alex waits, a wounded animal backed into a corner.

Michael enters the house, a look of pure disgust on his face.

"Get in the car."

"What?"

"I said get in the car. We have to drop off the drinks for Dave's party."

Alex feels his heart collect itself. Wasn't his Dad just about to drive to Willow Grove, never to return? He had spoken of running an errand for a friend earlier in the day, before the shootout occurred.

Alex does as he's told. Michael locks the door behind them, following Alex down the steps. Somehow, the normal routine, which had been so grandly shattered in the argument, returns to regularly scheduled programming.

"Are you still leaving, Dad?"

"I'm not sure." Michael says, entering the driver's side of the car.

"I'm sorry."

"So am I."

———

Hammond studies the boy sitting in front of him on the couch.

"So what happened after you got to the reception hall to deliver the drinks?"

"We talked a bit more," Alex says. The confrontation with his father had been three days ago.

"And you patched it up?" Hammond's face creases with concern, his hands gripping each other tightly.

"Yeah. He apologized, I apologized. It was terrible."

The child sitting in front of him now resembles Michael less by his good demeanor, and more via the barren look infringing upon his essence.

Hammond assures him, "I'll have a talk with your dad."

"Thanks," Alex says. "I'd appreciate that."

By the corners of his leaking eyes, Hammond knows Alex speaks with meaning.

13
June 14, 2010

For many people, the window, which looks to the outside from the corner of the hospital, is the last thing they witness in life. So many moments had they spent either in motion or sitting still, looking at different slices of the world, only to end their existences as an audience to a single portrait. Every moment in their stories leads into the next, building and compounding with each step and second, only for the end to come through a panorama of their history.

The window itself isn't special—it's simply a pane of glass, set into three panels, which allows sunlight to enter, or be blocked by curtains. When it rains, the glass protects whoever lies or sits in the bed, flanked by either loved ones or the space of decades. The resident of the bed might want to feel those drops of water for a final time before their residency ends, with their journey either completed or just beginning, depending on their beliefs.

Cynthia McGregor believes she hasn't reached the end. She can't say as much, with her hands folded over the thin sheets and her garment-adorned, baby blue covered body hiding in the warmth. This species of temperature in the room is not the kind of atmosphere felt in her home with her husband; this temperature is as synthetic as the partitioned and planned meals which travel to her every day in the cycle, as well as the fluids keeping her sustained. The drinks she receives do not hold the same coolness as the water she can siphon from the tap at home and place down her throat voluntarily.

The last time she'd felt authentic, she'd been cutting food for the night's meal in her kitchen; she's been artificial since the point she'd woken up on the floor, with the paramedics rushing in with their stretchers and their steeled faces. She doesn't remember calling the emergency services, or how she had mumbled out the address as the feeling in her face disappeared. Now, instead of waking up daily and seeing the love of a couple engrained in the boards of her home, she sees the window stretching out to the places she's known before.

Each day she awakens with her speech restricted, with her body suddenly trapped in partial functionality, with only the ability to croak out a few words whose sensibility is left bouncing around inside her own skull. She's someone who assesses all she receives with the eye of a sculptor molding a statue out of clay, forming her own judgments, creases, and curves. Her independence is now as intact as the hip she fractured falling to the floor, or as her son's marriage. While those two entities are able to mend with time, the infliction of the stroke is eternal. Surgery is imminent. Her once dignified, silvery hair is gone, covered instead with a bandage marking the place where they'd siphoned the blood from the accident. Such an action saved her life, but it bears a cost. How long shall she hang in limbo, with the synthetic fluid, the forced smiles, the non-existent speech, and the shitty food? She can't even read. She has to watch the television in the corner of the room, hanging from the ceiling only a few inches away from the window.

When she watches the local news, the same message screams at her—*you've been out here with us, but you're probably not coming back.*

The only solace Cynthia receives is when the ones she left on the outside come to visit. Today is an important day; it's

Alex's graduation from 8th grade. Inside her chest, Cynthia's heart attempts to hide.

The boy is growing up in the spitting image of both her husband and the boy's own father. She should be there, sitting with her book tucked under her arm, her hands clapping together, a look shining on her face of a frequency only grandparents can transmit. The boy's parents are imbeciles, and now she, his grandmother, is only causing everybody more stress and raising nothing but questions.

When are you going to get out? and *How are you feeling today?*

The answer to the first question is something she dares not attempt to verbalize. The end doesn't come grandly; the veil between the earthly world and the existence known to the other side is delicate. The only difference is, through the window that looks to the surrounding area, Cynthia knows the sunlight is real. She knows the other side is calm, and while she does not fear what awaits her, she does fear the passage and its residual effects. While it is not yet time for her to pass, her heart, for all the love it has given, the children raised, and every single "I love you" it has ever spoken, knows.

———

The auditorium at Freedom High School's size far exceeds Alex's expectations. The continuation of the past shackles the future. At a ceremony dedicated towards advancing in his education, he sits on stage between Luke Marsden and Justin Mencotti, thinking not of walking into the high school as a new student, but how his life prior to May 19 will return out of the nether to be his reality once more.

Alex can see his family in the audience. Their faces break out of the monotone wave of spectators. His father is a mannequin, prepared for public appearance as a model for a photo shoot, his soul airbrushed. The debilitating lung disease stays persistent, only barely budging backwards, somewhere under the nice collared shirt and the clean-cropped face. Nobody can see the fountains of pain, the source of the bubbling blue of his eyes. Nobody can tell how the sturdiness of the wedding band on his hand is made of fool's gold, the silver a Band-Aid to a sickness stemming not from the stillness of his hands, but the downward trajectory of his heart.

Harlan sits to the right of Michael, a different gleam radiating from his presence. His spectacles shine, polished with the light reflecting off his grandson. Harlan knows the eyes of Cynthia are probably looking through the pane of a window, completely alone. The shoes Harlan wears, rugged and worn, do not represent the steps he's taken to arrive at this night.

A woman sits to the left of Michael. She drove a rental car to the ceremony tonight. She wears a bright blue dress, choosing to look her best for the first time seeing Alex in almost eight years. Her golden blonde hair is neatly laced into a pony tail which reaches down to her upper back, age no match for the benefits received living in a consistently 80 degree locale. Her eyes sparkle like her brother's and father's, with a newborn hope and a familiar sadness seen throughout the generations, the glint seeming to reverberate off her quaint earrings. If Alex were closer, he could've seen that her eyes contain knowing blue and softness superior to any hardship, filled with both electricity and genuine compassion. Sitting next to her brother, Eve McGregor seems complete. She's a week returned from California.

The Great Fake Family, fully operational, but with a piece missing.

Alex pushes his mother out of his mind as if suppressing

vomit; he told her two days ago not to attend. His achievements are valid, and the emotions the three adults in the crowd are displaying mean the world to him, but they do not alter the plasticity of the surroundings. Mom and Dad don't talk, they argue. Grandma's still in the hospital. Alex's fear remains in close proximity, a wolf tracking a sick animal.

Alex shoves a grin forth as his principal takes the podium at the front of the stage. He is but a puppet, and the entire charade hangs on invisible strings controlled by mysterious hands.

Alex himself broke the totality of the synthetic flow. His mother had promised she would sit at the opposite end of the auditorium. Alex instead told her to sit at home.

The principal says words along the lines of congratulations, and recycles wisdom for their future endeavors in high school. There will be 'challenges' and 'obstacles', but Alex's class has 'every opportunity' to be **great**.

Great.

———

After the ceremony, the McGregors convene in the lobby. Alex stands for pictures, one with his proud Aunt, one with his beaming Grandfather, and a Kodak moment with his father. They are weather vanes in the midst of a tropical depression, an eye of balance and extraordinary achievement. The kid graduates in the top 10 academically, and is the 2010 Freedom Middle School Social Studies Student of the Year (with a trophy to prove such a feat, which will end up tossed inside a container and lost in three weeks time). Now, the true test of his life awaits him come September, with an entire summer to experience first.

Michael looks him in the eyes, standing on the steps of the high school; the stone is cracked, but still functional.

"Congratulations, Alex. I knew you could do it."

"Yeah," Alex laughs, the cliché of his father's words erased by the uniqueness of his voice. "Every time you bitched at me to do my homework, it really paid off!"

Michael chuckles wryly. Eve beams. Her brother today is an entirely different creature and, concurrently, the same as she remembers him.

"Congratulations, Alex!" She echoes, giving the boy a hug.

"Thanks, Aunt Eve. I'm really glad you could be here."

"Of course. I'm just sorry I couldn't have been here sooner."

Is that why you never sent me a Christmas card? Alex returns her smile.

Eve had sent many Christmas cards. Eve had said she would come and visit; she would've come to visit her family in Pennsylvania every year, had it not been for the fact she hadn't touched the East Coast in 8 years until the past weekend.

Michael had been careful to throw each red, pink, or blue envelope from California into the black hole of a trash bag that resides under the stove in the McGregor kitchen. Michael feels no remorse as he stands alongside Eve and Alex. He'd been protecting his son. Eve could be a manipulative bitch, which is probably something she learned dissecting and seducing juries in law school before she had gotten married to a wealthy man named Roger Bennett back in 2001. She had rubbed her filthy money in Michael's face, and he had told her where to put it.

Obviously, her unchanging and complete devotion to the idea of money equating to happiness is absolute in her persona, and Michael is smart enough to be the only one who realizes such thinking is toxic to Alex's view of the world. Therefore, whichever stupid words she'd sent in those lovely cards are lost in the trash, just like the value of her alleged superiority she'd rubbed in Michael's and Lauren's existence.

Eve had called Harlan crying on multiple occasions, apologizing for moving cross-country from her childhood home. She'd tried writing, she'd tried calling, and she'd tried emails. Eve is one of the most humble people Harlan's known in his entire life, but when words and families mix, the potential of harm is equal to the risk of hurt. Michael always blames Eve and burns it to the ground rather than spend valuable time making repairs.

A state of limbo resolved the issue, communicated by a standard of sibling silence. The only reason Eve's returned is due to the illness. Cynthia's surgery is four days away. Michael accepts Eve's reintegration, remaining silent. As tragedy tears his life to opposite sides of the galaxy, a long forsaken, forgotten star returns to his orbit.

Michael and Eve pose for a picture; Eve is unable to hide her crying eyes, clutching her brother, his arm around the waist of her blue dress. For a moment, they could've been a couple. The moment passes, and Harlan's smile is as long as an interstate highway.

Now they're going to the hospital, with seven years of non-communication and assumptions serving as backseat drivers, with a bunch of days and hours of broken relationships spinning under the wheels.

Such is why Alex McGregor thinks a lot.

14
June 20, 2010

After her surgery, Cynthia transfers out of the hospital to a facility in Allentown specializing in stroke rehabilitation and advanced treatment. Walking into the lobby, Alex considers the giant effigy hanging on the wall of a glorified stick figure holding a cane. He reads the curly, cold text:

Greener Pastures Rehabilitation

Michael, Eve, and Alex wait for the elevator to reach the lobby, preparing to be herded into the next stage of life. The smell of trapped people moving together to another floor wafts out of the elevator, with an elderly man emerging and the family moving inside. Whoever is directing this entire show should be fired for their bullshit script. Alex feels no different from the dumb sheep displayed on the sign of the facility, his master whipping him in circles. As the family ascends the floors in silence, Alex wonders whether whoever leads him is striking him with their staff towards salvation, or off the edge of a cliff.

The first thing Alex notices when the doors open are the screens displayed promptly near the nurses' station. Gone is the namelessness and essence of quick transfers; the residents in these beds, with their glass doors and standardization, are either long-term guests or permanent residents. Alex examines the names, moving closer to the large television mounted on the spicy, mustard colored walls. He vaguely notes how, next to their vital signs, each one of these people are missing pieces in others' lives.

Such are the thoughts of all the family members who enter through those elevator doors towards the kiosk of activity, no matter their origin, their appearance, or their differences. Everybody comes through and exits via the same hallway. Tragedy doesn't discriminate.

Gary Bartholomew. Sally Burns. Keith Daniels. Victoria Edgemont. Genevieve Lorton.

Cynthia McGregor.

"She's in room 213."

His father walks back from the nurses' station. Harlan nods, and Eve walks next to Michael as the group moves towards their new destination. Alex traces the blinking names and the beeping vitals of the station, with the lives and life spans of the patients marked down to units. Part of how things as vast and reaching as lifetimes can seem as small as to fit on the monitor stuns him.

Alex never imagined his grandmother in a hospital before. She's always the person who floats around on her own air, spreading comfort to everyone she knows. Grandma is the one who's used to building other people up and fostering love, attention, and care.

Each too-far bed adjustment sends a young nurse running to make sure Cynthia hasn't fallen. Her family members stay up by the phone at night to make sure she doesn't call to tell them she's leaving them forever. All these aspects make Cynthia want to scream.

Alex's grandfather, his mother's father, had passed away back in 2005; he had been a short man of few words, but also capable of great care. He had made his mistakes in life, for he was human, and Alex knows he found atonement for his sins. Alex had never gotten to know him. Alex had cried at the funeral, for he still loved him, the kind of love which is not admitted, yet is constantly present.

He can't imagine repeating the same process with his father's mother, a woman who he's grown close to through her visits and her unique humor. Now she is far from the image in his mind, and seeing her after the surgery is going to bring a sharper dichotomy to life. *More doctors, just like Dad's.*

Turning into the room, Alex notices the bandage around his grandmother's head. Instead of being quaint, they now threaten to swallow her. Her hair's shaven, her face slumps, but she's awake. Cynthia could've lit up the room under normal circumstances, but she's a firefly trapped in a jar, with the lid slammed closed by a stupid toddler who doesn't understand the majesty of the smallest lights.

She peers at them with a tired expression, her eyes speaking volumes; for the rest of his life, Alex will never forget their apology.

There's also a tube coming out of her throat.

It's blue, curvy, and akin to a vacuum cleaner crudely trying to suck a dust bunny out of the corner of a couch. Instead of pointing to a bag, its sinews lead to a machine next to the bed, which purrs like a massive feline. Its color is darker than the liquids filling the bags around Cynthia's space. Her appearance is the same as the sound: no more floating, happy breaths, just respirations of conscripted air.

They'd told Harlan about the ventilator, but they hadn't told Michael.

———

"Had you ever seen somebody like that before?" Hammond asks, his hands draping over the sides of his chair.

In each of the six sessions he and Alex have shared, Alex

hasn't seen him write one note. Alex's eyes dart around the room momentarily. Hammond's college degrees reside over his desk in an alcove of the room. Odd memorabilia from around the world inhabits the corners of the office. Books countering the stigmas surrounding mental health, about different methods of cleansing both the mind and spirit, and the entire collection of a man named Eckhart Tolle perch on the top of the wooden workspace.

"I've seen people in hospital settings before." Alex responds, thinking back to the day of his father's bronchoscopy.

"Did it bother you?" Hammond asks. He's wearing one of his typical sweaters and dress pants.

"A little bit, I guess." Alex casts his vision down to the floor, which he's made a habit of studying frequently.

"It must've." Hammond places a hand on his chin.

"What do you usually do when things bother you?" Hammond switches positions. His movements and tonalities are different parts of an orchestra.

"Do you talk to people about it, do you exercise?"

Alex folds his hands, the jagged stubs of nails crossing each other.

"I write."

"What do you write about?"

"Usually, it's just about how I'm feeling."

"Poetry? Prose?"

"Actually, a lot of lyrics. I've already written something like eight collections of stuff."

"Do they have music to them? I think you told me that you play guitar."

"Some do, but most of it I haven't written down, since I don't really know how to play that well."

"I used to play acoustic, I never really got into electric."

Hammond walks over to his desk. He grabs a small yellow packet and tosses it over to Alex

"What are these?" Alex asks.

Hammond pops open an identical pack of his own. A small gummy creature, strawberry red, in the shape of a fish, falls from the bag into the counselor's mouth.

"You've never had Swedish fish before?"

Alex laughs. "Not until now."

"They're pretty good. Try one."

Alex opens the plastic. They taste unique, and nothing like fish, but good.

"Not bad, right?" Hammond says. He could've been another 14 year old, talking to Alex over lunch.

"Yeah, not bad at all. Are they actually from Sweden?"

"Are all Irish Setters born in Ireland?"

"Point taken." Alex chuckles.

"So, when you don't have the chance to write," Hammond asks, his smile stepping back to allow room for his questions. "How do you deal with these things? Do you think about your parents fighting when you're at school?"

"Nah, I can't think about them then." Alex asserts, popping the fish in quick succession into his mouth.

"Why not?"

"I wouldn't be able to focus on school. School has been a big deal to my parents, if you couldn't tell from talking with my dad."

"They both just want what's best to you."

"Usually, I can just block it out and not think about it, but then other times, usually when it's quit, it slips out."

"What do you mean, slips out?"

"I guess you could say I'm trying to lock it all somewhere

where I don't exactly have to deal with it."

"Taking it one day at a time?"

"Yeah, exactly. I can't do anything else."

"You talk to your Dad about this stuff?"

"All the time."

"From what you've told me, you were involved in their arguments a lot."

"Yep. I usually played mediator."

"Why did you do that?"

"I feel like I have to—almost like if I don't, they won't be able to take care of it themselves." Alex shifts on the couch.

"I've stopped a lot of arguments between both of them, and it's usually turned out great."

Hammond's lips suddenly parse instead of smile, the look of a melancholy passenger on a train realizing it's about to rain.

"I really don't mind it." Alex continues, eating more of the fish. "It hasn't really affected me in school, hasn't affected me dealing with my friends. I argue with my mom when I talk to her, telling her how Dad's sick and she needs to come back, but she won't even talk to him unless it's some sort of shouting match."

"Your father is getting frustrated?"

"Yep. I feel bad for him. I figure if I can keep it together, it's the least I can do ... something else he doesn't have to worry about."

"Alex, it's his job to worry about you. My kids are 18 and 21, and I worry about them all the time. They're grown men."

"Yeah, but he's got a lot of other stuff he has to worry about."

Hammond nods, trying to weed out potential rocks and specs of dirt from a cool stream of water like an archeologist.

"Have you ever tried to break a diamond, Alex?"

"No, I don't think I've ever seen one broken, either." Alex lets a look of puzzlement encroach upon his face. *This guy.*

"I haven't, either." Hammond shifts, his pants shuffling slightly over the material of the cushion.

"When I hear people talk about them, all I ever hear about is how diamonds are beautiful. How they shine. You ever heard the phrase 'diamonds are a girl's best friend?'"

"Of course,"

"Or how about," Hammond makes an emotional face, turning his eyes to the ceiling, his hands strumming an imaginary guitar. "'Lucy in the Sky with Diamonds!'"

Alex laughs, the noise a strange texture in his mouth.

"Yeah?" Hammond finishes his serenade.

"Yeah. By some band called the Beatles."

"Good, your dad taught you well." Hammond clears his throat.

"Well, some people in society value diamonds because they sparkle, because they shine. People are attracted to those types of things. People use them to show off, to use them as a symbol of wealth that they purchase; God knows how much money people spend on them. Diamond earrings, necklaces, bands, and a whole bunch of other shit that I can't even name."

"But the fact that a diamond shines is not what makes it so valuable, right? The wealth has to come from somewhere, to make a diamond a diamond, and not just some other rock like a sapphire, emerald, or ruby, whichever. The true value of diamonds rests in the fact they're so hard to break. You can take a diamond, a good-sized rock, and it would take some extraordinary force to crack it. It's almost like a gold—or diamond—standard for breakability. When somebody says it's hard as diamond, that's a true compliment. A diamond is just a stone that followed its dreams, or something like that.

"When you tell me you want to go out and look like you're doing well, or you're worried about being a burden, that isn't going to make me or your father any happier. We want to know if you're genuinely upset, or if you're thinking about parts of life, with worries, or even fears. You've got a whole lot going on right now, Alex. And let me tell you something: with enough polishing, and enough trickery, somebody can make something shine as bright as a diamond. But you see, what makes a diamond a diamond is not how it looks, but its strength. So when you go out saying that you want to appear like you're alright, that you want to make it seem like you're fine, there's really no value in those actions, because the true worth of what you can do for this situation lies in being genuine. And let me tell you, I've learned from my line of work, the first thing that somebody has to do if they want to just live better—forget fixing anything—but if they want to *start* trying to develop as a person, they have to be honest. The only way to be truly strong is to be able to admit when you're weak.

"I think your father would like it a lot more if you just tell him when you're upset with what's going on, or with whatever you're feeling, because he cares enough to ask and he cares enough to know, no matter how sick he might be getting. That's why you meet with me. So if you're sitting there telling me that you're good on a day-to-day basis, and you actually are, then that's great. But if you're not, your dad will think a lot more of you if you show him that it's in your strength, not some synthetic shine, where you find your pride."

Alex sits back as Hammond finishes. The pack of fish is empty.

15
June 23, 2010

Home once was a fulfilling place for Lauren. Feeling the
turn of the key, removing it from the Corolla, letting the metal
whisk across her palm as the ridges hungrily searched for the
lock instead of the ignition. There had been slight anticipation
as the smooth grey interior of the door opened with a click,
knowing that when she carried herself over the pavement to the
front door, and up the three steps, either her son or husband
would be waiting. They'd kept her from delving into the
darkness, the necrosis her parents had shown her in her youth
and for which her brother gave his life. Her son and her husband
had been the spark in the blackness, and she hadn't savored their
heat.

Now, she's spent the entirety of her life demolishing the
place she again calls home with emotional dynamite and the
misunderstood napalm of maturation. At the current step in
her journey, she suddenly finds herself relapsed into her past,
confronting an identical door; she knows the person who waits
for her behind the peaked angles of the roof and the whiteness of
the house's exterior is born from nothing but shadow.

Home is a place where nothing but childhood memories
and simple hope should exist; a return worth the effort, never
out of reach. She and her brother, swimming out back in the
old aboveground pool demolished decades ago; the entire family
taking walks down the road, far away from the city, close to
nature; her senior prom, which had been spent with the darkness

almost totally suppressed, a beautiful green dress upon her shoulders, both parents looking on from the background of the still shots. All those small memories earned fostered a marriage and a child that brought clean air to her smog on the bad days.

Instead, the happiness she recalls is but a stab of pain as she closes the door to her car. It twists in her soul as she views the porch in front of her, with its small awning shielding the deck chairs from the sun. A set of chimes hangs from the roof, swaying as if to soar. Lauren herself might as well be glass shards floating in the wind. She'd broken free of those restraints and flown high, from the steps of the church where she and Michael married to the hospital room where Alex was born, to the yard of the Palace.

Like all things which ascend to the sky, she too eventually fell, and on her way down the light above her faded slowly, until she finally hit rock bottom and shattered into innumerable pieces.

Lauren slowly approaches the small front door. Her keys jingle not in a carefree gait, but with the tremulous quality of the muscles in her hand. After two attempts, the key fits into the lock, and Lauren turns. Mom isn't home; she's rarely in the house, with her glowing social life and group of friends who detest her daughter. Mom hates her daughter, too. Lauren hadn't shown the promise of Jim, hadn't shown the effortless smile, the athletic prowess, the image of gold. She's always been the younger sister, the one who needs a little more work. Dad hadn't minded. Jim had been the malleable model of potential actualization, and Lauren was the clay only fit for being a base on which someone better should stand.

Their golden boy had been broken, and no amount of Mom's glue or Dad's determination fixed him. The statue of gold

melted down into death, and Mom's husband had followed.
All that remains is the cracked platform as valuable as a broken
record playing the music of parental failure on an endless loop.
It's surprising Mom's allowing her to reside in the house, but she
also senses it's only a matter of time before she finds herself out
with the rest of the trash.

She pushes the door shut, the once delicate fingers closing
the lock. A staircase winds its way up behind the wall next to
her. Lauren doesn't bother to follow the stairs, for they only
ascend to different levels of regret. Every step on the floor
creaks under her feet as she makes her way to the kitchen. The
Cheshire cat nips at her heels, its demented face enjoying every
reaction. The Cheshire now exerts free reign. She's been walking
around this old war zone for the past month, among the waylaid
dreams and stillborn aspirations that constitute the foundation.
The entire house breathes via noises in the walls, of the squirrel
trapped in the boards and the dead moments of her past.
Occasionally she thinks she should follow Jim, for if nothing
else, the blackness will be steady and absolute instead of this
Parkinson's syndrome of life, watching the entirety of her and
her husband's monuments crumble and fade.

Lauren reaches the kitchen table. A shudder envelops her,
propelled by a chill that does not originate in the temperature
of the air. It races up her arms, whiter than they've been in her
entire life, arching through the elbows and up to her shoulders.
This coldness is not a physical beast; it is an intrinsic force,
coming from the same station in her head controlling the
Cheshire cat, and the walls, and the desire to follow Jim into
eternity.

Pulling out a chair from the kitchen table, scraping the
wood of the floor, Lauren folds, her fingers finding her hair.

They steady among the locks, but now it's the eyes' turn to shake, not with muscular reactions, but with the tears tracing familiar patterns on her face. Hitting the wood one by one, some dam inside her head seems to spring a leak, and now the river Styx of emotion flows freely. If her soul is truly visible through her eyes, whatever shards remain, it surely drowns in a wave of its own inability to compartmentalize the calamities.

Lauren weeps. She cried more often than she had let Michael or Alex see, but this is an advanced form of sobbing. This isn't a cry out of desire, or a cry for attention; it is a cry rooted in need. The release is not manual, or routine, but systemic. A few inches away from her place at the table are the papers she knows she will have to sign during the next week—if she doesn't want them to be late by Michael's standards.

A divorce needs two signatures, just like a marriage needs two hearts to begin. They joined at the start, and so they shall be together at the end. The little words printed on those white sheets of paper should never have to exist in the world outside her walls. Instead, she's in the middle of the same place where her Dad tried to kill himself, finding exactly where 'forever and ever' ends.

The dick, the bastard, the cocksucking son of a bitch. He knows exactly where to stab her; her desire to rebuild all they've torn apart, how much sending divorce papers takes her fragility and jaggedly deepens the wounds. Every conversation since the 19 has been destructive, signs pointing to a future of non-existence. Alex maintains a sanction on seeing her if she doesn't try to resolve her problems with Michael. The poor kid is under his spell, some horrible substitute for the man who possessed so much light back in 1991. One would've thought the stupid bleb inside his lung, filtering the daily smoke, would've made him less apt to argue, or to fight, or to make motions towards ending their world. Yet here are those fucking papers, which arrived while she'd been out working.

This is death. The obituary, the death certificate, makes its home on the table. Dad had tried to leave her, Jim had left her, and now Michael looks to take and toss her out like the garbage her mother claims her to be. The Cheshire cat purrs as it shifts around her feet, the Fear and Hurt consuming. No miracle resolution, which served as an ending to all the other dumb arguments, can alter the outcome. All she needs to do is endorse the one agreement she promised never to bear, but now sits alive inches from her face.

For a moment, as the tears slow and the shaking stops, she considers signing the papers. She could sign the documents, and go buy a Cadillac Escalade and ride off into the sunset of a sealed room. Or hell, maybe she could even go and buy a shitload of gasoline, drape it over the house, and let the feeling inside of her, the smoldering wreckage of her marriage, become tangible. She could go down in the flames, and then she could tell Jim what an idiot he'd been for forgetting her here, leaving her to deal with the fallout. The pen lies only a few feet away, in her mom's holder she uses to fill out her obligatory birthday cards and manufactured well-wishes society tells her to send. She can grab the pen and fill out this endorsement with the same sense of stupidity and obligation every fiber of her heart tells her is wrong, but that every logical portion of her brain tells her is the only end to the agony.

But what of Alex? She wouldn't hurt him in that way, by following Jim, no matter how much peace it would bring her. The kid is blind thanks to Michael's manipulation: the man's sick, and can elicit sympathy from the wandering eyes who aren't observant enough to know the truth. The little bastard argues like his father, and Lauren can hear the same bullshit Michael says coming from the pained, sweet voice Lauren's reared from infancy. Hammond has to be out of his mind if he isn't telling Alex to call his mother during those sessions. If that counselor isn't *making* Alex call her, then maybe he's lost in Michael's sympathetic whirlwind.

They're all probably ready to take another spin at her expense. They'll all get together and laugh at her, just like the kids during high school, just as her Dad must've when he tried to use those pills to get out of this house, just as Jim did as the last of his soul filled up with that stupid gas, and just as mom must be, out with her friends, her daughter sitting in the same house with the Cheshire cat chortling under her chair.

Lauren walks over to the phone hanging on the wall. Michael will stop laughing at her now. Michael most certainly won't be getting his divorce agreement, whatever proceedings he wants, because Lauren is going to stand. The cat's grin grows wide as it hears the words, the smile on Lauren's face cracking with pain and the depth of her scars.

"Hello, you've reached the New Life Center of Quakertown."

She's dialed the right number.

———

Harlan sits on the love seat in the living room, looking at his son sitting in the corner of the couch nearest to the wall. The latest report on the MAI's progress has arrived: the disease is deadlocked with the medicinal efforts. No decrease, no increase—the battle has reached a stalemate.

"I can't believe this, Dad."

"I know, Mike. I never would've thought in a thousand years…"

"She just up and quits her fucking job."

Harlan sighs, wincing.

The cigarette in Michael's hand is nowhere near the window in the kitchen.

"I can't do it, Dad." Michael coughs, taking a drag from the white stick.

"Yes, you can."

"How am I supposed to pay for the mortgage?"

Harlan casts his eyes to the floor, the carpet underneath absorbing his gaze as if he's spilled a drink.

"I don't understand it, Dad. I don't understand any of it. I don't understand why this disease is still inside me, I don't understand why mom's on a ventilator, I don't understand why my wife just quit her job when she knows I can't work, and I really don't understand the concept of how I'm going to explain this to Alex."

"Explain what?"

Alex emerges from his room.

Michael sighs, laughs, and cries in one release of breath. Harlan looks up, giving Alex a pained smile.

"Come here and have a seat, Alex." Harlan pats the cushion next to him. Michael watches the blank television sitting near the wall. The pink tinged wood seems to be fading to pure white.

Alex walks over and sits down, the cushion sinking to accommodate.

"Alex," Michael says, the smoke trailing the words from his mouth.

"I've never tried to sugar coat anything with you. I've always been honest; I've always valued the fact we can talk about things. We aren't like your mom, we can be completely open. You can tell me anything, I can trust you with information."

"Right," Alex's pulse accelerates in tune with the response.

"Well, your mom quit her job today." Michael claps his hands together.

"What ?Are you serious?"

"Yep. I have a friend who works at the same place. She told me how she'd been spreading rumors about divorce before anybody filed anything."

"Tiff?" Alex asks.

"Yes." Michael sniffles shortly, cleaning his airway.

"Tiff told me that your mom called in after work today and quit. So, I called your mom. She didn't answer me, of course. But then she called back a couple minutes later, and she told me yeah, she quit. She didn't want spousal support on the divorce, so for the good of money, she quit. And guess what? Now, if we file for a divorce, I'm going to have to pay *her*."

"But Michael, the courts are going to know what she's up to."

"She's clinically fucking depressed! She can make an argument that she's sick too, Dad. According to Tiff, she caught her flushing the pills down the toilet in the office the other day instead of taking them at lunch, and then she decides to quit, claiming her mental disability is too much for her to deal with right now. Do you realize how that looks? It makes me seem like *I'm* the one abusing her!"

"She's living in a house that's paid for." Harlan adds as he shakes his head.

"So you're saying that we're not going to be able to pay for the house?" Alex's tears have found their way out of the desert of his facade.

"We can't." Michael says. "We're heading for foreclosure."

Alex knows the word.

"We can go for probably three months before they come and take it." Michael explains. Three months before the big, scary, evil bank steals his home.

"That's just until the start of high school." Alex whispers.

"I'm sorry, Alex, but it looks like we're gonna have to move, all because your mom quit her job."

"You aren't moving." Harlan coughs.

"What?" Michael looks at his father as if reacting to a punch. "Dad, we can't pay for this house if Lauren isn't working, this is a fact."

"We'll find a way to pay for it." Harlan replies stoically.

"No, Dad, I won't let you do that."

Harlan looks at his son, the weight and wisdom of his years rising to his face.

"It's not a problem, Mike. We can at least hold it over 'til you find another place in the district."

Alex studies Harlan.

"Alex needs to stay in the same school." Harlan says with a tone of finality.

Michael sighs, putting his face in his hands as if to pray. "I just can't believe she'd actually quit her job just to spite me."

The phone rings. Alex is sitting inside a high-pressure tube, his very ability to breathe becoming suspect.

"Hello?" Michael talks into the receiver as he bums his cigarette where the clock used to sit on the table.

"The doctor wants to see us? At this hour?"

Harlan is already on his feet.

Alex feels his soul shift.

"We'll be over in fifteen minutes."

Harlan and Michael share a quick glance.

It's warm enough outside for a cricket to chirp in the distance, just as it plows itself into the home of a spider, its fate sealed inside the beautiful spindles of a web.

16
June 23, 2010

A window resides in Cynthia's room at Greener Pastures, but it's unlike the one holding the promises of the hospital pane. The second window guarantees even more, because the purpose of her treatment facility is to heal the afflicted and send them back into the world. Many came into those rooms and then are able to either be pushed, helped, or even walk out of Greener Pastures after a certain amount of time.

Cynthia McGregor will never walk again.

Chairs align as a bedside council. Harlan has slept in one with a pull out footrest. Another accommodates Michael and Alex; it rests in front of the window. A final seat, made of tan leather, houses the figure of Eve. As they conglomerate around the foot of the bed, the ventilator puffing in and out, Cynthia's eyes closed, they study the woman as if she is a work of art.

She's the person who always used her time to ensure the safety of others, because she understands how the kindest ones are those who have known neglect. In Harlan's hands, he holds a small sheet of lined paper Cynthia requested a few days ago, prior to the surgery. On it, in her familiar, grandmotherly penmanship, are the words 'I love you.' Harlan holds the paper close to his chest. Even though she sleeps, he knows she can feel his grasp. Harlan seems to be out of tears—he sits gridlocked, weighing a decision.

The family knew prior to the surgery of this potential outcome. Random acts of happenstance seem to occur to the best of people, just like how the dedicated father had received a pulmonary infection; he's looking at his mother with tubes blossoming from her throat, feeling more hollow than an abandoned church at Easter. The damage is final, and no correction by either doctors or surgeons can mend the wounds of time. A woman who had not been at a great risk of stroke still suffered one; a person who had never acted in malevolence now stands outside the doors of tragedy.

Do they choose to reach the end, with peace?

Michael puts an arm around his sister's shoulders. Only a few moments ago, back at the house, the possibility of recovery still hid in the false promise of the undefined. They would've walked in the room, and she would've been standing, a twinkle in her eye, talking to them in her familiarly soothing voice as to how they could all go home.

Silence accompanies Eve's tears; Michael's stay suppressed only due to the proximity of his son. His marriage shattered, the mortgage failing; his lung throbs internally with infection. His own mother lies dying in front of him on the same machine his best friend had left behind.

"I don't think we should do it." Alex says, his shorts providing a rest for his arms, which in turn offer a platform for his head. Memories flash in front of him like channels through a cable box. Walking in the park in his youth, next to the big wooden castle with the arrows painted on the side of the structures like Native American art; the way in which she always asked him the same questions in a way so holistically pure it made him warm in the middle of winter. Alex wipes his eyes as his father turns to him.

"Alex," Michael says, "We don't want her to suffer."

"But what if she gets off the ventilator? What if she gets

better? She could walk again, she could recover."

"She wouldn't be able to talk."

"I know."

Harlan silently peers down at the face of his wife. Her morphine induced sleep alleviates the agony Harlan feels behind her mask. The peacefulness is haunting. As the seconds pass, he sees no rest in the silence, no true stillness, for there is a soul trapped underneath the machines, somewhere below the needles and the bags of fluid.

Part of Alex mutters about how there's a shot she can be Fixed, just like how he's Fixed things before. Death is not something to be Fixed, for at any given moment, anyone on the earth can die.

Harlan is going to keep the note he clutches to his chest in his coat pocket. Her handwriting covers his pages; her script imprints his soul.

Eve walks to the side of the bed opposite her father, taking her mother's free hand in her own. She hadn't come to visit when she'd been well, because the scene playing out in front of her eyes could've never happened. Time would just go on forever, with lives rotating in distance and routine without an end. She clutches the hand of the woman, the biologically separate but familiarly loving mother, who had saved her and her brother. This woman is the architect who rebuilt her father— now sustained by the gentle fade of technological support. Every time she hadn't called, every mile she'd moved to get away from memories Cynthia hadn't caused, expresses itself in every cipher of fluid flowing down the tubes into Cynthia's bloodstream.

"I love you, mom." Eve speaks into her ear, just below the bandage.

"I'm sorry I moved away. I'm sorry I fought with Michael."

Her lip quivers, but the emotion of the years breaks through her mouth's limitations.

"I know you aren't my mom by blood. You didn't need to be."

"I remember, I was eighteen. My own mom had just passed. You sat me down. You told me that even though you'd just met me, I was your daughter. Mike and I, we're your kids, and you're my mom."

Eve finds the betraying, soft blue of her mother's sheets blotching with smaller, darker spots.

Harlan gazes at her from across the bed.

"Eve?"

Eve's irises are barely visible through the shroud of the water.

"Don't be sorry. It's meant to happen."

Eve returns her vision to the sheets, a couple more tears falling out in response.

"I could've called. I could've stayed closer. I could've been less of a bitch to Michael and we would've talked! I would've been able to come over and see you, see Dad, see all of you, spend time together, just like the stupid portraits all those families take."

Harlan's face is a synthesis of a smile and a grimace.

Eve's emotions pound on her teeth, but only three words emerge in a choked voice that could belong to a six-year-old child.

Those three words, just like on the paper, "*I love you.*"

Michael rises from his chair. He pulls the seat behind him as he goes, and offers it to Eve, clouds obscuring the entirety of her vision. She releases Cynthia's hand, and Michael picks it up delicately. It's soft and wrinkled, but still comfortable and strong.

"I'm sorry, too, Mom." Michael says to Cynthia. "I'm sorry

this happened to you."

Michael feels another chair at his back. Alex has followed him.

"You told me something when I was about twenty-six years old, I think. I was a man on paper, but still a kid." Michael studies her, all the familiar features and beauty age hasn't spoiled. The ventilator hisses at him, but not even its noise can over-talk his words.

"You saw what happened between my other mom and Dad, what happened to me." The choking sensation rises again, transferring from Eve to Michael in a few short steps. Michael pushes it down, clearing his throat.

"I asked you, I think, why my mom had been an alcoholic, and why my parents fought. I asked you, 'Cynthia, why do bad things happen to good people?' The fact I even asked it made me feel like I was an eight year old. And you told me something that I'm never, ever going to forget. I loved my mom, but you were more of a mother to me in more ways than she ever could've been, and this was one of those times.

"You said, 'Michael, if you're living, you've got problems. The world isn't meant to be nice, it isn't meant to give you things that you don't work for. You might get lucky, but generally, it's going to give you a bunch of 90 degree turns, good and bad. You can't predict the future. The only thing you can do is work hard and be a good person. Michael, you aren't afraid to give or receive love, and that makes you extraordinary.'

"You told me, mom, 'We can't have happiness without sadness, Mike. But it's the happiness you can find that makes the hard times worth living. People are put here for a reason. We don't know why, we aren't meant to know why. But there are going to be people in your life who are meant to help you, who are going to be there for you through those bad times, people who you can have the honor of saying you love, and who love you in return. They can be family, friends, but the best part of it is, you're never going to tell when one is going to come into your life. It could be at some point when you're down, when life has beaten the hell out of you, when you're left lying on a cold floor alone with nothing but the place from which you fell hanging over your head. But these people will try and help you stand. They'll tell you that you can make it, even when you think everything is lost, and that even in the darkest of times, there is some light out there to be found. You just have to know where to look.'"

Michael feels his composure breaking. Just before he allows the release, he lets out a few more words to Cynthia's ears, believing with every fiber of his being that she can hear him.

"You are, and forever will be, one of 'those people' for me."

He kisses Cynthia on the cheek softly, as if too much pressure will scrape the skin, before leaning back and putting an arm around his sister, whose smile has been born from the warmth radiating from the words Michael's lungs, infected, blackened, and dismayed, still defiantly speak with hope.

Alex doesn't have a speech to give. All he leaves as tribute is a small kiss on his grandmother's forehead, just underneath the white of the bandages.

After either minutes or days, Harlan looks at his two children.

"Are you ready to call the doctor in?"

Michael and Eve nod.

Harlan stands, tucking the piece of paper in his pocket.

Cynthia McGregor is relieved of the ventilator.

Three days later, she passes on, a smile imbued in her face.

She makes it through the window after all.

———

Lauren doesn't attend Cynthia's funeral.

———

July 6, 2010

Jack Hammond attended Cynthia's service. Sitting in his office, he surveys Michael McGregor carefully. It's been two days since the burial, and Michael reeks of both tiredness and absence.

"How are you and Alex holding up since the funeral? It was a beautiful event." Hammond's voice is careful, as if a loud syllable might accidentally be a step on a covered explosive.

"I think we're all stunned, Jack. My Dad's not trying to show it, but he just doesn't seem to have that light about him anymore."

"With how close they were, I'd imagine it feels like half of him is gone."

Michael laughs—an expression of grief, because he's either going to laugh or break down, just like in the hospital room when the damn tube finally left her throat.

"The day she passed—it had to have been like 3 in the morning, Jack. I'm sleeping on the couch, Alex is in his room, my dad is staying where Lauren and I used to sleep. We got a call from the woman at Greener Pastures, telling us that she's slipping away. So I went to go tell Alex, ruffled him out of bed and all. Alex was fast asleep, but when I went to wake my dad, he was already dressed. I turned the corner to knock on his door, and he was already standing there, looking in the mirror we have in our room. I told him that the woman from the rehab place was on the phone, and he just nodded. I've never heard my father that quiet in my entire life, but the entire ride over, with the sky peaking in the middle of the night, there was nothing but stars and silence. All those years they spent laughing, talking, the way those two acted together; it was as if they were traveling in the lack of noise. Alex was listening to his music, because what else is he going to do? I can't explain the feeling I had, the sense of both loss and defeat, but in that silence, I also felt a kind of calm. It was one of the weirdest moments, because it felt as if my dad spoke to me."

Michael takes a breath.

"We got to the hospital, rehab place, whatever you want to call it, and we took that same dumb elevator back up to her floor. Her name was usually on this board that the nurses used to keep track of the patients. It wasn't there anymore. We walked down and turned into the room, and the nurses, you know, they wear that sympathetic face, but is it genuine, Jack? These people are used to saying those words of 'we did all we could' and 'I'm sorry', and I'm sure they mean it, but I always stop and think about how many people have heard those exact phrases. So she directs us in, and she was lying there.

"There were no more machines, no more bags of fluid, no more ventilators or different mechanisms keeping her alive. At the end she had started to lose bladder functionality; she lost her ability to speak first, she couldn't even communicate with us. The sort of peace that I saw in her face, Jack, the way she was just lying there. They always say that stupid bullshit about how she could be sleeping, but I knew that wasn't true. My 14-year-old kid standing behind me certainly didn't think she was asleep. He didn't really know what to do, and really, neither did I, but my Dad still treated her like gold.

"We left the place after like 30 minutes, and we knew we weren't going to be sleeping. I drove them into Quakertown, to this diner, and I looked at the sky. It had to be almost five in the morning at this point, maybe closer to six. I had never seen such a beautiful sunrise. There wasn't anything special about it; really, it looked like the sun just breaking through the clouds. But we're sitting in this booth, and there are probably five employees in the place, and I'm looking out the window, and it was just the way the sunlight peaked through the sky. There has to be a certain slant of light that reaches your sight after somebody passes, and I hadn't seen it in years. I saw Alex looking at it, and I knew he was seeing the same thing I was, but when you see it for the first time out of a diner window eating some omelet at five or six in the morning, how do you move past that? I saw it for the first time when my biological mom passed, but I saw it come from street lamps casting their beams through some soft rain when I was driving. It comes in different ways, but I hadn't ever expected it to come for my son in that moment."

Michael pauses again, and then looks directly at Hammond.

"I'm getting worse, Jack."

"What do you mean?" Hammond asks.

"Something inside of me. First, it was the diagnosis, then the disease isn't getting any better; it's staying the same no matter how many of those pills I shove down my throat. Then Lauren moves out – she didn't come to the funeral, by the way."

Hammond's eyes light up, rudely jostled.

"Really? I thought she had a great relationship with Cynthia, from what you told me."

"I thought I had a pretty good marriage too, Jack, but I guess I was wrong. Lauren moves out, my mom has a stroke and passes away like this, my house is gonna go into foreclosure, and my kid, Jack … my son."

"Your son is extremely smart. He knows that what's going on isn't going to last forever. It's in his blood; he has an extremely tough father."

"I don't know how much more I can take. And like I said, I'm not getting better. This shit is flying around inside of me, I haven't been resting, and now I'm a couple days removed from a funeral which I haven't even acknowledged."

Hammond ponders the words like a scientist classifying a bone.

"I'm going to make sure Alex is ok, Mike. Here's what I'm going to do for you: every time you come in for a session, you pay me. When you bring Alex, don't."

"Jack, you don't have to do that."

"That's not the point. Put the thirty towards your mortgage."

Michael sighs. "Thank you, Jack, really."

Hammond stands. 60 minutes have passed.

"I still can't believe Lauren didn't come to the funeral."

"Neither can I. I don't even know who she is anymore."

In truth, Michael is losing sight of himself, and Hammond sees him drifting further and further away.

If Michael's doubt roots itself in this session, it's about to be extrapolated past anything he thought possible; no discounts will be able to balance the cost of what is about to be threatened.

17
July 16, 2010

Alex has aspired to be a lawyer since the start of 8th grade. The idea of working with people and being able to apply writing in his job appeals to him, and the pay is supposed to be excellent. The career has many species: personal defense law, trial attorney, corporate law; the opportunities abound. Alex can't see himself stuck behind a desk, a slave to the grind of a clock, and he finds himself unable to imagine defending somebody he knows to be guilty. He's heard that the relationship between an attorney and their client is one of the most important bonds in the entire legal world, and if the client and the lawyer are on opposite pages, then the synchronization between the case and the desired outcome is rendered nearly impossible to procure.

One part of law Alex could never manage, he knows, is divorce law. Yet now he finds himself at the center of a completely different breed of case, one involving a familiar buzzword:

Custody.

With Cynthia's death only days removed, Lauren called them not to offer condolences, but to threaten Michael with a potential custody suit. Michael raged at her, and only quick intervention by Harlan stopped him from wrecking another one of the house's phones.

Alex waits in the lobby of an office in Quakertown. It's a small place, situated near the town center. Its stone architecture is in close proximity to the Sines 5 & 10 diner. From his father's explanation, the escalation of the divorce proceedings is now a disaster that nobody, not the Fixer, not God, not Satan, and definitely not any miracle, can correct. If legal proceedings continue to the point where custody is a question—finances and custody are two separate issues, but they're both as daunting as shark fins in a pool full of children—then counsel shall be necessary.

Alex hears the pulses of his father and the lawyer's voice through the glass of the office door. His name is Mr. Niles Rogers; Alex half expects him to prance out of the entryway and start singing about what a wonderful day in the neighborhood it is, now give him three thousand dollars. The receptionist at the door seems adept at acting robotically pleasant, but Alex hears the turning of the gears through the static of peoples' personas. Reconciliation is a foregone conclusion, and he's going to end up as nothing but the product of another broken home, just like a main character in a Green Day song.

The third ticket to the concert now belongs to Eve, who is an extended guest at the Hotel Pennsylvania. Alex sees all their colored and creative masks, with their smiles acting like a cotton swab on an amputation, and he remembers Hammond's words about sources of strength and the value of honesty. If the axiom is true, now all these people have turned from shiners into a masquerade of happiness, about as authentic as the silicone implanted and injected into people proudly displayed on the cover of the magazine folded in his hands.

The door to the office opens, and Michael emerges first, sickness in his steps. Alex places the magazine down, and walks past the sticky chairs of green leather scattered about the waiting area to shake the hand of Mr. Rogers.

Alex barely hears the man's words. He's dressed in a nice

suit, his black hair combed with gel and streaks of gray. Rogers speaks of how he's going to be helping both of them, and how he's impressed a person of Alex's age is already leaning towards a profession such as law, because, he assures Alex, it's a profession that requires durability and malleability.

So is having your grandmother die, your father sick, and your mom turn into a raving lunatic in the space of three months.

Lauren's stopped paying the essential heat and light bills her paycheck is meant to cover. Now it's up to Michael to whore himself to his family for the money. From the chatter, Alex hears Aunt Eve is paying the mortgage for August. He feels grateful in his father's shame.

Mr. Rogers finally stops talking, patting Alex on the shoulder, and returns to his office. Alex considers how no amount of mercenary help will be able to affect the outcome, whether it be provided by a lawyer, a counselor, or the friends who are surely tired of his incessant bitching about his life. Maybe he should just move away, and let Aunt Eve keep her money.

He follows his father out to the parking lot, determined to look forward instead of allowing the rear view mirror to act as their windshield. They have a concert to attend in a few weeks, and a school year beyond the summer. Walking out the door and onto the street corner, Alex looks over at Sines. His family had visited the place frequently before his life was a caterwaul of constant upheaval. The place will stay the same for a hundred years, but Alex feels as if the every second of stability comes with a cost.

———

Two days later, Alex awakens to find his father in the

kitchen, talking on the new, shiny, silver receiver. Harlan has moved out of the Palace to live back at Willow Grove with Eve, whose husband knows his wife won't be home for at least another month. Mr. Bennett is content, due to the fact he's on an endless rotunda of business trips. He aids from afar, delivering remorse for his wife through financing the mortgage for the Palace. For the time being, father and son are alone. Roxy has decided to stay as well, with the authorities rejecting her request for a more stable environment based on the fact she's a dog.

"It's gotten larger?" Michael asks, cigarette in hand, the water from the tap dripping onto the metal of the sink.

"Unfortunately," Dr. Fost says. He examines the results of Michael's latest chest x-ray like a preacher reading from scripture.

"Are the drugs working?" Michael notices Alex's silhouette in the doorway to the living room.

"Possibly. But from the results, it seems as if the bleb has burst."

"Burst? What the hell does that mean, Richard?"

"It means that, due to the infection, it seems to have spread past its boundaries to expand further into the lung. You really need to rest, Mike. I don't know what you're doing to yourself, but whatever it is, you need to put your own health first."

"How the hell am I supposed to do that? I have to work, I have a father who is going insane with grief, and I have a son to raise."

"I know, I know. But you can't expect to beat this disease if you don't concentrate more of your energy towards recovery. I understand the circumstances are less than ideal."

"That's the understatement of the year, Rich. My mom just

died, my wife has abandoned us."

"All I can do is report the results of the tests, Mike. That's my job, and I wouldn't be doing it well if I don't try to steer you in the right direction."

Michael takes another puff of his cigarette.

"Are you smoking?" Fost asks.

"Yes." Michael replies, blowing towards the window.

"Well, cut that out. This situation isn't terrible, but it's definitely not getting any better thanks to smoking. It's not good for your health."

"I know." Michael lights up another cigarette.

"Let's keep track of it, but you really need to rest more, ok?"

"Ok, Richard. Thanks for letting me know."

"You're welcome."

Michael hangs up the phone and places it down next to the sink.

"Dad?" Alex asks from the doorway. "Who was that?"

"Dr. Fost."

"What did he have to say?"

"The results from the latest x-ray are bad."

"What does that mean, exactly?"

"Well, instead of shrinking, the bleb has decided to expand."

"How much?"

"Not by a lot, but it's starting to get worse. It's because I've been too active."

"You've been doing a lot."

"I've had to, since your mom won't."

Silence.

"How are things going legally?"

"Mr. Rogers says that we're due for something called mediation, so I'll get to see your mom face to face. She's decided to represent herself."

"Represent herself?" Alex chuckles. "She's not a lawyer."

"Well, she doesn't want to pay." Michael bums the cigarette in the ashtray.

"She also doesn't want to work, or do anything except wallow in how much she feels I've hurt her. She won't call anymore, she only sends these cryptic emails where she cancels bills and pisses me off. I don't think we'll have to worry about it if she tries to make a case for you."

"Good, because I definitely don't want to go with her. Never in a million years."

"I'd never let you go with her in a million years, either, Alex. You need to know what's right and what's wrong, and everything you're seeing her do is completely the opposite of how a rational adult should act. I'm not saying I'm perfect, but she thinks she is. You know, you've tried talking to her."

His mother talks about how she's forced to live in someone else's home, how Michael initiated the divorce proceedings, how she'd been told to leave. Alex had followed his father to one of the mandatory pulmonologist meetings with Dr. Nicholson, and argued with his mother whilst his father received his check up. Alex won't entertain his mother with another volley of shouting.

Alex embraces his father, standing in front of the kitchen sink, the same place where Michael had yelled and called him Lauren only weeks ago.

———

In the evening, when things become darker and the distractions such as friends, the computer, games, and general interaction all set with the sun, Alex usually lies awake in bed. In his younger days, he considered life to be a television show;

what happens after the end? The credits will roll; a funeral—
just like the one he attended for his grandmother—will occur
with tradition, but will there be a sequel? His friends obviously
believe in heaven. Staring up at the at the Eagles helmet poster
his Uncle Jim installed over eight years ago, Alex knows he's
never seen heaven through the ceiling. He likes to hold faith
in the items he can touch, and the surrounding people. The
two most important figures, his parents, are now the source of
the problems. His friends are the ones who hear of the micro-
tragedies taking place on a daily basis, of the legal developments,
of the fact that his father's illness is a wildfire in a dehydrated
forest.

Alex rolls, the white blue of the sheets following his motion.
He reaches to the bottom part of the nightstand, where he
knows he will find the familiar plastic of the pen waiting for
him, along with the small book of paper. The small books are
an upgrade from the pads. Since the end of seventh grade, the
lyrics have evolved from simple tunes into grander mediums of
conceptual expression, mostly centering on the way in which
he can't talk to people, even as he interacts with dozens daily.
He's collected, yet so broken; so introverted, yet so friendly.
He doesn't want each passing glance to look at him as *the kid
whose parents are divorcing* or *the kid whose father is sick.* The page
doesn't judge him, and as his fingers guide through the contents
of the book, he reads the words that hold the quiet truths of his
simple world.

By the light over his bedside table, he dissects one of the
pieces he wrote back in June. It doesn't speak to anyone in
particular, but if he's going to believe in heaven, he might as well
make it rhyme.

"I Need an Angel"

Alex smiles fondly. He wonders at the possibility of telling somebody, besides Mr. Hammond, his inward thoughts and notions of life.

I need an angel, I need a soul,
To give me direction, to take control.
I need a savior, to get me through,
I need a hero, can it please be you?

Alex knows others face much tougher tribulations, but he doesn't evaluate for severity; he seeks similarity in a world of people who all walk by him as if he's a brick in the walls of the high school—by his choice.

Do you understand? Do you contemplate?
Is it too early? Or am I too late?
I'm free falling, losing all my days,
I need a voice, I need to hear it say...

Here comes the chorus, Alex thinks, with a mock sense of achievement

I'm here to lend a hand.
Yes I, understand why it began.
I will help you any way I can.
I saw you when you ran,
You needed a friend,
Let's run through this land,
I will help you make a stand.
Where is my angel?

He isn't the type of person to pray, but any time God feels like sending somebody down to help him, Alex will be waiting with an open heart. He flips the pages again. There's the one

wrote on the way to the hospital to see his grandmother for the
final time. It's called "Spirit."

Cynthia had specifically signed papers saying she didn't want
to suffer. Even though such an outcome was the antithesis to
everything Alex considers moral, he knows it was her decision to
make. He keeps waiting for another kiss on the cheek.

Reading all of "Spirit" would take a lot of time, but he loves
the chorus:

And you know I can see,
The darker side of me.
Why'd you have to be,
So cold and lonely?
Why can't you comprehend?
It's hard to understand,
When you are as lost
And hopeless, and dark as I am.

Alex wants to reach out to whoever's hand wrote those
words. The life on the pages belongs to a stronger person, who
can be solid like Hammond wants and shine like his father
deserves. When school arrives on the autumn wind, he'll have
to be at the absolute top of his performance, to prevent adding
unneeded stress while his father tries to rest. The fact his father
hasn't left rolls over him in a wave of injured gratitude. He
doesn't miss his mother enough to abandon the people who truly
work for him, in exchange for the one who claims to miss him
while she stays on the backside of Bethlehem.

Closing the book, Alex puts the trap over the emotions, a
Greek hero sealing the winds of the world in a mountain with
the tip of his spear. It's two weeks until the Green Day concert.
Aunt Eve will tag along, and he'll probably have a lot more fun

with two people who want to be there, not with someone who took defusing a situation as a way to leave forever. He won't quit, drifting off with his own words in his mind, no matter the consequence; he's sticking in it for his father's sake.

Alex would love an angel right now.

18
August 3, 2010

The action inside the Buick LeSabre makes the drive to New Jersey seem extremely short. The blaring music, the combined chatter of the three passengers, and the miles away from the battlefield known as home allow the past year to fall into an illusory backdrop. If Lauren were in Eve's place, everything would be normal. Instead, brother and sister, who've hardly found time to grieve in the past month since Cynthia's death, are looking forward to the waiting brightness at the venue. The mile markers passing by stand out of the foliage like hitchhikers. Alex doesn't keep track of them from the back seat. He's focusing on the words of his Aunt, his earphones resting limply in his lap.

"So you went and saw Phil Collins together?"

"Damn sure did!" Michael says, keeping his eyes on the road.

The kid has been looking forward to the concert for months, and the fact they're getting out for a night is a blessing. A normal summer day consists of random visits from the Pocks down the road, Harlan coming over to possibly cook his world famous beef stroganoff, Eve assisting with groceries, his friend David selflessly providing essential items and services, and Michael feeling like the largest collection of worthlessness on the face of the planet. He can feel the breaths getting shorter, the sleep growing deeper. Between Alex's needs, counseling appointments with Hammond, meetings with the lawyer, and preparation for the mediation with Lauren waiting for him in early September, every step is part of a mile that keeps growing in length.

"And that was before he retired?" Alex asks.

"Yes it was. It was on his farewell tour, sometime in the 90's." Eve replies. A skirt and a nice red top, which fits her figure and contains the pain from her mother's death, have replaced her love of dresses. She's never been a mother before. Bennett hadn't wanted children. As she hangs her elbow out the window, the wind kissing her arm smoothly, she feels the marks Father Time painted on her starting to recede as they draw closer to the venue. Green Day's "Holiday" blares on the speakers.

"He was still really, really good." Michael assuredly states. "The place went absolutely ballistic when he played 'In the Air Tonight.' That's a weird song for our family, though. It seems like something bad happens whenever we hear it unexpectedly."

"Oh come on," Eve says, her laugh laced with a teenage note. "You don't believe that what you hear on the radio can really predict how your day is going to be?"

"I feel more like we're on the 'Boulevard of Broken Dreams.' I'm apartment number 48." Michael replies, a tinge of humor in his voice. He wants his wife. He wants to hug her and kiss her and bring her to this concert, so she could stand next to him during any love songs they're going to play; instead, he'll be a baseball player in an empty outfield, trying to catch the pieces of his broken heart flying towards the fences.

"I wish Mom could've been here." Alex says.

"Yeah, well, that's her fault." Eve says. "I'm not complaining! I love Green Day!"

"Band wagoner." Michael mumbles, pulling into the massive parking lot of the stadium.

"I'm not! I moved to California, remember, and they're from that area. I loved *Dookie*!"

"That's disgusting, Aunt Eve." Alex laughs.

"You know what I mean."

"You certainly smoked a lot of weed when we were teenagers." Michael chortles.

"Hey!" Eve smacks her brother.

"Not while I'm driving!"

To onlookers, they very well could be a married couple—they walk closer to each other than Lauren and Michael used to during family excursions. They stroll towards the venue through the tailgating fans, playing music and singing along to everything from *International Superhits* to *Shenanigans.* It seems as though the family demons are banned from the venue for being too drunk on the negative aspects of life.

The stage is designed perfectly; even in their seats near the outskirts of the venue, the family can see the face of the drumhead clearly. The opening act is a band called AFI—A Fire Inside—whom Alex knows thanks to their song "Miss Murder", but not for much else, except for possibly "Girl's Not Grey." Their music is faster and louder than Alex's usual taste; they're a great accent to the experience.

As the McGregors take their seats, die-hard fans of both bands file in, with guitar shaped bottles of alcohol colored as if it's Christmas, vibrant combinations of lime green and succulent red filled to the foam with punchy, riveting taste. Alex doesn't understand why people need such gratuitous amounts of alcohol to enhance the drug of music, but he doesn't understand a lot of things anymore. He stands in the middle of his father and Aunt, enjoying the excitement captured in the anticipation.

Eventually, Davey Havok from AFI emerges, signaling it's time for the crowd to either sit down and listen or to stand up and cheer.

AFI don't use many pyrotechnics, instead utilizing the bare minimum to accent their powerful vocals and resounding bass lines. They aren't the main stage, and after about 30 or 40 minutes, they clear down with thank-yous and appreciation from the still-building, yet absolutely raucous, crowd.

If Alex were musically talented, there's no doubt in his mind the stage would serve as the pulpit for his dreams. He could write a song, but he hasn't been gifted with the ability to craft magic. Instead, he relegates himself to writing lyrics for music he produces in his mind, without translating their sound into tangibility, due to lack of interpersonal charisma and the lack of drive to develop greater skills. For now, he'll project his aspirations via the energy of Billie Joe.

A few minutes later, a man in a rabbit costume wanders onto the stage. Eve laughs hysterically.

"Is that the lead singer of Green Day in there?" she asks.

"Probably." Alex replies. Billie Joe is eccentric, and Alex wishes his personality could emulate those actions. Armstrong projects his soul through his lyrics and music; Alex knows thousands of people will probably never shout the words he writes at night back to him in a massive stadium. Alex doesn't mind the fact he's unique, but part of him, probably the naturalistic teenager, still wants to be bland and normal. He pays attention to politics; he values intelligent conversations, isn't apt to go partying, and puts forth a shy demeanor. He's afraid of opening up, especially when the interior of his life is even uglier than his outward appearance. Nobody wants to merge with such a corrupted existence, one which originally contained so much promise, but now is seemingly ready to collapse at the faintest August wind.

The lights dim. The sun is already almost beyond the

horizon; it knows the level of excitement coming for the 14 year old and his family is going to be too much for a simple star to withstand. As the first notes of the intro theme roar to life, Alex, Eve, and Michael are on their feet instantly, as the surging fans await the entrance of the band. For the next few hours, all of the hardship is about to be blasted away by anthems Alex listens to repeatedly, not just as music, but as therapy for his soul even Hammond can't duplicate.

The lights fly up, and Alex cheers as he receives a slice of pure salvation.

———

The sun shifts behind the clouds; a child, hiding from the monster in the closet, stays underneath the sheets until sleep finally arrives. In his younger days, Harlan himself feared an unseen monster lurking in the shadows. Now he walks through his home, closing out the remaining lamps, knowing the daylight brings the true terrors of the world. The darkness doesn't hold a candle to the tragedies that are illuminated and bare, and the beams can't blot out the emptiness from the type of cold that thrives despite the heat. The kind of blotches resonating in his soul are internal, and even if he walks into the kitchen and uses one of Cynthia's knives to slice open his arm, reality won't bleed out of him. He's shaken the hand of Death once more, and this time, it's taken from him not just a partner, not just a soul mate, but also his savior.

Death has followed him since his childhood, when his own father dropped in the middle of a Saturday haircut. His last moments had been among rows of shaving cream and conditioner as his heart burst on a barbershop floor. Now Death returns, and it doesn't care how much Harlan hurts or how much it seems like Cynthia will be waiting around every corner—she's now a tenant of a different house. Harlan couldn't bear watching her wilt away like a flower plucked out of the ground, so he'd finally let the petals turn to dust.

Harlan monotonously walks from the kitchen into the living room, sitting down on his favorite chair in front of the television. Across from him rests a fraternal leather twin. Harlan's chair is black. The other is white. Both are of exceptional quality, and are only a few years old.

In a couple minutes, Cynthia will come floating in from working in the kitchen, or from reading in the bedroom. She'll fold her nice dress or slide her pants across the leather and prop her feet up, and the two of them will watch the evening news, or maybe just chat about the day's events. Eventually, she will get up and walk across the carpeted floor to the receiver on the wall to call Michael, or maybe Eve, or perhaps even her friend Dorothy who lives in Florida. No distance can separate her from her children, and no way in hell will the fact their daughter lives in California, or that her friends live in other states, stop Cynthia from being the loving, upbeat, cheerful, sanguine, protective, gorgeous –

Harlan stops. He can almost smell her cooking drifting out of the kitchen. Using his jean-clad legs to push the footrest back underneath the chair, he rises. He walks with legs untouched by Father Time, but with a heart so tinkered and tampered, he can hardly breathe. This isn't grief. This is a cold, hard slap of truth so forceful it sends him to bed in the middle of the afternoon. The sun doesn't shine as brightly; the kids who play a couple yards down don't seem auspicious anymore. They're all going to die someday.

Harlan opens the fridge, seeking to fill the holes inside

of him with a little bit of sustenance. During his residency at
the Palace, everything seems to have expired. Working his way
down the glass shelves of the fridge, he tosses out some of the
spoiled amenities. Cynthia will never buy anything for him
again, whether it's food or another anniversary gift. Now, the
anniversary will turn from being a marker of progress and the
future to being a lingering reminder of an absence. Out goes a
block of cheese, previously prepared for a salad jointly eaten. He
discards mayonnaise used to construct sandwiches; he empties
the entire fridge, except for a little glass tub hiding at the
bottom. It's cold, and Harlan picks it up with both hands.

A small note sits on top of the lid; it's pink, and written
in the same scrawl as the paper folded in the chest pocket of
Harlan's coat in the closet, close to his heart but distant.

Just in case you get hungry ☺—*Love you.*

They're cookies. Chocolate chip cookies.

Harlan drops the glass on the ground. It rattles, but doesn't
break. And there, on his kitchen floor, does Harlan McGregor
cry, the loneliest man in the universe.

————

Three hours after the glass touches the floor, Green Day
finishes their concert. Alex, Eve, and Michael walk into the
parking lot together, waiting for the crowd's flow to take them
back to their vehicle. The band's set stretched from the early
days of their catalogue to their most recent releases, which Alex
will keep replaying until his ears bleed. When he goes to see
Dr. Nicholson with his father, he soundtracks the journey with
American Idiot. When he wants to get in the mindset for the
next day at school, he plays *21st Century Breakdown*. When his
parents argue, he plays "Boulevard of Broken Dreams" on repeat,

until eventually removing the earphones and morphing into the Fixer.

Since the Fixer is apparently dead or in a coma, he can listen to even more Green Day, Ozzy Osbourne, or Aerosmith. Songs are his prayers, lyrics his psalms, and he's just attended the best church service in the history of his life. Even Michael, who is a fan of classics as opposed to the contemporary, revels in the glow of the outstanding show. If he had been smart, he never would've given up his musical pursuits, and he would've gone to see more concerts. Since he's a genius, he'd given it all up for marriage, a career arc which seems to be heading for the autopsy table.

While Eve swells with joy at the sight of her excited nephew, one part of the experience causes reservations in her thoughts. During one song—near the end, so probably something from *Dookie* or *American Idiot*—she noticed Michael sitting down while everyone around him had been dancing and singing as a pulsating chorus. He'd said he simply didn't have the air to stay on his feet; so drained was he from the medicine, so hampered was he by the encircling situations of his life, he couldn't stand during the modern day rock opera. He asked Eve to drive home. Within the first 15 minutes of being on the road, Michael's fast asleep, the music of Eve and Alex's conversation acting as his lullaby.

Eve talks from the driver's seat, making occasional eye contact with Alex by using the rear view mirror. Michael's entire soul is askew. Is the MAI really hitting him that hard? Or is it that every time he looked over to his sister, he wished he saw see his wife dancing beside him instead? His son's mental state and the possibility of such a vision occurring decline in tandem with each day. Perhaps it's better to sleep, for in sleep, upon waking, at least the nightmares are left behind; if one is attempting to sleep in the nightmare of life, sleep is the only place to which dreams can escape.

Eve drives, Michael sleeps, Alex talks about the band. The grace period from the darkness is over. It returns from the depths of Harlan's fridge.

19
September 4, 2010

When Alex wakes up at 5:30 in the morning on September 4, he doesn't cherish the last fading hour of summer. He wishes to forget the heat. He rolls out of bed, the sheets falling easily off his body, planting his feet on the lukewarm carpet. He's only stolen four hours of sleep from the night, and he doesn't plan to return to the scene of the crime.

The hole in his father's lung is becoming aggressive. The mediation between his parents had been expensively futile, the genesis of further conflict and division. Lauren isn't coming back, Michael continues to fight; Lauren wants to see Alex, Alex has no reciprocal emotions, and Michael will continue paying Nile Rogers to try to procure a happy day in the neighborhood.

Aunt Eve is a frequent fixture around the Palace, driving down from Willow Grove on a daily basis. Instead of music and benevolence, days have been filled with doctors' appointments, pulmonologist visits, driving Alex to guitar, driving Alex to friends' houses occasionally, and trimming the fat of the family's financial demands. Before the world exploded, such pursuits had been trivial, but by the time Alex rolls over and silences his alarm, the problems have outlasted the summer.

Alex takes his morning shower in silence, allowing the water to cleanse the grime of his soul. He dresses himself stoically, the expensive clothing covering the span of his emptiness. His motivation for rising so early is lost in the annals of the night.

When he exits his room, it's only 6:10. He has another thirty minutes before the bus arrives. It'll be bus 13 this year, just as it had been in 8th grade; he'll see Kenny with his antics, Leigh with her music, Paul with his 'being a Junior' shtick. Every other year, two parents had seen him off with their handkerchiefs of hugs and mementos of well wishes.

In the kitchen, Michael waits, standing by the window, a cigarette in his hand.

"Good morning, Alex." His happiness is flagrant, but anorexic.

"Hey, Dad." Alex walks over to the cabinet next to his father, grabs a bowl, and then crosses the kitchen to the pantry.

"You ready for your first day of High School?"

"As I'll ever be. I was talking to Zach about it yesterday, and we've all heard some really funny things."

"I'm sure you'll be fine. I never entered a High School, you know."

"I remember you telling me. Was Temple similar to how you pictured High School?"

"They didn't offer anything like a GED, so I had to show up for those classes. Universities are usually adamant about attendance."

"Why don't I just drop out while I'm ahead and just go straight to college, then?"

"Because you're smarter than me, Alex."

Alex is a boxer, and Michael is Muhammad Ali. Alex sees his father by the sink, the unquestionable expression of a proud parent on his face, disease constricting his smile. Gratitude unfolds in Alex's heart for the man he's known all his life, but is only starting to understand.

"You'll do great. You were what, ranked 7th coming from the middle school?" Michael tosses the cigarette into the ashtray.

Another five minutes trickle off his life.

"Yep, something like that."

"I'm sure you'll stay up there. You're really smart, Alex, smarter than me, smarter than your mom. I feel really lucky to be able to call you my son."

Alex smiles into the coldness of his milk. Isn't cereal technically a type of soup?

"I feel lucky to call you my Dad."

Alex still has another twenty minutes before the bus arrives. He walks out of the room and packs his bag with a binder for each subject, loaded with loose-leaf paper and a closeted aspiration for teacher-pupil connection. Alex loves learning every aspect of his English courses, and detests almost every Geometric formula in existence. Alex fights the urge to apply the wisdom of his home to his classes. He can't let the two worlds cross; if they do, disaster shall be imminent.

The bus arrives in a puff of auspicious, tree-killing smoke. Alex gives his Dad a hug, grabs his key, and walks down the porch. His music player is equipped for the ride, a smile on his face, and the tiredness chasing his stolen slumber catches him. Alex walks to the end of the driveway, the pavement crunching under his sneakers. He's wearing a new hoodie bought by Aunt Eve, with the same jeans and shoes from last year, with a tee shirt underneath adhering to his figure and his basic sense of style. He quarantines the embarrassment, the pain, and the isolation like a virus.

The bus rolls to a stop, and the doors welcome Alex to the next stage of his life. It's still mostly dark, and he takes the stairs hesitantly. Scanning, he sees Kenny sitting on the left side, his headphones draped over his head, listening to some new kind of music called dub-step. Leigh sits across from him, looking out the window. She gives Alex a quick smile as he walks to the back, which he returns. Alex sits in the seat in front of Kenny, and looks out the window as the Palace falls out of view. His father watches from the window next to the front door; Alex knows he's beaming. His father is a tempest of pain, yet his silhouette stands alone against the window. Kenny and Leigh notice him, and then their gazes leave the Palace as the bus trundles down the road.

20

September 23, 2010

It's around three in the morning, and the sun is shining.

It doesn't peak through the windows like a bold burglar. It does not warm Alex, for he can only see a sliver of light from the hallway. It is not going to cultivate or produce, for the source is illumination, not energy. The drowsiness of Alex's chest houses a singular tenant of emotion, as if the bottom of his stomach is going to collapse into his waist. No sunlight touches the hour of 3 AM, except if reflected by the moon or trapped in a star. Some say the hour between three and four is when the veil between this world and the next is the thinnest. On this night, the night where the beams from the lamp in Michael's room catch Alex's eyes, Alex shall cross the borders of possibility.

Alex wakes up thirsty; dinner last night was bite-sized potatoes, filled with clusters of salt and spice. Alex turns to the clock, and notices there are three hours before school starts. As Alex rises from the bed, he notices the light. Thirst doesn't drive Alex.

"He's probably just in the bathroom." Alex says to himself. A sensation runs up his arms, racing through his neurons towards the conclusion.

Pushing the blackness aside, Alex walks across the cold whiteness of the floor outside his bedroom. Alex opens the door, and walks through the living room to the fridge in the kitchen. His hands grip the cold water bottle, chilling on the upper shelf, and drinks hungrily. This triggers an urge to use the bathroom.

The toilet sits right next to his bedroom, so as Alex trudges back, still half asleep, the uneasy feeling sits upon his shoulders like a seatbelt on a rollercoaster.

Alex uses the restroom, and recedes into the familiar darkness of his room. Alex notices the light in Michael's room still lit. The forces of irrationality are suddenly pounding the gates of his mind. The 'what ifs' float around, prodding his brain like syringes trying to draw blood, pulling the organ from the refuge of sleep into reality. Suddenly, the light draws Alex, for finding his father will allow him to flee back into sleep. He hears the door to the living room open, and after waiting another minute, he walks towards the source of the noise, past the door and into his father's room.

The sheets on his father's bed are ruffled. Alex goes back into the living room to continue searching, and he finds the refugee.

Michael sits on the couch, wearing his bedclothes. The light resonates from a lamp sitting on the table next to the couch. Alex is overcome with the urge to eradicate each bulb in the house, stalling the heroic vehicle of sleep.

"Come here, Alex." Michael says. His voice is staggered, subdued by quick breaths.

Alex senses each abnormal respiration, drenched in pain. Alex has found his father, and isn't going back to bed.

"I think," Michael says, staring past the floor. "I think my lung's collapsing."

"What?" Alex replies.

"I think the bleb either burst, or my lung is collapsing."

"How long have you been out here for?"

"An hour."

"Holy shit."

"I tried going back to bed, but I came out here a couple

minutes ago. I heard you go to the bathroom."

Michael pants like a parched dog, and then wheezes more words.

"Maybe it was what we ate for dinner, but I don't think its heartburn."

"Maybe."

Perhaps, possibly. Every hypothetical solution now pounces on Alex. Michael's breathing continues, labored and wet.

"I can't even walk, it hurts so badly. I think we're going to have to call an ambulance."

If they call the ambulance, it will serve as an admission of the terrible state of their lives. If they don't call the ambulance, a fatal error may be committed. Rationality leaves the McGregor household in an instant, launching itself through the window next to the front door leading to the yard.

"I was trying to see if it would go away. If we call an ambulance, your mom can make a case that I can't take care of you."

"Dad, we need to call somebody."

"It might go away."

"You've been awake for an hour and a half."

"I know, but give me a few minutes."

The new golden clock on the table ticks away the seconds.

"Dad, you could be having a heart attack."

"I'm not having a goddamn heart attack," Michael snarls. "It's in my lung, not my heart."

"You're holding a spot right next to your heart. It could be the lung; it could be both."

"Alex, I'm telling you, if your mom hears about this, I might lose you."

"That won't matter if you're dead."

Michael cracks a smile, as the pain in his chest threatens to tear him open like a badly built doll in the hands of a toddler.

"Either way, we're not calling an ambulance. I'll drive if I have to."

Alex's temperature drops. A current infuses his blood.

Stealing a glance at the clock, Alex notices it's 4:10 in the morning. 40 minutes have been spent waiting, and talking, and observing. The breathing becomes spectral to Alex; no miracles are working to let him go back to sleep, to let everything be fine for another day.

Michael coughs, a ratchet and coarse sound.

"Dad, if you're not going to call that ambulance, I am."

"Just," Glazed sweat permeates Michael's face. "Just let me see if it'll calm down on its own."

Alex rushes over to his desk. He picks up his phone, the same keys he often uses to text his friends, with a savior on speed dial.

"Don't do that, Alex." Michael looks to him. "Don't do that to me."

Alex hesitates.

"Go get me the phone from the kitchen."

Alex does as his father tells him. His feet mutely whisk across the hardwood floor.

The lines on Michael's hands are tributaries of precipitation.

"I should just drive. It's not that bad."

"Dad, I am not letting you drive to the hospital."

"I don't want to lose you, Alex."

"I don't want to lose you, either. That's why your ass is staying on that couch until you dial the ambulance."

"Don't be smart with me."

"I'm being smart enough to make sure you're ok, Dad."

Michael sighs, still clutching a lump of his chest. The pain refuses to flatten, throbbing. It pulses like a parasite filled with blood, not a pump meant to sustain a life. Michael's responses are slowing. His voice is fading like the end of a song.

Concurrently, the possibilities stab Alex. *Heart attack. Collapsed lung. Irreversible illness.* In all outcomes, Alex sees a piece of his nightmares coming alive in every breath his father cycles, every remark of pain he makes, and every drop that slides off his face. Michael's hand now rubs his jawbone.

"Fine." Michael finally picks the phone off the couch and dials three numbers.

The Fixer is back. The Fixer is on *fire*. He's closing the game like a pro.

Michael describes his symptoms to the voice on the other end of the line. Alex realizes he's getting out of school in the morning.

At the conclusion of the call, Michael hands the phone back to Alex. The solution shall arrive in the form of an ambulance, which will come to the house in silence. 10 minutes.

"Let's go get changed, then." Michael rises from the couch slowly, flinching with each step on the familiar floor.

Reaching the room he used to share with his wife, Michael walks through the doorway as Alex turns on the light in his own adjacent room. Walking to the closet, with its dumb white sliding doors, Alex throws on a shirt and a pair of jeans. He doesn't bother to put the sliding doors back into place. Alex walks back into the hallway with the light turned off and the right hand side of the door left dangling from the metal sheath on the ceiling.

Cautiously, Alex enters his parents' room. His father's bed *(if he lives to sleep in it again)* is covered by a maroon bedspread of warm fabric. Alex remembers how he'd hide under those covers as a child.

Michael walks out of his closet, wearing a pair of jeans and a loose tee shirt.

"I have to use the bathroom." He declares, each breath manual.

"Ok, I'll be waiting right here."

With each exchange, Alex can keep a grasp on the world falling away from him. If something happens to his father, all the blame will fall to the Fixer. The Fixer has been battle tested for these high-pressure situations, but has never experienced this severity in his line of work. The situation is solely his to command. Every step he takes could be leading him one more mile away from resolution. Even in his glory, the Fixer feels the fear.

Michael limps over to the bathroom. Alex stays around the corner, watching the windows, waiting for the headlights.

Michael finishes his business.

"Ok, Alex, I'm done, we can talk more now." Finally, he's playing into the plan. The conclusion is near. The Fixer will get a medal.

Alex turns the corner and peers into the bathroom. When the house had been a church, the room served as a baptismal chamber. The floor is tiled and white, and two navy blue rugs adorn positions in front of the sink and the bathtub. The toilet sits in a small alcove in the wall. A pillar supports the ceiling adjacent to the toilet.

Michael leans against the pillar. He's standing up straight, his jeans buttoned. He seems to be staring at the mirror, his hand hugging his chest.

"Are you alright, Dad?"

Michael doesn't answer.

The mirror is shiny.

"Dad?" Alex takes a step into the bathroom.

So shiny.

"… Dad?"

"Lights." Michael mutters. Father Time stands still.

Then he falls.

Michael hits the blue rug like a collapsing tree in the forest.

"HOLY FUCK!" Alex screams. His father slams into the carpet, rolling on his back, clutching his chest.

"He's dead! He's dead! I can't believe it, he's going to die!" Alex cries hysterically, bending over Michael. His eyes are barely open, with the lids covering the blue Lauren stared into on their wedding day.

His chest still rises and falls, his hand limply placed over the side of his chest containing his lung, his heart, and his mortal soul.

"Dad? Can you hear me?" Alex asks, too stunned for tears.

His father mutters an unintelligible word.

Kneeling over him, they could have been wounded comrades in arms on a battlefield, ducking in a foxhole.

The Fixer hadn't broken the fall.

"Alex." Michael says, his eyes still half shuttered.

"Dad!" Alex crouches. The ambulance. The long shot. The miracle.

"I'm alright," his father whispers. His breathing is shallow. Fluid envelops his face. His hand flutters close to his heart.

"I'm completely fine."

Alex runs into the living room. The front door is already open. He lurches into the foyer and sees the two EMTs walking up his sidewalk. Alex bursts into the chilly night air.

"My dad just collapsed on the floor. I think he's having a heart attack."

Their faces are blurry, as if covered by mosaic. When Alex tries to recall them later, it's as if they're frames cut from a strip of film. Their speed increases as Alex delivers the news.

The trio enters the house. The male EMT walks over, and helps Michael sit up. Michael vomits into the toilet, blood mixing with the bile.

Alex goes and puts Roxy in the kitchen. Alex makes sure he has his phone and his key. Alex turns out the light next to the couch, resisting the urge to punch it through the wall. The Fixer is officially retired.

The two EMTs load Michael onto the unfolded stretcher. A portable oxygen tube hooks to his mouth and nose. They wheel him down the stairs leading from the front porch. The open back of the ambulance waits in the driveway. Alex shuts the door behind him and locks it, rushing to see where he's going, not just for the next few hours, but also for the rest of his life.

As the EMTs lift Michael into the back of the ambulance, he speaks four words:

"I love you, Alex."

Part III

September 24, 2010 — February 17, 2011

21

September 24, 2010

Alex awakens cradled in an armchair in an adjunct room
of the hospital, down the hallway from his father. He notices
stiffness in his back, and the hoodie he wears is no longer in
condition for school. The ambulance raced to Doylestown
through the drizzle and barriers of the morning sun. Alex moves,
and his neck grumbles in protest, the muscles annoyed by the
fact his four hours of sleep were spent hanging over a chair like
clothes on a line.

In all her years, Eve never expected her brother to have a
heart attack. Harlan sits in a familiar position next to the bed.
Michael complains about how the lingering pain in his chest,
and how the drugs the doctors provide him only agitate. During
the panic of the night, Eve called Lauren and informed her of
the situation. Lauren had immediately asked why Alex hadn't
called her, to which Eve offered an answer. In Alex's view, Lauren
engineers her absence to cause destruction, so they shouldn't
allow her to keep the rubble as a trophy.

Alex only fell asleep after establishing his father's residency.
Stumbling back into the hospital, Alex sees doctors flocking
around the entrance to his father's room like vultures.

"It's a 95% blockage in the artery." One doctor proclaims,
his silver hair draping over the sides of his glasses. He's dressed in
a white coat; his beard is long and neatly maintained.

"Oh my God." Eve says, looking at her brother. Michael
stares back, his eyes glassy and void.

"Most likely, it's caused by smoking. How long have you smoked for?" A second doctor asks.

"Around 40 years." Harlan answers.

"40 years for you or 40 years for him?" the first doctor asks.

"40 years for me." Michael says. His voice is a moisture deprived choke.

"But you're only 49." The third doctor says quizzically. She's a young woman in her mid thirties, with shoulder length dark hair and a wedding ring on her left hand.

"And?" Michael responds. "I had a stressful childhood."

The three doctors share a look. Harlan sighs and wipes his face with his palm. Eve looks down. Alex shifts into the picture, sitting on the opposite side of his father's bed with his Aunt. Michael's essential organs seem to be revolting, with the lung convincing the heart to join in the overthrow of health.

"We'll have to implant a stint." The second doctor says, a younger man in his 40's with cropped black hair. He looks a little bit like Misha Collins, Alex thinks.

"What does that entail?" Eve asks.

"It's a pretty minor surgery, actually. It doesn't require a large dose of anesthesia. It's basically non-invasive." The female doctor explains. "We go into the vein and open the flow, allowing the blood to circulate properly."

"Had you been feeling fatigued lately?" The silver haired doctor asks.

"Yes, but I think it's from the battery of drugs that I swallow every morning which aren't working at all, not this." Michael replies.

"Mike, try to be cooperative." Harlan's voice is muffled by his hands.

"Speaking of things that don't work," Michael continues.

"What does Dr. Nicholson have to say about this?"

"We've been in contact with his office." The second doctor says. "He'll be paying you a visit either later today or tomorrow."

"Maybe we can ask him why the drugs that everyone is saying should cure me only cause more problems, and now I'm in the hospital." Michael's agitation roots itself in the reddening of his face.

"Mr. McGregor, we honestly can't determine the effectiveness of anything at the moment. Were you scheduled for any other surgeries?"

"Yes, actually." Eve says. "They wanted to perform a bronchoscopy on him, since the results from the x-rays have been mixed in regards to the MAI." She sits motionless, the stress of the situation flowing around her like water around a rock.

"I don't believe we're going to be able to facilitate that at the same point as the corrective surgery for the stint. It may need to be delayed."

"Great." Michael says, coughing to punctuate his sentence.

"Would it not make more sense just to get it done now?" Alex asks.

"Unfortunately, with the condition your father is in, it would be a mistake to try and do too much at once. A bronchoscopy isn't as simple as it sounds." The Misha Collins lookalike doctor replies.

"How long will we have to wait?" Harlan asks.

"I'd say probably three weeks, if not longer, depending on the recovery from this." The same doctor adds.

"God dammit." Michael mutters.

"What do we do in the meantime?" Eve ignores her brother.

"Well, he should stop smoking, for one." The female doctor

says.

Michael stares at her through his haze of medication. *Assholes.*

"Rest needs to be a priority." The older doctor says. "After this surgery, inactivity will be imperative. He's very lucky that this heart attack wasn't severe."

"He's lucky Alex was there to take care of him, too." Eve smiles, casting an eye to her nephew.

"We'll try to see him once more before the surgery tomorrow." The doctor concludes. The three coats bid the family adieu, and move on to spread more good news down the hallways.

"You did a great job, Alex." Eve says. "I'm so sorry you were alone."

"It wasn't a problem; I did what I remembered to do." Alex replies, brushing off the compliments and condolences with numb fingers.

"Should I tell Mr. Hammond you aren't going today?" Eve asks.

"No," Michael says. "No, he needs to see Jack, even if he's not going to school."

"What do you want to do, Alex?" Eve pats Michael on the arm.

Alex thinks.

"I'll go, definitely."

"Alright, I'll drive you when its time. We still have a couple hours, so let's go and get something to eat." Eve stands, looking at Harlan. Harlan moves in from the outskirts, filling the chair at Michael's side.

"You did great, Alex." Michael says as his son reaches the door.

"Thanks, Dad. I'm just glad you're alright."

Michael coughs, his surrounding apparatus shaking slightly.

"You'll be fine." Harlan says.

"That hurt." Michael states dryly.

———

Eve and Alex walk down to the food court through the halls. The sponsors and great figures of the hospital's history adorn the walls like a hall of fame. Alex doesn't want to work in a hospital. He's supposed to be in school. He could go home and attend his appointment as usual. Instead, as he and Eve reach the food line, he selects the most processed looking hospital sandwich on the face of the earth, along with a bottle of water. Eve pays. The two walk through the tables and chairs to the outer edge of the food court, where they can still pretend to be part of the outside world.

"I'm sorry I wasn't there." Eve unwraps her sandwich. It's small, portioned to satiate.

"Why did you move away from here?" Alex asks.

"Well, I'm sure your dad has told you about our mom, your Grandmom." Eve replies, taking a bite.

"Some stuff. He said that she drank a lot."

"She did. She would drink seemingly as a hobby, trapped in the house all day. She would go down into the basement and chuck the empty bottles against the walls; we could hear her clanging at all hours of the night. It was scary." Eve doesn't feel as though the delectable hospital sandwich will fill her stomach.

"It's really hard, living with someone with an addiction. My dad wanted to help her, but he had to work. With us two kids, he sometimes had to work more than one job to keep the bills paid. We never wanted to put our mom in treatment, but there were times when the two of them would fight and your dad would take me upstairs to call the police when I was only six or seven. I think it's why he moved out when he reached 16."

"It was that bad?" Alex cuts in.

"It got violent. My dad had no idea what to do really. We didn't want anybody at school to know about it, either. It was embarrassing, with my mom drunk and my dad lost in a job with no idea how to help her. And yet there your father and I were, trying to grow up in the middle of it. Your dad's older than me by about seven years, so he probably remembers a lot more."

"What do you remember about it?"

"One time, mom got drunk." Eve swallows.

"She was telling me to either clean my section of the kitchen or to run the vacuum, and I refused. I had to have been about eight, maybe nine. She was raging and cursing, and I guess the fact I mouthed off to her made her mad enough for her to take a green bottle and slap me across the face."

"Wow." Alex replies, his sandwich forgotten.

"She was really lucky it didn't break, but it gave me this massive welt on my cheek that I had to explain in school. She would beat us if we didn't listen, and my dad didn't know what to do. Eventually, it got so bad your grandfather and I had to move off old Wales road. I still call it that after all these years, mostly because it helps me forget some of the other events. I'm sure your dad will tell you more when you're older."

"Maybe." Alex thinks.

His dad isn't going to die. That's preposterous.

"How did you deal with having to go home to that, along with going to school?"

"It wasn't easy, by any means." Eve says, deciding to eat half of the sandwich. The dirt from the buried past seems to rise the more she talks.

"But we had to talk about it somehow. Our friends knew what went on, our other family members knew as well. When dad finally snapped and moved us out, your dad had already dropped out of high school and was working odd jobs around town en route to living with his girlfriend. It was an urban area, so he could find work in those days as a kid. Nowadays, you can't really do that. I must've been nine when enough was finally enough. I eventually grew out of the area, from that little house. I can talk about it now, but there are some things," Eve pauses. "I can't talk about some things, even with my husband."

"That's what happened to my mom, too."

"Believe it or not, Alex, your mom is a good person."

"Where is she, then?"

"She can't be here; your dad would probably have another heart attack. Every time I talked to her, when I came back to visit or saw her on the holidays, she seemed really nice."

"We all seemed really nice on the outside."

Eve's eyes bear compassion.

"Everybody has problems, but your family … the way your dad and mom argued, for hours on end, with the kind of anger they'd hold …"

"I know all about it, I was there." Alex picks up the nearest half of the sandwich and reluctantly takes a bite. "Why did you and my dad not talk for like seven years?"

Eve smiles. "That's just how your dad and I can be, I guess. He's a really stubborn individual."

"Really? I never would've guessed."

"I don't even remember what it was over, but he took me having a bad day to mean that I was out to get him or something."

"I know that feeling." Alex keeps chewing. He swallows.

"Both of them together are one hell of a match, right? I can't believe we held it together as long as we did, looking back now. My mom told me back in April we were probably heading for a divorce."

"Well, they did at least one thing right together, and he's sitting across from me."

Alex laughs.

"There were good times too, though, when we were kids." Eve continues. "There has to be."

"I had mine as well. A lot of the time, we didn't have to pretend too hard, but other times it seemed as if we would have to lie, even to people like you." Alex's food has vanished.

"I knew there was trouble going on, from when I talked to Grandma Cynthia. You just need to know that what happened, that's not how a family is supposed to be. That's not how people in a relationship are supposed to treat each other."

"I know that much." Alex wraps up his trash. "If I ever get into a marriage, I sure as hell won't repeat what I saw here."

"Do you have anybody you're interested in?" Eve asks wryly, changing the topic away from the minefield of memories through which they've been strolling.

"Yeah," Alex says. "I don't talk to her, though."

"Why not?"

"Who the hell would want to be involved with somebody in a situation like this, for one, and two, I'm really nervous. I guess I'm just sort of shy about the entire thing."

"You'll mature. Someone is gonna come along."

"Hey, you sound like me."

"What?"

"Gonna."

"It's a McGregor thing, don't you know. My last name may say Bennett, but you know I'm a McGregor, through and through. We all are, no matter what the papers say."

Eve pokes the wrapper of her sandwich with a finger.

"Listen, Alex, I may not have been here for the past years, but we have a lot of time to make up. I know it took your dad getting sick, but now that I'm back around, I'm not going to leave you again. Your dad wants me to be more involved, to help him take care of you. It's really hard being a single parent, and I might not be a mom, but I can be a damn good Aunt if I try hard enough."

"You're already a damn good Aunt." Alex says. "You feel more like a mom to me right now than my actual mother."

"Don't go that far. I'm sure she misses you."

"Misses me?" Alex replies. "She's sitting over in Bethlehem wallowing in her own pity. She doesn't give a damn what happens to my dad, and I guess I'm just more collateral damage to her."

"You're never, ever collateral damage, Alex. Not as long as I'm around."

Alex squeezes his Aunt's hand, their meals sitting neglected, half consumed.

"I might not be, but it sure as hell feels like I am."

———

Michael's surgery is a success. They implant the stint, and they clear him to return home on the weekend. Eve drives both Alex and Michael home from the hospital, stopping only once to let Michael get out of the car and smoke.

22
October 15, 2010

October will be the last good month for the McGregors.

After recovering from his heart attack, Michael resumes his daily regimen of shoving pills down his throat. Eve finances the mortgage, with Harlan paying some of the other bills. November shall be confronted when the calendar changes pages.

Alex knows, at least for October, he'll be staying in his school with his friends, in the same Palace, and his mother won't have a chance in the world of possibly winning the war. Going to school this morning, it's raining hard. Alex waves goodbye to his father and hustles onto the bus.

There's Leigh, giving him her friendly smile as he works towards his seat, the most consistent aspect of his life. Repeated motion traps his father. Court dealings, appointments—which now involve something called an EKG—consuming entire days, trying to maintain the house, walking Roxy, making dinner, trading emotional airstrikes with his mother. The divorce proceedings are stuck. According to the presiding judge, Lauren has "given up" on the situation. Alex doesn't need a gable or a robe to deliver a verdict of common sense. He contains his anger in the seat two steps in front of Kenny and Leigh.

Putting on his headphones, Alex hears the music start; he looks out the window. Gliding down the road, the rain seems to slide over the glass like racers shooting for the finish line, the trees still cast in the remnants of the night.

Green Day still holds at number one on the Alex McGregor

charts, but a particular song is starting to make gains, by a band named Linkin Park. Their latest album, *A Thousand Suns*, preaches of an environment shredded by conflict. Alex lives in the song "Waiting for the End."

The guitars soar to life at the beginning of the track, with an electrical beat pulsing in his ears, the strobe lights from the top of the bus flashing onto the trees cast a glow on Alex's prison; he feels as if Chester Bennington sits in the seat next to him, narrating Alex's timeline, with Mike Shinoda leading in.

Alex's words of joy are as hollow as the promises made by his mother. He doesn't feel like he's at the end of his journey. People will never know of his life's occurrences, the trials faced by his family, for they will make him appear weak if revealed. He doesn't care how Hammond rephrases the truth; the people in his school don't need to know. His friends are privy to only morsels of the agony.

Occasionally, as the bus turns a corner, Alex wishes he can just tell everybody. But he won't. Even those who sit near him on this bus won't know, who ride past the remains of the Palace daily but don't see the desolation inside.

High School is fine so far. He's holding his A's, and he's starting to talk to people. He might only be in the building until next month; he slaps the thought away as if swatting a hornet. He won't leave them. He's already making more friends than he ever thought possible, Kenny and Leigh included. They don't talk in the morning, but the afternoon guarantees hilarity.

As the thoughts flash in perfect synchronization with the white light on top of the bus, the rain continues to pour. It's Chester's turn. Alex wishes for nothing more than to control his parents, blocking them out or finally reaching a ceasefire.

Alex casts a glance to the window, and notices Leigh looking out into the rain, her hands in the pockets of her jacket, her pink earphones arching down. She's at least a year older than him; he's never considered having a friend outside of the grade before. Hell, he's never hypothesized having a friend who's a *girl* before her. But the more and more the group on the bus talks, the more she seems to navigate his stigmas. Does the fact he's now 14 constitute a world of difference, now that these people are the highlight of his day? Alex knows he's getting ahead of himself; talking to somebody on a daily basis doesn't mean that they're a friend. He talked to his mom for 13 years straight, and she's certainly not a friend.

The bus rolls to a stop, and Bobbie, the annoying sixth grader who never shuts up on the afternoon rides, joins the bus.

Alex doesn't have a mother right now. She's in some far off place beyond vision. Are all those dreams his parents fought for, which he argued for, really going to end with a move to Willow Grove?

"I'm not going." Alex mumbles. Kenny glances up, and then back down, the dubstep blaring from his ears.

The chorus repeats again, and then Shinoda shoots into the bridge. Alex grins. The bus cuts another turn, and then starts backing up. It has to make a turnaround from a road with no outlet.

The music unfurls into a symphony of sound. Alex's eyes start to tear. Day to day is one thing, but when simple survival becomes not a mode of operation and instead a litmus test for Alex's mental health, and his father is having random heart attacks in the middle of the night, how much can be consumed by the emptiness?

More than anything, Alex wants to fight for the life his parents have built and accordingly broken after the explosion of their critical mass. Deep down inside of him, Alex knows it's his fault. He'd been the subject of so many arguments. He's why his mother is a terrible example of a parent. If Alex can find a way to Fix it, then nothing will be broken.

The Fixer in him died when he Michael hit the floor; the rest is just the psychological autopsy. His father seems to operate reluctantly. The cures have yielded only new ailments.

If only Alex could sing like Linkin Park! He could turn the lyrics he writes into music. How many kids have it worse than he does right now? Some can't t even afford food. Suddenly, Alex feels ashamed of wallowing in his hardship. Alex changes the track to Green Day's "Longview" and puts the thoughts back in their places. He might consider smoking drugs, like Kenny.

"Why do I love everything I'm going to lose?" Alex whispers. He'll keep his grip, even if he dies in the process.

———

Alex gets on the bus in the afternoon quickly. With his earphones engaged, he ignores the laughter. An itch irritates him from underneath his skin. It started in the middle of English class, during a presentation by his friend Neil. He's written 176 lyrical pieces since 7th grade. He's starting to piece them together on his computer. If only he'd been born musically talented. The lyrics he's writing are the only escape from the hot, burning, destroyed, ruined —

"Alex?"

Alex removes his earphones. Kenny stares at him from the back seat, a mischievous grin on his face. His eyes are mirrors reflecting the essence of his soul.

"Yeah?" Alex replies.

"You're smart. Tell me if this will work." He holds up a

beaker and a hot plate, along with a coiled plastic tube.

"What … Kenny, what the hell are you doing?"

"I'm trying to make a vaporizer."

"What is that?"

"You'll learn about it more when you're a Sophomore."

"How am I supposed to know if that'll work if I don't even know what you're trying to do?"

Kenny puts the tube to his mouth, pretending to inhale, his eyes rolling in mock pleasure.

"Oh Jesus." Alex laughs. Leigh walks on the bus and takes her usual seat.

"Did you steal that from Mr. Barlow's room?" Leigh asks, noticing the contraption in Kenny's hands.

Kenny smiles, tossing the beaker and catching it with one hand. "He won't even notice, the guy's too tweaked out."

"Kenny, you're gonna get in trouble if you ever get caught with that." Leigh remarks, sharing a humored glance with Alex.

"He won't notice." Kenny shoves the chemistry equipment back into his bag. "I've taken all sorts of stuff from this school, and I've never gotten caught."

"Well, good luck with that." Alex says, turning back around. At least Kenny isn't coming to school high anymore.

A couple other kids meander onto the bus. Alex wonders, as they pass, if they see around his walls. He never has the courage to ask, so he relegates himself to sitting and imagining what it must be like for them. He's heard of terrible events in the lives of other kids – parents dying, drug addictions. One kid's house even burnt down. There is no luck in terms of tragedy, and he's finally fitting in as he's always desired.

"Does anybody have a pen?" Leigh asks.

"No, but I have a lighter if you want it!" Kenny replies,

flicking a Bic. The bus driver chuckles from the front.

"I do," Alex says. He's keeping one earphone dislodged. Alex reaches into his pocket and hands the pen to Leigh. She thanks him, and Alex goes back to his music.

Grandpa will be at the Palace when he gets home. Maybe there's a way to inherit his strength.

"Here you go, Alex." Leigh hands the pen back to him, along with a small addition in the form of what seems to be a miniature index card.

Alex puts the pen back in his pocket, and turns the other object over. Leigh's face smiles up at him from the picture in his hands, those same incandescent eyes set in front of a blue backdrop. *That picture really doesn't do them justice*, he thinks, looking back at her. She gives him the same dependable smile, and Alex flips to the back of the picture. On the white, she's written 'Alex', with a small heart drawn next to the name, and then simply her name, '*Leigh*', at the bottom. Alex thanks her, and safely stores the picture in the top part of his backpack, returning to his music as she does the same.

For some reason, the small action elates him. He'll have to talk to her more, now, instead of letting his music be the one to listen. She probably has a million other people to talk to, such as her actual friends, but maybe there's worth in taking his buds out more often.

Maybe.

———

When Alex gets off the bus, he quickly heads towards the Palace to show his father the picture. Michael and Harlan's faces are flush with color. Michael wants to stop taking the drugs. Alex walks in the door and hands the small object to his father, a massive smile on his face.

"Who is this?" Michael asks, an inquisitive tone in his voice.

"Her name's Leigh, she rides the same bus I do."

"Oh, I thought it was that Addison girl you said you liked." Michael jokes.

"Shut up, Dad."

Harlan laughs. Michael's illness alleviates every time he speaks to his son.

"She's pretty. Is she a friend of yours?" Michael asks.

"Yeah, I guess she is. I talk to her sometimes."

"Well, good. Like I've said, it's normal for you to expand your circle. High school has a way of doing that."

Alex isn't one to argue. As he takes the picture back, he gets an idea for a song. Thinking of the words in his head, he travels upstairs. He knows exactly what he's going to call the new collection he's crafting:

Working Miracles.

23
November 2, 2010

Michael McGregor tries to get out of bed, and he realizes he's practically immobile.

His right leg, at the joint where the hip and leg connect, sears with pain when he tries to swing it over the side of the bed. The sensation began as a nagging prod about a week ago, but now it's as if the bone will snap out of the socket and punch him in the kidney if moved. Such equates to his life since the end of October. Clutching the sheets, Michael moves the rebellious joint out of its frozen position, and he cries out as it passes over the side of the bed and hits the floor.

He's been careful – he's been dancing from Rogers' office, to mediation, to appointments, to walking the dog, but none of those should've rendered a great strain. Roxy doesn't pull when she's outside; a 50 pound Corgi isn't going to shatter bones. He's scheduled for a liver biopsy soon.

Could the MAI really be expanding so rapidly? The last chest x-ray was painted purple with the marks of the disease. Eve is paying the mortgage for November. Their income handicaps correlate with his deterioration. Thinking of Alex, Michael pops the pills down his throat, swallowing the water and suppressing his desire to find the nearest gun store, insert a barrel into his neck, and pull the trigger. Knowing his luck, it would fire a blank.

Michael drags his leg across the familiarly carpeted floor. Lauren is still playing poker against him with nothing but a pair of jokers. She's convinced Michael's 'mental state' is in decline, and that 'his decisions' are the roots of their issues. Michael scoffs, and tries not to vomit from the stupidity.

Alex says it himself: he cut communication after Lauren tried to cancel their electricity. She sued for custody with the belief Michael's harming Alex, with her non-existent income and demented bitch of a mother floating in and out of the house in Bethlehem. As he hobbles into the kitchen and skates across the floor, Roxy looks up at him from her position under the counter attached to the island. Michael's foot misses her tail by inches.

"Sorry, girl." Michael says, walking over to the fan and the merciful cigarettes. The dog is the one getting the worst from this entire ordeal. Mommy is gone, Daddy is crazy, and Alex is receding.

Alex won't move in with Grandpa. Michael coughs and takes another drag. As he looks out the window, he notices Eve's rental car pulling into the driveway.

This is a hurdle, this illness. If he gets over it, then he'll be in the clear. If he doesn't, he's going to die. He would've rather battled the ventilator than fade into nothing.

Bumming the cigarette, he hobbles to meet Eve at the door. It opens, the familiar chime of the security system filling the house. Eve walks up the stairs, and sees her brother wincing. She's wearing a light blue jacket, her hair pinned up, her fingers clutching a bag of groceries.

"You look like you're in pain." Eve says to greet him.

"I am. This leg." Michael turns back inside.

"What happened?"

"I guess I must've pulled it or something a couple days ago. It's been bothering me for the better part of a week now, and I can't remember what I did to it."

"You don't think it has anything to do with the MAI, do you?"

"No, the MAI is in the lung," *all over the lung.* "It must be just a sore joint or something. One more thing, right?"

Eve comes inside. "Where's Alex?"

"In his room. He's been talking to his friends for a bit."

Alex is on the phone with Dan and Zach, catching them up on the recent events of *General Gruversville.*

As if on cue, Roxy starts barking.

"Oh what the hell dog, I just talked to you. Do you have to go out?" Michael asks. The pain in his leg flares. He finds himself sitting on the arm of the couch, his bare feet pressed on the top of the heating vent on the floor.

"Alex!" Michael yells.

"What dad?"

"Come here and take the dog out, please!"

Alex tells his friends he'll call them back. Grabbing his cell phone, he throws on some jeans and a shirt and walks into the living room.

"Hey, Aunt Eve." Alex walks over and gives her a hug.

"Hi Alex. How are you today?"

"Good, I was just talking to some of my friends."

"Which ones?"

"Dan and Zach. They're the brothers, so I can talk to them both at once."

"You kids still do regular phone calls? I thought it was all about social media by now."

"I just got a Facebook in August, and dad won't even let me use my real name."

"I make him use it as Alex Stephen M." Michael says seriously. "You don't know what kind of shit could be out there on the Internet."

"We don't talk about it, it's a silly place." Alex laughs at his father. The man doesn't understand the tools in his hands when he uses the computer. Grabbing the rough leash from the side of the cabinet near the door, Alex calls Roxy over. It looks as though it's about to rain outside.

"I like that hoodie." Aunt Eve says.

"Some kids at school don't." Alex replies, opening the door.

"What do you mean?"

"I don't know, I just think that I look bad sometimes."

"Nonsense." Eve says, as Michael moves towards the kitchen. He's hunting for another elusive white stick.

"Yeah, I know." Alex pushes the screen door open. Roxy is ready to go.

Alex wakes up in the mornings and spends minutes trying to get his hair right, but it always ends up looking disheveled. As he walks down the stairs, he thinks of how he wants to change all the aspects of his appearance. It isn't the kids at school making him desire a new image, it's the departed voice of the Fixer trapped in his cranium.

Roxy does her business. It's starting to drizzle. The rain is liquid inspiration for Alex. Pulling his phone out of his pocket— not a smart phone, but not a dumb phone, either—Alex opens up a new message, addressed to himself. Standing underneath the tree, the dog tethered to his hand, Alex writes.

All of the things you like to say I'm not,
Down from my clothes to my train of thought,
You always were quick to criticize,
Said everything I told you was a lie.

Alex and his father have started to fight again, over the

stupid shit, like whether or not they're going to be moving out of the district. Now that he hasn't spoken to his mother in over two months, and now that his father is becoming more unrecognizable by the day, Alex realizes he's alone. He taps on the phone, his fingers flying over the keys, the rain misting around him. Alex's last lyrical collection is dedicated to a few friends and his father, because Alex still knows this is all his fault.

Your turn of anger and your hits of fate,
Never took the time to stop and think,
I had a feeling like everyone else,
You saw me as blank and took out the details.

Alex doesn't really like this particular lyric. It seems weak. It serves its purpose, however. He continues, now with a chorus line in mind.

And all of the things I won't get credit for,
I never was another mental whore,

Alex laughs to himself. He certainly never wants to forgo his mental temperance. He continues with the chorus section; it's going to be rather lengthy.

I was different in my own new way,
Yet you never found the things to say.

In their mediations, do his parents spread the pieces of Alex's life out on the table and pick which ones are worth keeping? His mom has to give a shit, but she doesn't talk to him, no longer calls, never even takes the time of day to look past herself and consider Alex's motivation for not seeing her in six months.

And all of the dreams and the shattered hopes,
Every creature on earth dies alone.

But I still have to carry through,
Everything I do I'm doing for you.

He wants to return his father to radiance. He wants him to get better; he wants him to win. Alex thinks of a particular picture hanging in the kitchen, a family on a dock on a school trip.

The picture frame tells me a tale,
A happy family just as well,
You helped me see all the things I've known,
And then you left me here all alone.

He's been left at home with a sick father, and a debilitating, costly Palace. Alex thinks of his guitar in his room, how if he learns to play he'll bring meaning to these stupid words nobody will ever read. Roxy pulls towards the door, but Alex stands still.

And a guitar it can tell a story,
To all of the people who thought they knew me,
When you don't know when your last day is,
It's so much easier to tell you this.

If they force him to move away, he'll tell his friends, and the kids on the bus, about the public details of his private struggle. He writes *(Chorus)*. He wants a small bridge section next. He thinks of the kids on the bus, of Leigh's picture sitting on his desk.

All of the people I've come to know,
Seen me fall down and seen me grow,
I'm not saying this is my goodbye,
But if it is then this is why.

Roxy starts to bark, her fur steadily moistening. Alex types faster, keeping the same structure as the chorus.

For all of the things I never got to know,
I can't thank you for the love you showed.

His friends, even those previously random kids on the bus, all have shown him love.

One thing I really wish I'd do.
Is tell you that I loved you too.

Maybe he will someday. It's getting dark for a Saturday morning.

And in this hour on my darkest day,
When all I knew has gone to stay,
I'm still hoping I can make it through,
And then maybe I can see me with you.

He hits the save button, staying under the character limit by a few words. He goes towards the house with inflection in his muscles. Right before he goes inside, a title crawls to life. He doesn't know how much he can take. Clicking the leash off Roxy's neck, he catches a small shower as Roxy shakes her puffing fur, her happy face panting at him. He walks over to his computer.

"How Much"
Verse 1:
All of the things you like to say I'm not,
Down from my clothes to my train of thought,
You always were quick to criticize,
Said everything I told you was a lie.

Verse 2:

Your turn of anger and your hits of fate,
Never took the time to stop and think,
I had a feeling like everyone else,
You saw me as blank and took out the details.

Chorus:
And all of the things I won't get credit for,
I never was another mental whore.
I was different in my own new way,
Yet you never found the things to say.
And all of the dreams and the shattered hopes,
Every creature on earth dies alone.
But I still have to carry through,
Everything I do I'm doing for you.

Verse 3:
The picture frame tells me a tale,
A happy family just as well.
You helped me see all the things I've known,
And then you left me here all alone.
And a guitar it can tell a story,
To all of the people who thought they knew me.
When you don't know when your last day is,
It's so much easier to tell you this.

Chorus:
And all of the things I won't get credit for,
I never was another mental whore.
I was different in my own new way,
Yet you never found the things to say.
And all of the dreams and the shattered hopes,
Every creature on earth dies alone.

But I still have to carry through,
Everything I do I'm doing for you.

Verse 3:
And all of the people I've come to know,
Seen me fall down and seen me grow,
I'm not saying this is my goodbye,
But if it is than this is why.

Chorus:
And all of the things I won't get credit for,
I never was another mental whore.
I was different in my own new way,
Yet you never found the things to say.
And all of the dreams and the shattered hopes,
Every creature on earth dies alone.
But I still have to carry through,
Everything I do I'm doing for you.

Chorus 2:
All of the things I never got to know,
I can't thank you for the love you showed.
One thing I really wish I'd do,
Is tell you that I loved you too.
And in this hour on my darkest day,
When all that I knew has gone to stay,
I'm still hoping I can make it through,
And then maybe I can see me with you

24
November 15, 2010

"I want to try something a little bit different today," Hammond says.

He's sitting in his usual attire on his chair. He's brought a stereo for today's session; the machine is older, but contains an auxiliary port for music players. Alex usually plugs his into the dashboard of the LeSabre during ventures to the store with his father. It's how he holds on to the lingering notes from the Green Day concert, which already have the same kind of worn, dusty appeal as every benevolent aspect of Alex's life. Now, in Hammond's office, Alex discards the memory, paying attention to the smiling counselor.

"I know, that's why I brought the cord and the music player." Alex returns the expression seamlessly.

"Good." Hammond clicks the stereo to life. It hums softly, waiting.

"You've told me you like music, so what we're going to do is this." Hammond rises from the chair and walks over to his desk. He picks up a pen and a pad of paper. Handing it to Alex, he returns to his seat.

"Pick a song that you have on your I-Pod or whatever that is - I'm an old guy so I wouldn't know. We're going to play it a couple times, and as we play it, I want you to just sit there with nothing but that song and write down whatever comes to mind."

"Definitely." Alex agrees. He knows the exact song he'll play. He's shown it to Lou in their Design Concepts class at school.

His dad loved it when Alex played it for him in the Wal-Mart parking lot. Taking his music player out of his pocket, the silver familiar in his hands, he flips through the artists. Green Day, My Chemical Romance, Genesis, Linkin Park. Finally, he reaches the bottom, and clicks on the name displaying 'U2'. They're one of his mom's favorite bands, Alex thinks with disappointment. Clicking on *How to Dismantle an Atomic Bomb*, he selects track three, a song called "Sometimes You Can't make it On Your Own."

"Ready?" Hammond asks, taking the cord and plugging it into the device. "Now remember, no noise except the song."

"Right." Alex closes his eyes, leaning up against the back of the couch.

"Go for it."

Click.

The song begins.

I'm imagining the rain on the windshield, dripping down slowly. My dad is sitting next to me in the driver's seat. He's talking to me about possibly getting back together with mom. This has to be sometime in October. As we're listening, he's telling me the lyrics are definitely relatable to what we're going through. We don't know who's going to be paying the mortgage, and I know that he's really sick. All I want to do is take that illness and beat it to death for him, to take it all away.

As it hits the chorus, I remember the lights from those cars passing us by. I always get the biggest amount of chills when Bono hits the high note. I've fought with my dad, and while it might not be all the time, I want nothing more than to just see him be happy again. He's gone through all these tribulations and trials, and if I could only find a way to bring mom back so they could reconcile ... it might all be better. If only I could find the kind of strength he has.

It hits the second chorus, and my dad is talking about how he misses mom, and how if only she could be more cooperative we might be able to fix this. He said he feels abandoned, and I agree with him. The bridge is coming; I know it's going to be great.

Bono is now talking about how they don't communicate, and I know the feeling. I just wish that my dad could hear me singing, because that would make the difference. The voice soars, and I'm frozen. My dad really is the reason I sing, I want to do well for him. I want to show him that we can beat this illness, against whatever odds. I just want to let my mom know that I haven't forgotten about her, either. I love both my parents, and I want her to come home. I want nothing more than for both of them to be happy.

When I look at myself, I can't understand what Bono is saying, but I see my dad sitting there on that October night, with a load of groceries and the rain pouring down, and I don't want to fake it anymore. I want to tell somebody, tell Dan, tell Zach, Lou, Neil, tell Leigh, tell someone what I'm dealing with. As the song fades out, my dad seems somewhat mad, because he knows that I'm hurting. All he ever wants to do is protect me. If only he knows how good a job I think he's doing…

The song ends. Alex opens his eyes.

"Alright, so, what were you thinking about?" Hammond asks.

"A lot, actually." Alex replies.

"Such as?"

"Pretty much how I want my dad to beat this MAI stuff." Hammond nods.

"I'm a pretty big fan of U2, you know." He says.

"Really?"

"Yeah. I'm not just all classical, you know. I try to stay hip."

"Don't embarrass yourself."

"In seriousness, I know Bono wrote the song about trying to connect with his father. Do you ever feel like you're disconnected from your dad?"

"Not so much my dad. My mom, yeah, definitely."

"When's the last time you talked to her?"

"Probably August."

"So it's been almost three months?"

"That sounds about right."

"Well, she's been here to see one of my colleagues."

"I know. My dad told me before how he'd talk to you and you'd say how she'd always come in for her appointments looking downtrodden and upset. But doesn't she have any conscious for us?"

"I'm sure she does. I'm sure it hurts her too, Alex."

"Right. That's why she won't cooperate, and keeps manufacturing stupid court moves."

"She doesn't know what to do, Alex."

"That's pretty apparent."

"I don't think anybody here expected this to happen."

"No shit, Jack."

"You know what I mean. So, you say you write lyrics, go ahead and tell me why this song has such an impact on you. I saw you look like you were about to cry."

"Well, the lyrics are talking about how you're seeing this person try to fight, this parent try to overcome. Bono wrote it when his dad was passing away."

"Do you think your dad is passing away?"

"I don't think it, but I fear it."

"Go on."

"Bono saw his dad trying to be strong, and he wished he could do something more. I don't know, Jack, I just feel so powerless in this entire situation. Almost like it's my fault."

"How could it be your fault?" Hammond asks. "You haven't done anything."

"I've told my Mom I don't want to see her, I've been mouthy at times, I've made my dad upset."

"You're 14. These are all parts of life, except not talking to your mom, that you're expected to deal with. All of this other stuff nobody predicted, but you're still working through it with amazing strength, Alex. I'm sure your dad is very proud of you."

"But before," Alex says, tears threatening the rim of his eyes. "I could always piece it back together."

"Listen," Hammond leans in. "You can't do that to yourself. This isn't your war to fight, it's between the two of them."

"But they put me in the center!" Alex's voice rises, a crescendo of suppressed indignation. "I've been in every argument they've had since I was seven."

"It couldn't have been every argument."

"Most of them. I heard things I wasn't supposed to hear, saw things I never should've seen, and now I feel like I'm supposed to fix this. I have to. They aren't, they have no idea what they're doing."

"Your dad has to have an idea."

"My dad does, but my mom has to be nuts."

"How would you know?" Hammond questions. "You haven't tried to hear her side of things."

"Yes I have. And when I've listened, all I've heard her say is how my dad is somehow unstable, how the disease is driving him nuts, and how none of this is her fault, because she was stepped on for the last nineteen years in their marriage."

"Do you see how she could feel that way?"

"No! My dad has always consulted her, he's even been angry

at how he's asked for her opinion on decisions ranging from money to what's good for me to what's good for the family to how they're losing 170,000 dollars on the house they want to sell."

"Alex, you need to let the adults be the adults."

"How, when they're arguing over my future in court like I'm some piece of fucking property?"

"You're never property, Alex. Both your parents love you very much."

"You say that, as the only thing they're doing is divorcing, and making our lives a thousand times worse. I feel like I'm completely alone in all this."

"But what about your friends?"

"My friends are probably tired of hearing me bitch and moan about how bad my life is all the time. Then, when I try to look on the bright side, something else insane happens. October was a good month, but now here we are a week into November and my Dad's leg is hurt for some unknown reason."

"Is that why he was limping today?"

"Yeah." Alex says, his voice lowering.

"I saw him walk in. He looked like there was something wrong."

"There's always something wrong. Nothing will ever be right again. We just need to find a way to keep paying the mortgage."

"Was that your Aunt Eve with him today?"

"Yeah."

"She's been helping you a lot?"

"Absolutely. She's been great. She's been absolutely great."

"Why do you think the two of them didn't talk for years?"

"I don't know. My Dad overreacted."

"How so?"

"He took some of the small problems and made mountains out of molehills. And don't try to pull your bullshit and say that's what he's doing with my mom too, or what he's done with her, I won't take that."

"Who's the therapist, here?"

"You are, but I think I might've found my calling."

"Listen, Alex," Hammond's voice is soft.

"You can't expect to be able to fix everything. You're a 14 year old kid who is going through a hard time. A lot of people have gone through hard times, and the way we work past them is by doing what you're doing, with the strength I told you about long before we got to here."

"My dad's making dinner, cleaning the house at random times, working, taking me places, and is sick with a disease that literally makes him limp, only two months after a heart attack, attending doctors' appointments nobody can stop, and taking drugs that make him feel like absolute shit. And here I am, just going to school and screwing around on the bus."

"You can't be a miracle worker, Alex. None of us can be."

"I could sure use one at the moment, though."

"Can't we all." Hammond looks back to the radio. "You want to play it again?"

"Sure." Alex replies.

———

Dr. Fost examines the paper in front of him, dated 11/04/10 - the results from Michael McGregor's liver biopsy. Its appearance is normal, except for one peculiarity.

One darker spot stands out on the black and white of the image.

For one, McGregor doesn't drink. For another, the disease

he's fighting is in his lung. What the hell is a dark spot doing there?

Fost's eyes widen. All feeling fades from his body, a paralysis ricocheting down his spine as if a bucket of ice saturates his back. An insane thought enters his mind.

He pulls out his folder on Michael, and dissects the x-rays from the past scans of the lung. First is the March report, with no growth and no shrinkage. May is next, with the disease beginning to spread. October follows, taken after the heart attack, showing corruption throughout the lung. The infection is completely unhindered by the salvo of medication.

Fost looks back to the results from the liver biopsy, the dark spot haunting him like an eyeball, piercing into the very depths of his soul.

He picks up the phone on the side of his desk, and dials a harried sequence of numbers.

"Hello, is this the office of Jeremy Nicholson? Yes, this is Dr. Richard Fost; I'm the general practitioner for one of Dr. Nicholson's patients. I was wondering if Dr Nicholson is available." Fost's chair stays still.

"Yes, Dr. Nicholson? Hi, it's Dr. Richard Fost, Michael McGregor's general practitioner. I have the results of his liver tests in my hands, and I'm seeing a random dark spot that's out of place. I'm guessing from how it looks that it's probably nothing serious,"

Fost's head is in his hands as he stares down at the papers on his desk.

"... But I wanted to know your exact opinion on the progression of his treatment."

"Right," Fost listens.

"Right, and then it started to expand."

"Ok."

"Yes."

"Right, and then in May it turned into this expansion we're seeing now. How typical is this?"

Fost pauses.

"Why? What are we doing wrong?"

"His wife left him, you know."

"Yeah, he's been raising the kid on his own."

The receiver pressed to his ear is practically weightless.

"Right, and then the most recent result is that this disease is out of control."

"You don't think it's MAI?"

Pause.

Fost pales.

"I think it would be best if we scheduled him for a bronchoscopy immediately, then? You're the pulmonologist."

"Oh, you were going to make that suggestion? Alright, I'll let you call the hospital, and I'll call Michael in a moment and tell him of the plan."

"Thank you very much, sir, I'll let him know."

Fost hangs up the phone. He sits at his desk, motionless.

"*Fuck!*" Fost screams, whipping his pen across the room. It skates to a halt by the wall.

Why hadn't he chosen the surgery?

The spot on the liver stares. Fost's brain works with almost incomprehensible speed.

Picking up the phone again, he dials the cell phone number listed on the folder next to Michael's name. His breath leaves him, and he keeps eye contact with the spot on the x-ray.

Fost recognizes those dark pupils.

———

Michael sits next to Eve in the lobby, reading a magazine. His leg has improved over the past couple weeks. His pocket vibrates, and he reaches down to answer the call.

"Hello?"

"Hey, Mike. It's Dr. Fost."

"Hey, Dr. Fost. How are you today?"

"I'm doing fine. We have the results of your liver test, and some further analysis on the results of your last checkup for the MAI."

"Alright."

"I talked with Dr. Nicholson, and we want you to go in for a bronchoscopy tomorrow."

"What? What the hell do the liver results have to do with this MAI bullshit?"

Eve looks up from her magazine. The beautiful people on the cover laugh at her.

"Listen," Fost says, his voice spreading thin. "We need to go in and do some more tests of to see what exactly is happening."

"Richard, what did the liver tests show?"

"I'm not as worried about the liver tests as I am the lung, after talking to Dr. Nicholson."

"Why?"

"Mike," Fost lets out a heavy sigh. "I don't think you have MAI anymore."

Alex and Hammond walk out from Hammond's office. Alex wraps his headphones around his music player. The silver glints in the sunlight streaming through the window behind Michael and Eve.

Michael's face turns paper white.

"What are you saying, Richard?"

"I don't know yet, Mike, the only way to test would be to do a full biopsy of the liver. I don't think that spot has anything to do with this MAI, Mike."

"I know." Mike says, closing his eyes. He sighs, and tears begin to form.

"Mike, let's not jump the gun. We don't know what it is."

"What do you think it is, Richard?"

Fost is silent.

"It looks like cancer, Mike."

"I'll do the bronchoscopy tomorrow."

"Alright. I'll be in touch."

Michael hangs up the phone. He looks into the eyes of Jack Hammond. Hammond appears puzzled. Michael does nothing but smile at him, but it's a downward smile, a smile of finality. He felt it when Lauren left, he felt it when the MAI started to spread, and now he feels it once more, sitting in the lobby, looking at the man who guides his son through the treacherous times Michael can't resolve.

"I have a spot on my liver."

25
November 22, 2010

Alex McGregor, Eve McGregor, Michael McGregor, Harlan McGregor, and Michael's friend David Waters gather around the island in the kitchen, a convening council of reluctant leaders. It's nearly 10:00 in the evening. The fan in the window doesn't spin.

"I'm telling you," Michael says. "They broke my goddamn rib."

"Mike, that makes no sense."

"Dad, I'm telling you, it's hurt to breathe for the past four days."

"That doesn't mean that the bronchoscopy broke your rib, Mike."

"Dad, do you think I'd lie about this?"

"Hey," David says. He's a man in his mid-thirties. His son, Nick, is one of Alex's best friends. Both of them have been enhancements to the Palace's care package in recent weeks, after David heard of the liver's black eye.

"Let's not fight about this. Mike is saying that he thinks his rib is broken."

"How the hell could they have done that, though?" Eve asks. She's wearing plain clothing, no need for dressing fancy any longer.

"I think they dropped me or something, or jerked me the wrong way." Michael's lost 50 pounds since June. The drugs are placebos. The MAI is out of control. The pain in his leg and ribs has reached the apex of his pain index.

"Well, we can go back in for x-rays, but the results of the bronchoscopy are due back soon. We can see what's going on and then take it from there." Harlan offers.

"Are we going to tell mom about this?" Alex asks.

"We might have to." Eve says.

"I don't want to." Michael replies, each respiration a nuisance.

"Neither do I." Alex says.

"I think we're past the point of being able to say what we want to do." Harlan finishes, moving from his position and into the living room. Everyone lets out a collective sigh, dissecting different spaces on the wall.

———

Hammond examines the familiar man sitting on the couch. Michael looks back at the man who has helped him navigate over the rough seas of the past months with as much fire and wisdom as possible, the North Star in a moonless sky.

Michael sighs. "Cancer, huh?"

Hammond looks down, his hands resting limply between his business pants.

"I can't fucking believe it." Michael continues.

"We don't know for sure yet." Hammond says weakly.

"Yes we do. There's a spot on the liver. If it's already gotten that far, we've already lost. I wonder how long I've had it for."

"We don't even know if you have it."

"What else could it be? What else will explain the drugs failing, or how the spots have done nothing but expand? The fatigue? This rib I've got now, which I'm sure they broke, doesn't add up, the leg doesn't add up, the heart attack was a nice icing on the cake."

Michael verbalizes the truth of his heart.

"I'm dying, Jack."

"Don't say that."

"I've been dying for a long time, since last September."

"Stop it. This isn't helping the situation."

"Alex."

That's all Michael says.

"Alex." Hammond repeats.

"Jack, this is gonna ask a lot of you, but I want him to meet with Lauren."

"Alright." Hammond agrees.

"Can they do it here?"

"Of course."

Hammond rises, and walks over to his desk to examine his calendar.

"How long has it been since they've seen each other?" Hammond asks.

"May."

"Oh my God. That's almost six months."

"It's over six months. Alex counted it out. If they meet on the 2nd, it'll have been 197 days."

Hammond surveys him, scanning like a surgeon.

"You need to go home and rest."

"I might not be able to come here much longer, you know. I might not be doing anything much longer, come to think of it."

"Stop it." Hammond's voice crescendos.

"Look at it," Michael says, coughing. He pauses, whistling in pain.

"I'm falling to pieces. That's all I've ever been good for, falling to pieces. That's all I ever did when I was a kid, all I ever did in my first marriage, now in this marriage, and with my kid."

"Alex has been handling it beautifully."

"But how do you handle this?" Michael responds. "How do we tell that amazing kid that his father has cancer?"

"Stop!" Hammond stands. "Alright! You don't have cancer!"

"Yes I do, Jack. The liver."

"We don't know anything for sure."

"Jack, I need to ask you something."

"What?"

"Take care of Alex for me."

Hammond sighs. "Jesus Christ, stop it. Listen to yourself."

"Please, Jack. You have to promise me. If I'm not here, you'll take care of my son."

Hammond feels a tear rush to his eye.

"You'll be here to take care of him." Hammond urges.

"And what if I'm not?" Michael's voice quickly rises. He stands on his wounded leg, his rib pounding in protest. "What if I drop dead on the floor, what then?"

"How am I supposed to tell your son that his father has cancer?" Hammond asks. "How can you expect me to do that?"

"I'm not asking you to do that. I'm asking you to help him through it if I can't beat this, Jack. This is my last hurdle."

Michael's demeanor softens. He lays a hand on his friend's shoulder.

"I've got to get over this. Whatever this," he gestures to himself, wincing in the motion. "Whatever this is. If I don't, I need to know you'll keep seeing Alex. You talking to him, you helping him, that's been one of the only reasons we've been able to hold it together. That's thanks to you."

Hammond's supply of advice is depleted. He hasn't felt such wordlessness since his own childhood.

"Thank you, Jack. For everything."

"No, Mike. Thank you. What the hell are you doing? It's not even time to go yet." Hammond asks with a smile, his own tears leaking out of his eyes. *They're* supposed to cry during the sessions.

"I feel if I stand or sit here any longer, my rib is going to pop out of my chest." Michael turns to the door.

"Please tell me you aren't driving." Hammond says, following him.

"No, Eve's taking me. She brought me here. Remember what I said to you, Jack."

Hammond follows him down the hallway, and watches as Michael limps over to his sister. She helps him out the door, and as he exits, Michael smiles back at his counselor, his comrade in the fight, the end to which waits just over the horizon. For a second, he appears new, confident, and whole. In the next, he's faded and cracked, a memory neglected and forgotten in history.

"I'll see you soon, Mike." Hammond says.

When he returns to write his notes, the therapist is the one who cries.

———

Lauren sits on the couch her husband occupied not two hours earlier.

Hammond studies her carefully, his eyes completely dry, the streaks on his cheeks covered. She's wearing a sleek black jacket, her hair framing crescent circles underneath her eyes. Her face is a dichotomy of sickness and health, occupied by both a smile and a bubbling grimace that threatens to break the surface of her irises.

"So," Hammond begins. "What have the past few months

been like for you?"

Lauren smiles. "Hell. Utter hell."

"How long will it have been since you've seen Alex?"

"197 days."

"Why do you think that is?"

"Every time I would call him, we would fight. Michael would say that I was hurting him, and then he somehow convinced Alex to send me this ridiculous email."

"Which one was that?"

"He sent it back in June, claiming how all of this was somehow my fault, using his father's words, and how he wanted nothing to do with me."

"I tried to get him to call you, Lauren."

Lauren scowls. This is her first meeting with Hammond. He's an agent of Michael's bullshit.

"But I have to ask, why have you acted the way you have? Off the record." Hammond asks.

"What do you mean?"

"Quitting your job?"

"I wasn't going to get served divorce papers, get kicked in the heart, punched in the teeth, and then told to bow to that bastard." Lauren replies. Her mother has been talking to her a lot. Her mother is right.

"Please, no name-calling."

"But he calls me a slut, a whore, every other name. Why can't I call him a bastard?"

"I wouldn't let him call you any of those names if he were here."

Hammond shifts in his chair.

"How much do you know about what's been going on over there?" he asks.

"I know Eve's probably been paying for the house. Or Harlan."

"Ok. What else?"

"I know the MAI results haven't been particularly positive. But what could I do? I got kicked out and completely cut off."

"How so?"

"What do you mean 'how so'? It's pretty simple. I was asked to leave, thrown out of my own house."

"You left voluntarily."

"I told Michael, after the massive fight where I moved out in 2009, that if I was ever asked to leave my own home again, the one that I was helping to pay for, doing a bunch of tasks he promised to do at the start of our marriage, that I wouldn't come back."

"Not even after his mother had a stroke?"

"No. Because that's what happens, Jack. We get into a crisis situation, where everything is fine, but after the crisis passes, we're right back to the kind of abuse that he's been giving me for the past 19 years."

"What kind of abuse is that?"

"Mental. He's threatened with leaving me before, with taking Alex away from me, which he finally accomplished, with not trusting me with money. He's just completely lost it from this disease! I think it's because he's never dealt with his childhood. I'm sure he's told you."

"I can't tell you, but I also wasn't aware that his wife is an expert in mental health."

"I'm not, I'm just telling you what I know. I think he has borderline personality disorder. I read it in a book my therapist gave me. I pegged him as having at least four out of the seven traits for it. I think he's a very fearful person, to be honest."

Hammond stares. His words are slow to rise to his mouth.

"So what exactly have you been doing for the past six months, if I can ask?"

"Well, after I quit my job, it was more about going to therapy and studying the sort of law that we've been dealing with in court."

"Yeah, I think Mike told me you were going pro-bono."

"Yes. I was living off my Mom enough; I wasn't going to have her pay for a lawyer. It's really not that hard to be a lawyer, you just have to be very professional and follow a certain set of procedures."

"Right." Hammond suppresses a cough, and then continues.

"So then, what stopped you and Alex from talking?"

"Michael." Lauren replies. "Easily. He corrupted him into blaming me."

"Well, Lauren, if you had problems that you hadn't resolved from before with the way Michael treated you, whose fault is that?"

"Mine. I'm coming to terms that I probably shouldn't have continued this marriage after the late nineties based on the way he's treated me."

"But how did you treat him? I don't know specifics, but I've heard something about money managing and something about IOUs in an envelope?"

"That was in 2003. I haven't acted as a saint. I've made a bunch of mistakes, but I still don't deserve to be called names during an argument all the time or have to walk on these eggshells to avoid pissing him off. It actually felt kind of liberating, being free from him for the past six months."

"Have you used that time to work on yourself at all?"

"Yes, definitely." Lauren quickly replies. The Cheshire cat sits on top of Hammond's head, laughing at her fibs. Its tail curls around the counselor's ears.

"Well, that's good." Hammond sits up straighter. "On the 2nd of December, Alex is going to be here, and as long as you're alright with it, we can use that session as a reconnection for the two of you. Michael is not in good health."

Lauren's expression fades.

"What do you mean?"

"I'm not at liberty to tell you. I'd recommend calling Eve. To be honest, the only reason any of this is happening is due to the fact Michael's in decline. They're worried about how the MAI's progressed. He actually went in for a bronchoscopy a couple of days ago. If we're going to pull this off, and you're going to be put back into the loop, you need to be integrated back into the system. Mike can't do it, but Eve can."

Lauren nods. The fire she's been kindling over the past six months is gone. She suddenly feels barren.

In bad health?

———

Alex lies on the bed, looking up at the ceiling, with no intention of falling asleep.

Cancer.

His mind relays back and forth in slow motion. A spot on the liver? The doctors all agreed it was MAI, MAI, definitely MAI.

But there had been a small chance …

All he knows is falling. It might not be cancer. It might be cancer. There's a spot on the liver. There's a broken rib, most likely a broken leg. His father is the walking shell of a superhero, down to the very depths of his soul. His idol now struggles to walk, his breaths short and rigid. The foundations are crumbling to dust, and he can't see the beauty in the remains.

Alex imagines his brain to be a room. There is a man who sits at a table in the room, near a door. The door is closed. Behind the door lies everything the man fears, with words like *biopsy* and *ventilator* and *MAI* and now *cancer* banging at every hour. Behind the door is every lost chance to talk to a person he's thrown away. His grades in math have started to drop, and they slip out from behind the door. His friends have started to notice his seclusion, and they escape from behind the door. He hasn't been talking to the kids on the bus, and they too metastasize from behind the door; shadows, the spaces between the entrance and the floor pathways for the drafts of hell.

What will happen when the door opens? Will the official documents declaring the end of his parents' marriage emerge, or instead a testimony in regards to where he'll have to live, in Willow Grove or Bethlehem, as his home is scorched to the ground? In reality, Alex knows what's behind that door; he knows what stands behind the wood of splintered dreams.

He's heard stories of cancer. He's heard of the ways it ravages the host like a murderer in a packed hotel. He knows the way the malignancy bustling under the door carries the death and destruction of all he holds dear. His life doesn't flash before his eyes; it blinds him. The forgotten freedom of the air seeks to suffocate.

There is no greater fear to a child than seeing a parent leave their home. Will they ever return? Who knows, for a child doesn't comprehend what waits beyond the curves of Keystone road. They haven't seen the majesties outside the gates of the Palace. Alex has heard stories of murders on the news. Alex sometimes worries that a man in a mask will break in and kill his family. Alex also got scared as a child that when his dad went out to see friends or his grandparents, he'd die in a car accident.

Eventually, his dad is going to go to bed and never wake up. He's eventually going to go and get some news about how *cancer* isn't a hunch; it's absolute. A storm shall descend and swallow the defensible planks of the Palace and steal Alex's future. All those happy memories with his father, all the pictures, and all the frames they've tried so hard to turn into reality—they'll shatter his life into a million tiny pieces.

Alex starts to cry. He hasn't cried like this in years. There had been the time, after talking to his mother, he'd broken down in Hammond's office. This is a different flavor of crying, one not of anger, but born of fear and hurt. Alex thinks of his father limping, his father complaining of the pain in his rib, his father, his dad, Michael McGregor, the man who'd promised to protect him at all costs. He thinks of his mother, too, with how he used to come home and hug her. He wants nothing more than to piece their picture back together and make a happy family once again.

Instead, the door grows closer. He can't put enough distance between himself and what lies beyond, the truth that lurks under his bed at the very second and makes him want to vomit and cry and scream. No lyrics can give it a name; no fingers can pull out its face from where it hides, because as it lurks, it consumes the man Alex is supposed to become.

Cancer cancer cancer cancer cancer.

26

Eve eases the car into the parking lot; Alex unbuckles his seat belt. In the window, which peers into the office adjacent to Hammond's, sits the woman whom he hasn't seen for a total of 197 days. Her hair falls over the back of the couch. On the bus, they'd asked him about his plans for tonight. He said he has a lot of homework.

Yesterday, his father checked into the hospital for dehydration. He came home screaming at six o'clock in the morning after his friend, David Waters, went and retrieved him. The bronchoscopy results are due back in a couple days. Completely ignoring the doctor's advice, Michael now sits under Harlan's supervision at the Palace.

Alex went to bed on November 30 praying for a better December. So far, it's shaping up to be absolutely spectacular.

"Are you nervous?" Eve asks.

"Nope." Alex replies. He has to collapse to save himself from the falling wreckage. His friends still own a window to his world, but to the people on the bus, and to his teachers, he's gone silent. No more need he pretend to shine. He's going to let everything go; the weight of the world will crush him to peace.

As they exit the car, shutting the doors behind them, Eve puts her arm around Alex's shoulders. The slight kisses of the rain in the evening sky cannot cover the sound of her breaking heart.

Hammond waits at the top of the stairs, his light of the

building outlining his figure. He greets Eve, and then shakes Alex's hand.

"How are you feeling?" Hammond asks.

"Just great." Alex replies. "Let's do this."

Hammond leads him down the hallway to his office. The door separating him and his mother remains shut across the hall.

The actors move to their usual positions, to the chair and the couch.

"How's your dad been holding up?

"Well, we took him to the hospital two days ago because of the rib, and then, once he checked in, he refused to take his medication and checked himself out at around six yesterday morning, because his friend drove him home."

Hammond's eyebrows rise.

"What? That's insane."

"Yeah, it's something my dad would do."

"Have the results from the bronchoscopy come back yet?"

"Not that I know of." Alex says. He doesn't dare to verbalize his premonitions.

"Well," Hammond stands up slowly, a whisper of an apology on his face.

"I'm going to get your mom. You stay here." Alex's gaze follows him, as his muscles tense.

Hammond knocks on the door to the neighboring office.

"Lauren? There's somebody here to see you."

The door opens.

There she stands, in all her glory.

Lines of sickness don't streak her face; her eyes still appear as vibrant—maybe even more vibrant—as they were in May. She wears the same brand of jeans, with a tee shirt adorned by a feminine suit jacket. Her hair is nice and beautiful, and she's wearing earrings which match the memorial necklace gifted to her by her brother.

She wears no wedding ring.

Her hug shatters his powers of observation. 197 days of no contact whiplash into the moment, and for as much as part of him resists, he returns the hug forcefully. The savior releases him. She's crying now, with a smile on her face as wide as the past six months have been long.

"Hi, Mom." He says, his voice attempting to steady as it cracks.

"Hi, Alex." The tears flood her cheekbones.

Alex starts to cry, his hostility evaporating, and he embraces her again. The war is over, but there shall be no victor.

Hammond watches the scene; his tears remain locked inside of him. If Michael weren't so sick, this scene wouldn't be occurring. Michael's health is indeed past a point

cancer

where such things like the reconciliation happening in front of him, such a sight which Michael has prevented for the past several

cancer

months, are coming to fruition. Alex and Lauren release their embrace. No matter how many hugs they share, irreversible scars exist,

cancer

hiding deep beyond the fold of arms or the connectivity of mother and son, scars which threaten to end the world

CANCER.

Hammond coughs. Lauren and Alex take their places on opposite ends of the couch.

Congratulations, Jack. You're a hero.

Hammond wants to crawl under his desk in the fetal position.

Instead, he places on the smile, and opens his mouth.

"You seem happy, Lauren." Hammond says.

"It's been a long time." She wipes the tears from the sides of her face, a painter correcting angles on a canvas.

"Yep." Alex returns to stoicism. His right leg folds over his left. His eyes avoid Lauren. The manufactured homecoming is now a parlay to conclude a bitter conflict. They haven't warred with guns, bombs, and planes, but instead with legal moves, heartbreak, and now the inclusion of a third party seeking to overrun the world.

"Dad's not doing well, Mom." Alex says.

"He's been running around trying to take care of the house mostly by himself, and now he's got this spot on his liver that might be cancer."

"I know." Lauren replies, her index finger tracing the indented skin of her ring finger. "I talked with him earlier yesterday, I think it was."

"It couldn't have been yesterday, he was just getting out of the hospital."

"For what?" Lauren asks.

"Well, we took him in for the pain in his rib, which apparently is broken, and then he checked himself out with the help of Dave."

Lauren doesn't reply.

"Why didn't you come back, Mom?"

"Your father wouldn't apologize."

"Neither would you."

"I don't believe I have anything to apologize to him for."

"That's a load of bullshit, mom. You two own equal parts of

this."

"I was minding my own business and then he did what he always does. He made a mistake and then tried to blame me. He's obviously not thinking in his right mind because of the MAI."

"I think it's fair to call it 'cancer' now, Mom. You left him when he was sick. You left him with me, and you forced me to be responsible when he had a heart attack."

"You should have called me."

"I should have called you? No, you're the parent; you should have gotten past your stupid egotistical bullshit and made up for the sake of the kid. Both of you acted like such idiots, and now here we are, sitting in Jack's office, with you saying you still don't need to apologize."

"Alex, for 19 years I've been the one saying I'm sorry. After every argument, I always had to apologize for crimes I didn't commit, or else your dad would threaten to leave. I never stood up for myself, and then everybody was finally surprised the bitch finally fought back."

"Well, I'm glad you had your little revelation at the same time as he's falling apart. He can barely walk, he's in pain all the time, and he's still taking those stupid pills. He's supposed to be resting, but he had to work after you quit your job."

"I quit my job because he tried to sue me for divorce! I was never the one who wanted to split, he's the instigator."

"Because you walked around your work saying you wanted a divorce."

"I said that it was 'looking' as if we were heading for a divorce, living at my mom's, still working, practically homeless, not able to see my son—I'm so mad about that, you can't even begin to realize, Alex."

"I'm madder than I think you'll ever realize too, *mom*. I don't know how many hundreds of dollars we're going to have to pay Mr. Hammond here, but I don't even care right now. All I care about is what's going on with my dad."

"Alright," Hammond interjects. "The two of you arguing is never going to be productive. Alex, it's good you realize that you're angry about a lot of things, and your mom is very angry too."

"Why didn't you ever have him call me?" Lauren quips.

"Lauren, I tried, but …" Hammond starts, but Alex leapfrogs him.

"But I didn't want to. All of the things I said about this, the email I wrote you, the phone calls we had, that was all me talking, Mom."

"Bullshit. Those were your father's words, not yours. Talking about me 'manipulating the situation to fit my needs', calling me selfish,"

"You are very, very selfish." Alex says.

Lauren sighs. "So is your father."

"Bullshit."

"Enough." Hammond says, his tone cracking like the tip of a whip.

"Enough. This is not what we came here to do. What we came here to do is to try and find a new situation that would be best for what *Alex* needs, Lauren." Hammond punctuates his words with a sharp glance.

"That's all I've tried to do for the past six months!" Lauren replies.

Alex laughs, a barren and emotionless sound, rattling with days of regret and maturation.

"Well, now the way to really do that is by having you move

back in with the family at Alex's – well, your, house." Hammond reasons.

"I'm willing to do that, but I still want an apology from Michael."

"Well, that'll come with time. It'll all come with time." Hammond says.

"For now, let's take baby steps. We can't afford to start introducing a bunch of arguing and nonsense into the house like it's May again. It's not fair to you," he gestures to Alex. "Or you," he motions to Lauren. "And it's not fair to Michael. From what I know, he's in a whole different kind of fight."

"I've already stopped my side of the court proceedings." Lauren says.

"Oh yeah, how was it, playing lawyer?" Alex asks. He stares at Hammond.

"It really isn't that hard." Lauren explains. "You just have to be extremely respectful, address the judge correctly, and have a general idea of what you're talking about with the way proceedings work."

"Oh, maybe you could've earned some money doing that then, but instead you quit your job and almost made me lose my house."

"Alex, stop it." Hammond scolds.

"That was your father's decision. He could've easily gotten out of that situation." Lauren's voice arcs.

"When are you going to admit that some of this is your fault? You and Dad are the exact same way, both of you say that it's all the other person's fault, but we're all losing. Here I am, I haven't talked to you in months, and now I'm about to be told that my dad has cancer." Alex sniffles.

"We don't know that, Alex." Hammond's words are soft.

"Yes, we do. The spot on the liver confirms it."

Lauren silently watches the Cheshire cat on Hammond's windowsill, its demented face smiling back at her. It's shoulders are spring-loaded in anticipation.

"All we can do is wait and see." Hammond examines the clock.

"I don't think it would be a good idea for Lauren to go back tonight, but tomorrow, maybe you want to start reintegration – slowly, deliberately."

"Of course." Lauren says. "All I wanted was to see my son."

"Well, you did that much." Alex gets up and leaves the room, slamming the door as he exits.

The Cheshire cat glows.

————

December 11, 2010

Over the next nine days, Lauren acts on Hammond's advice. She starts visiting the Palace, and talking to Harlan and Eve. She and Michael keep their distance, with Michael now confined to the bedroom they used to share. Lauren crashes on the couch, away from the sickbed. With his leg only starting to mend and the rib still broken, Michael doesn't want to move. The MAI runs rampant, and the spot on the liver still slums in the darkness of obscurity. Perhaps it's just a benign growth, along for the ride. The answer reveals itself today.

Michael, Eve, and Harlan all take the ride they've experienced many times before for checkups and menial tasks. As they enter Dr. Fost's office, the room seems warm, a familiar setting in strange times.

Michael's decided to make the trip. He wears a heavier

jacket, for it's beginning to grow cold around Coopersburg, and his limp isn't as noticeable under jeans. His rib constantly throbs, the medication provided by the hospital not enough to completely drown the pain, or for him to drown himself. Lauren is back home with Alex. Lauren's going to work, the mortgage satiated. Eve's signed on to sponsor the Palace until Alex's graduation from High School. To Michael, it's as if the last of the bombs from the planes is set to fall, the final salvo before the armistice.

As Dr. Fost enters the room, he's retired his smile. He provides a weak substitute, a performer whose character is broken, just in a white jacket. He shakes Harlan's hand, along with Eve's, and he gives Michael a pat on the back before seating himself in his chair that shall not move today.

In his hand, Fost holds a manila folder. A sigh slips through his lips, and he looks into Michael's eyes.

"The results from the bronchoscopy are in." Fost says.

The words pass his lips with no great announcement, just through a simple motion.

"It's cancer."

"What stage?" Eve asks, her soul drifting to pieces.

"Four." Fost says.

Harlan's eyes widen. Eve puts a hand to her mouth.

"W-what?" Harlan stutters. "What do you mean stage four? Stage four lung cancer?"

"Yes." Fost continues robotically. "It's everywhere in the lung."

Michael says nothing; he bears a sad smile on his face.

"If I had to hypothesize," Fost says. "The MAI contained the cancer. When the bleb burst, the cancer must've sensed the weakened immune system and subsequent entryway as the

237

opportune moment to strike. Cancer is a very smart disease, and … due to the stress he was facing with the home life and the separation, we couldn't monitor the progress with precision. We wanted to do this bronchoscopy earlier, but the heart attack and the dehydration pushed it back."

Lauren is going to burn in hell for this.

"What about the rib?" Michael asks.

"When cancer spreads to the bones, it causes them to become very brittle." The words come out of Fost's mouth; he doesn't feel them pass over his lips.

"Due to the fact your immune system was diverted in performing those stressful daily activities while the drugs commandeered your strength, the cancer spread. It's in the liver, in the lung, in the rib, and probably in your leg too, Mike." Fost isn't supposed to show this kind of emotion with patients. That's how the machines, which will eventually replace him, shall be superior. He can't contain the tears that invade his eyes, joining the agony shedding from Eve and Harlan. Michael sits perfectly still.

"How long do I have?" Michael asks.

"I can't say for sure." Fost manages. "According to the preliminary oncology reports, with the proper treatment, it could be as long as two years."

"*Two years?*" Harlan says. "You mean he only has two years to live?"

"At most." Michael says.

"I'm so sorry." Fost chokes. The words on the pages in front of him are swimming now, trying to loosen the constriction of the margins.

"It won't be that long." Michael says. "It's already in the lymph nodes. It's everywhere, it can travel. If it's in my bones, from what we know … what did the oncologist say was the bottom end of the range?"

"Two months." Fost replies.

Eve shakes. Michael winces and covers her with his arm.

"The oncologist wants to meet with you tomorrow to discuss treatment options."

"Alright." Michael says.

"Thank you, Dr. Fost, for everything."

27
December 13, 2010

Hammond, for once, cannot conjure a single word. Pulling syllables from a secret reserve, he opens his mouth.

"When did they figure out that it was cancer?"

"Two days ago." Alex's pack of Swedish Fish sits unopened next to him.

"He went to see Dr. Fost, who then referred him to an oncologist named Dr. Welsh. They met yesterday. There really isn't a lot they can do, since my dad doesn't want treatment. There's no other way to put it. He has cancer, and my dad's gonna die."

"We don't know that yet."

"Right. Just like we didn't know if he had cancer in the first place, or how we weren't sure if my mom was going to continue being a bitch or not. It's fine. I've heard it all before, Jack. That's all they ever tell me: we don't know the outcome. I know what this outcome is, Jack. My dad's gonna fucking die."

Hammond's backup speech, the emergency generators, fail. The sun shines on outside.

———

Lauren sits at the kitchen table. This is everything she's wanted. To come back to the Palace in triumph, knowing she's always been correct and that she deserves an apology from her husband. But this doesn't feel like a win. Instead, it's a larger defeat than just about anything she's seen in her entire life, except maybe when they told her Jim killed himself with the fumes from his goddamn Cadillac. The end approaches in plain sight. Stage four lung cancer. Two months to two years. Michael isn't going to treatment. All he does now is stay in his room or wander to the living room to watch television. The fan no longer sits in the kitchen window.

This is my fault. This is my fault just like Jim's death was my fault, and daddy's suicide attempts were my fault, and now whatever Alex is feeling is my fault. All of it is my fault.

The Cheshire cat is dead; it has killed itself from overconsumption of agony, torment and pain. Everywhere she gazes, it's all the same blackness, same darkness, same desolation, and same undeniable notion that *all of it's her fault.* It's as if the very air her lungs need to breathe looks to asphyxiate her instead. It's all meant to end this way for her, she knows, with her past mistakes ignored, all of the potential resolutions unrealized. With the official news of her husband's cancer, they've finally caught her.

Alex probably hates her, and such is his right. But it's all Michael's fault? She'd avoided working through the problems, wallowed in her own self pity down in Bethlehem for the months since the 19, with her mother feeding her the addiction of being able to call herself the victim. The real victim is her son. 197 fucking days.

Well, she'll be seeing him a lot more now; she's the parent without an expiration date. Lauren lowers her head to her hands, her fingers kneading the brown locks. Her eyes close. Tears aren't enough; they'll need to invent a vehicle of the soul of greater expression to mitigate this breed of horror. She casts a glance to the white dresser situated next to the entrance to the living room; family pictures adorn the top shelf. No longer are they memories, but memorials. There will be no more family trips, no more days on the beach spent in sunlight, no more gatherings with Harlan and Cynthia. All those recollections will remain in the beauty of the frame, searching in vain for another moment.

Harlan and Michael argued, with Harlan screaming for Michael to take the treatment. Michael refused. Stage four is final.

He spoke of dignity.

He spoke of pride.

He doesn't want his hair falling out, doesn't want to be reduced to a skeletal hundred pounds.

Alex should remember him by the pictures, not by the disease.

Lauren wishes, with all her might, to crawl inside Roxy's house and sleep. All of her ghosts circle her, as if suspending her with a hook through the back of her neck over a barrel of emaciated sharks.

It's all her fault.

Welcome home.

———

Michael's seen the world outside the window on fire, but now it's peaceful. It hasn't snowed yet this winter, and the outside looks comfortably warm. Through the haze of smoke around him, he imagines running through the front yard one final time, dashing through the expectant grass, his bedclothes falling behind him in the freedom. They're telling him to be careful walking, because the bones are so brittle they might snap if he moves too quickly.

Alex.

He'd never wanted his son to hurt. He'd spent 14 years sheltering him, talking to him, getting to know him, telling him more about himself than he'd ever admitted. As he peers outside, the only remorse Michael really feels is that he'll look down on his son, see him devastated, and won't be able to comfort him.

He tried to jump the hurdle, and he missed. This is the last step of the hard way back to heaven he's driven out of Willow Grove. He'd seen the end prior to May 19, known he'd been sick long before September of 2009, because something had been lost which cannot be replaced. The bedroom window might be the final thing he sees before it's over.

But not yet. I have something that I still have to do.

It's a beautiful day.

———

Alex doesn't talk on the bus rides in the afternoon anymore.

Kenny and Leigh maintain a respectful distance. Alex has taken to sitting in the back seat of the bus, the last full seat available, watching the sights fly past. If they study him long enough, they can discern some of the blemishes. He's a nice kid. He doesn't talk about his personal life. People don't speak about the private, at least not in the public sphere. Alex is most certainly similar to millions of people in the world, especially those similarly aged. Leigh and Kenny figure he'll eventually snap out of it, and go back to joking around with them in his humorous, awkward way.

He's *such* a nice kid.

On one ride home, Kenny listened to his music; Alex wanted to talk. Leigh never minds talking to him, even though he's a year younger. In her experience, interacting with different people is the only way to learn. That particular day, they talked about music—My Chemical Romance. Alex said he'd gone to a Green Day concert in August. Leigh likes some of their music too. They talked about how *American Idiot* is a phenomenal album.

Alex uses such conversations like painkillers. He always wants to say more, but he never does. He'll either plug in his earphones, or change the topic the same way a press of a button changes a song too emotional to hear.

Leigh sees it in him, but never digs. Part of her wants to walk back there and tap the kid on the shoulder, and ask him if there's a song behind the silence. Instead, he keeps talking to her occasionally, and she enjoys talking back.

One day, he stops.

The rest of the bus group carries on with their shenanigans, with Kenny and his lighter almost setting the bus seat on fire. Leigh loves music, but obviously not as much as Alex. Part of her wonders.

What they don't realize is that Alex is telling them everything.

———

Alex sits at his computer. He's spreading the news to his good friends.

Yep, stage four. Merry goddamn Christmas, your parent has cancer!

Yep, there aren't many treatment options.

Nope, it hadn't been detected. God bless modern medicine.

Alex walks through the hallways at school, his home life's fate becoming crystal clear. Every lie aspires to become the truth.

His dad doesn't have cancer. His mom isn't in denial.

Deep down, Alex knows nothing will ever be fine again.

In his lyrics, night has fallen. Opening up a document, he reads a piece titled "Tropic of Cancer"; it describes his new home, with a different kind of heat pressing down upon him constantly in the December cold.

> *You'll never have a friend quite like cancer,*
> *It holds your hand through night day and life.*
> *You'll never be in need if you have cancer,*
> *And then you'll realize that cancer isn't alright.*

> *You'll never find a day without good old disease,*
> *And you will breathe just enough to bleed.*
> *You'll never need a friend except your illness,*
> *And the illness is all you'll ever feed.*

Besides conversation, writing is his alleviation. Talking to his friends increases the distance between his thoughts and his life, but they can't halt Father Time. It wouldn't be fair to trap his friends in his existence.

He wants the kids around school to ask him for a full disclosure as he neglects them; he really wants to tell Leigh and Kenny he isn't ignoring them. He hides in his music as an excuse not to speak, but at the same time, he wants to talk more than he has in his entire life. He's living in paradoxes.

His parents are back together! But his dad's going to die.

He wants to talk to nobody! But he wants to reveal his secrets.

Doctors still propel his life! But the doctors fucked up.

In all their teaching, they'd collectively missed detecting stage four lung cancer. The disease snuck in and now shall steal his father from underneath their noses in 'two years.' It won't be two years.

———

Lauren makes dinner, but Michael doesn't eat much of the food. He claims that if he eats, sickness will ensue. Harlan tries talking to him, his own food sitting lonely on the plate.

"What the hell are you doing?"

"I'm just living, Dad."

"You need to eat so that we can fight this, so that we can start moving towards radiation."

"I'm not doing radiation, Dad. It's in my bones. It's in my liver."

"So what? We can still fight it!"

"Dad," Michael puts the small part of his sandwich down.

"All I've done my entire life is fight. From the point where mom drank, to dropping out of high school, to earning my degree in sales, to living with one wife who I divorced, another relationship where I didn't keep a child, to this 19 year union with Lauren only whole again due to my illness. I fought the MAI, I fought in court, I've only ever lived in times of war."

"I'm tired, Dad. I'm really tired."

Harlan shakes his head.

"You can't give up on me. You can't give up on Alex."

"I never left this house, Dad. You know I never, ever wanted to leave Alex. But I know. I've known since at least September, after that heart attack, this is my time."

Harlan relents.

———

Lauren and Alex stand outside. It's stopped snowing.

Roxy laps a bit of the fallen crystals off the stacks covering the grass, waiting for a carefree child or teenager to disassemble the mounds.

247

"Mom," Alex says, kicking a part of the frozen driveway. "Why doesn't Dad want treatment?"

Lauren sniffles. Her black jacket no longer warms her. The echoes of her eyes look to the frozen field across the street.

"He thinks he's already too far gone."

"Something can be done, right? Chemotherapy?"

"It could be. We can't force him. He's refused every treatment option offered to him."

"I don't understand. How can he just give up like this?"

"He's had a really hard life, Alex."

"But that doesn't give him the right to quit. We've been through so much, and now he's just going to let it all slip away?"

"He's not thinking right. The only drug he's accepted so far is morphine, and it messes with his head."

"That's a cop out, Mom."

"I know."

Alex spits onto the pavement of the driveway.

"He's like a child. He has a bunch of toys, and he's playing with them all at once. But what he doesn't realize is that he's sitting in the middle of train tracks. You, me, grandpa, we can all tell him that the train is coming, but he refuses to move. No matter what I tell him, what you tell him, he refuses to believe there's a train coming for him. What do we do when it hits him, mom?"

Lauren blinks.

"I don't know, Alex."

———

Hammond and Alex are silent. Every angle has been dissected, the paths they've hypothesized all crossing into a solid conclusion.

"What have you been doing to cope with this, Alex?"

"I've been writing lyrics. I've been telling my friends the details, but I'm just trying to take it one day at a time."

One day at a time. Look at it all without emotion. The only way to keep going is to compartmentalize. Do what mom did. She's been successful, she's made it this far. It's easier locking it away. That's how tons of people deal with things.

The door in Alex's mind is almost ajar.

"I need you to keep talking to me about it, Alex. I work with many kids who go through similar experiences. It's my specialization."

"I know." Alex says.

One day at a time. Don't talk to them. Don't burden them.

There isn't a single cloud in the sky. It's a beautiful December evening. Alex thinks it should be raining, but rain won't fall tonight.

"You can get through this, Alex."

"I know. I already am."

One day at a time.

"You're doing a great job."

One day at a time.

But for what?

———

Later, all the sessions have ended. Alex sits down at his computer. On a document, he writes every thought leaking from his wounded mind:

Leigh and Kenny, why I don't have success, why I can't step the fuck up, doubt that I'm not good enough, unfairness, the good times in with the bad, simple conversations, why I don't know how to talk to anybody, clichés and the breakings of, if only you knew, I'm different, how I just want to say what I feel, why I can't express shit, why I can talk to everyone else about anything but what I really want to say, what I go through with insecurity, pressure, scrutinizing, not good enough, what can I do better? Why can't it just happen? Finding yourself in all around you, standing up, and the loneliness of being you.

Then, he writes.

———

"Pride"
How much is one person supposed to take?
How much pressure can you put on me?
Here I am, this is me breaking.
Is this really what you wanted to see...

Verse 1:
I've spent three whole years looking at your face,
Making memories that never took place.
I spent my time thinking about fantasy,
I took myself and I raped reality.
I'm floating in nothing and I look to you,
After all the bullshit and pain that I've gone through.
I can't tell you any of this,
Because I now know how ignorance is bliss ...
I took the pills of faith and hope,
I put up with the pressure and tried to cope.
Well can you see the cracks in my face?
Am I like you, now, in faith?

Chorus:
Am I like you, so perfect, so saved?
I feel lost, destroyed, and faded.

Am I finally there? Is this my heaven?
Why do I feel so angry, hurt, and jaded?
By a loving God, who took away my life,
He has left me changed, unholy, and I am alive.
You can take my mind, my body, my spirit and my soul,
But you will never take my pride.

Verse 2:
Re-reading all of the letters I wrote to you in my head,
Filled up with what I spoke, but didn't have the courage to send.
You can try to roll with the punches, well how about a bullet?
You can scrutinize me all you want, somehow I'll get through it.
What if I can't, what if I'm not good enough?
Grin and bear it, boy, you've got to be tough.
You walk away and go and play your games with yourself,
While we sit here, the nation of everyone else.
I saw the light coming back from the abyss,
I never thought that we would act like this.
So happy, and so car free,
Are you really talking to me?

Chorus:
Am I like you, so perfect, so saved?
I feel lost, destroyed, and faded.
Am I finally there? Is this my heaven?
Why do I feel so angry, hurt, and jaded?
By a loving God, who took away my life,
He has left me changed, unholy, and I am alive.
You can take my mind, my body, my spirit and my soul,
But you will never take my pride.

Verse 3:

I am not like you, pristine, and holy;
I am imperfect, cold, and lonely.
Distraught, askew, and ugly,
But you will never break me.

Bridge:
I may bend and I may fall,
I'll get up again in the midst of it all.
I can take your hate, and still love the world,
Look at me now, what do I have?
A life falling apart, you'll look and say 'that's sad'
If only you knew,
If only you knew.

Am I like you, so perfect, so saved?
I am lost, destroyed, and faking,
This must be heaven, because it's not right;
Can we please just go one more night?

Bridge 2:
If I could talk to you, I'd say,
I would ask how you were on that day,
And maybe yesterday, we'd be together,
But I can't see through the never.
The sun hides just behind the clouds,
We've gone up above, here we come down.
Life is not fair, life is not your friend,
But if you need someone then here I am.

Am I like you, so perfect, so saved?
I may be lost, destroyed, and faded,
This is it for me, this is my prayer,

If he dies tomorrow, will you still be there?
I see a loving God, who controls my life,
Give me pain, hate, and suffering, I'll take it in stride.
Defile me, destroy me, and mock my voice,
You may break me down but you will never break my,
You will never take my,
Pride.

28
December 24, 2010

On the days following Christmas, Alex McGregor's best friends visit the Palace. Zach, Dan, and Brian all come to pay their respects. Nick, David's son, is a presence that aids Alex tremendously. He spends the time with his friends, but is absent in spirit. He's tired of believing the lies he's using to cope, and tired of hearing his father admit defeat.

On the 21, Mike starts to hurl; blood, fluid, a cocktail of liquid agony. He lies in bed and vomits the entire day, unable to keep water down. Harlan convinces him to go the hospital.

Harlan drives him back home on Christmas Eve. Michael is now an outline, a remnant of a great work of art.

Michael is bedridden. The house is turning into a vigil. Family members and friends receive phone calls. Alex will later remember sitting at home on Christmas Eve making a call to a woman named Rachel Maria Edwards. He's heard of her before, but memory doesn't find much enjoyment breaking through the isolation. Time simply passes, it doesn't linger to create.

On Christmas, a tree adorns the dining room of the Palace. Alex goes out with Mr. Waters and Nick and cuts it down. They lug it into the house and decorate every branch. They take a picture of Roxy in front of the presents, looking her best and perfectly photogenic. The dog's going to outlive his father.

Instead of having Michael come to the living room, in his sick clothes and his brittle bones, Christmas moves to the bedroom. Harlan makes his son a tinfoil hat; Michael wears it proudly as he opens the gifts. It's just Eve, Harlan, Michael, Alex, and the Waters unwrapping presents.

Alex won't remember his gifts in a month's time. The isolation is working. Animalistic stability overwrites normalcy. He has a smile on his face as his father, drugs of salvation lapping over his mind, opens his gifts. Lauren's card is thrown into the nearest trashcan by Harlan.

Around the same time, a man arrives to the house and delivers an item called a 'hospital bed' to the family, received through the door to Michael's room, which used to lead to the front porch of a church. It's a wonderful Christmas gift, courtesy of the medical insurance and another small part of Alex McGregor's soul.

Late Christmas night, Michael flies into a rage. David took Alex out to get sandwiches from Subway, and Harlan and Eve hadn't told Michael of their plans. In his paranoid haze of the cancer, Michael came screaming into the living room, cursing at both his sister and his father about how they'd lost his son. David isn't family. Why had they let him go? He calms down when the two return home.

At around eight, another car pulls into the driveway. It has never touched the driveway before, but it's reached the correct destination.

There's a knock on the door after the driver ascends the stairs. Alex answers, stealing a glance through the same old window in the foyer that looks to the yard. Opening the door, he's unsurprised.

"Merry Christmas, Alex." Jack Hammond says, shaking the boy's hand.

"To you too, Jack." Alex opens the door wide. "Come on in, we've got Subway sandwiches."

"That's alright, I've already eaten. I just came to see how your dad's doing." Hammond walks inside, wiping his shoes on the carpet. They're the same shoes he's worn to every therapy session, his black pants tired out from a day's work, his dark jacket flecked with dots of former snowflakes.

Harlan and Eve watch the news in the living room. Lauren sits across from them on the love seat, looking at the television. David decided, after the Subway rage, to take Nick home for the night. Hammond greets them all, offering Eve a hug, Lauren another embrace, and Harlan a gaze of compassion.

"Where is your Dad?" Hammond asks. Alex leads him to the back of the house.

Reaching Michael's room, Alex opens the door. The smoke hits Hammond instantly. It curls around the air and flies up his nostrils with the force of a gas, a lingering presence as he walks across the battlefield.

Michael sits straight in his hospital bed, watching the door. Hammond stops at the threshold, as the sight in front of his eyes slams him in the chest like a strong wind.

"Hey, Jack." Michael croaks.

His voice scrapes like bones. He wears a t-shirt as pale as his skin, with food residue patterning the bareness of the fabric. Monitors flank the sides of the bed, their remotes nesting near Michael's fingers. An empty bucket sits within arm's length by Michael's left side, an ashtray adorning a table a few feet away, along with a picture of Alex.

"Merry Christmas."

Alex leaves the room. He closes the door behind him, and walks back to the sound of the television. They're watching a Lewis Black special.

Hammond's voice is a whisper.

"What happened to you, Michael?"

"Life." Michael replies, his grin a faded trademark.

"I knew from talking to Alex the other week it was bad, but … Jesus Christ. You're …"

"Dying." Michael concludes.

"I've been dying for a long, long time. But you helped keep me alive, you know. Every time I had a problem, I talked to you. I have friends, I have a sister, I have a father, but you helped steer me straight. All those visits to your office, the innumerable ways you've helped my son, what I asked of you the last time I saw you for a session – you made it possible for me to live. I can't ever repay you for how much you've helped me."

"I didn't know you were this sick, Mike. I would've come sooner."

"Nobody knew. I tried to tell them, but they didn't listen. Only you ever listened, and I can't thank you enough for that."

Hammond's wall of composure, built from over twenty years of solving problems and raising solutions, crumbles.

Hammond pulls up a chair and clasps the hand of his friend. Michael doesn't cry; he looks at Hammond.

"You know, Jack." Michael says. "I don't think, after all the times I've seen you, you've told me a lot about your wife. I think you mentioned that her name's Natalie?"

"Yeah." Hammond replies, using the arm of his jacket to wipe his face. "Yeah."

"Do you love her, Jack?"

"With all my heart." Hammond says, still sniffling from the debris of his fallen barriers.

"Let me tell you something then, Mr. Hammond." Michael squeezes his hand.

"Don't you ever let her go. We can make the most money

imaginable in our lives, we can find fame, we can find amazing material items, but we can only truly keep that which men cannot steal, and that's those who we love and those who love us."

Hammond laughs, his shoulders shaking like buildings in an earthquake.

"I'm supposed to be the therapist." He mumbles.

"Hey," Michael says. "I'm your friend. You aren't here to see me as a patient, I'd hope. I've had enough hopeless experts in lab coats telling me shit; I don't need you to do the same."

Michael releases Hammond's hand.

"How is Alex doing?"

Hammond clears his throat, and sits up straight in the chair.

"I haven't talked to him since a couple weeks ago."

"You keep talking to him, Jack. You need to help him." Michael's gaze is made of steel. "I know Lauren's back in his life, but you've been more of a parent to that kid than I could've been recently."

Hammond shakes his head, words rattling around inside his skull.

"No, Mike, you've been amazing. The things you've done here, what you sacrificed for that kid, nobody will ever forget."

Michael nods his head, the tubes that pierce the veins on his arm bobbing.

"Thanks, Jack. I'll never forget what you've done for me, either."

Hammond stands to leave. For an instant, Michael is the same man who came in for marriage counseling over a year ago, looking for self-improvement. Momentarily, he's repaired, and he'll be getting out of the bed any second.

Michael waves slightly, and says,

"You're a great man, Mr. Hammond."

Hammond tries to speak. All he manages is a choked goodbye.

Walking out, Michael watches Hammond's coat pass over the threshold.

———

January 1, 2011

As the ball drops in New York on New Year's Day, Michael McGregor, Lauren McGregor, and Alex McGregor all watch the small television from the bed that used to belong to the couple in a far off universe. All the happy people cheer as it falls.

Alex hadn't wanted to sit with the two of them, but Harlan, who watches with Eve in the living room, told him to go in with his parents.

Alex sits in the center, Michael propped up to his left, Lauren, with her hands folded over her jeans, to his right. 2011 officially begins.

Alex turns to his parents.

"I love you guys."

29
January 11, 2011

It is Tuesday.

Alex rides the bus home. Leigh and Kenny talk a couple seats in front of him. Kids meander back and forth, and occupy space. Eventually, the bus rolls to a stop in front of his house. He'll remember later that Leigh's wearing a nice black dress, and Kenny has on his usual jeans and blue hoodie. He doesn't say goodbye to them today. It looks like it's going to snow more, with the ground already covered. The sky is clear and gray.

The day before, the Hospice nurse visited. Alex asked her how long it takes people to heal before they're taken off Hospice. She'd smiled at him sadly.

His dad is now a constant fixture of his bedroom, emerging for the last time a couple days earlier in another one of his manic bursts of energy. The last thing he told his son, sitting there on the edge of the bed, talking to Lauren, who had been sitting on the floor, was:

"Everything is going to be ok."

Alex comes home and goes on his computer. He talks to his friends. The Hospice nurse had told the family that his father only had about a week to live, since his last burst of energy happened a week ago. Now Michael lies in silence in his room, not in the hospital bed, but in the same bed he and Lauren shared for countless nights prior to May.

They'd wanted to send him to a hospice facility. He refused to leave the house.

Lauren sits in the hearth room, in the chairs people never use, watching the fire in the wood stove. She's off work. The chairs are the sentry post, observing the soundless Michael via a mirror designed to fit him in view as he lies on his pillows on the side of the bed closest to the door. His chest rises and falls.

The priest visited the house around noon. Eve could've sworn she saw her brother mutter, "Thank you."

At quarter to five, Lauren gets up from the chair in the hearth room. She walks into the room she and her husband used as the catalyst for their family.

Her husband lies on the pillows, under the same burgundy blanket. The past six days have been nothing but sleep.

Now, his chest is still. The ghost of a smile remains on his face, and his eyes are turned towards the door.

Peace.

Tears streaming from her eyes, Lauren walks to Alex sitting at his computer. Harlan appears from the kitchen, his eyes dry. He strolls slowly to the bedroom.

The body of his son stares back at him from the wine-colored sheets.

Alex bends down and whispers into his father's ear.

"I love you dad."

Flurries fall outside.

Eve arrives fifteen minutes later, bringing dinner from Wendy's. Alex walks down the sidewalk, taking the food, and offers a small hello. She walks up to the porch to her father, who embraces her, and says,

"He's gone."

The nurse from the hospital arrives two hours after Michal's passing. Michael McGregor is at rest, his vital signs gone, his spirit finally free. The nurse disposes all of his medications—for the MAI, his anxiety, the futile cancer battle—by placing them in bags of beans.

The undertaker pulls into the driveway fifteen minutes later with his helpers, dressed in the blackness. Alex, Harlan, Eve, and Lauren all watch as the body of Michael McGregor leaves his room for the final time. It's already yellowing with the early stages of decay. As they move him off the bed, Alex meets Death for the first time. He is a cold, harsh truth.

Harlan chokes up and turns away. For the remainder of his life, the closed eyes shall inhabit his soul. It should've been him on that stretcher.

Michael finally leaves the Palace.

———

The funeral home sits only a few miles away from Gruversville. The building is extremely appropriate for Michael's service, with enough parking to accommodate every year unrealized due to the events of one day, and the actions of a group of people.

Alex wears his finest suit, his mother her finest dress, and Harlan the wear and tear of a bunch of failures patched together. The inside of the building is styled nicely, with chairs laid out in rows and pictures of Michael sprinkled around the casket on the dais. The pictures show him with his band mates, with his father as his college graduation, with a younger version of Alex. No pictures of Lauren, Michael, and Alex together are included.

Over those two hours, Alex stands alongside Harlan, Eve, Lauren, and his friend Nick at the front of the line, shaking hands and receiving sympathy from people who he doesn't know. Family of a man named Thom come to visit Michael. Michael's boss and a slew of his coworkers arrive as a pack. The teachers from Alex's school come to pay their dues. Alex's friends Neil Pock, and the twins Dan and Zach, turn out in support. Nick stands with him the entire time, with David Waters out among the slew of onlookers viewing the end of the world, with Genesis and Stevie Wonder playing in the background. They're the soundtrack for how the future becomes the past.

Michael McGregor's face is frozen atop the sheer white of the fabric underneath his body. Not a single hair on his head is out of place. He's perfectly washed, and dressed in a black suit.

Walking over to him, Alex slips an envelope beside him, like how a parent hands a stuffed animal to a frightened child. In that moment, when the crisp whiteness of the envelope falls into the casket as everyone in the room watches, Alex knows he's alone.

He should say something; he should read the contents of that envelope.

Instead, he stays silent, giving his father a kiss on the forehead.

His father's skin is as cold as marble.

The priest comes and says words about God. Alex won't remember them later. He sees his mother crying, perhaps for her own guilt or for her husband, maybe both. Alex does not cry. Instead, he watches, and he listens, and he feels the words: all of the condolences, the repetitions of 'I'm sorry', the blessings placed upon to him to prevent a tragedy already realized.

At the end of the service, Eve is the last to leave. She promised she'd never leave him alone again. Crying hysterically, Harlan eventually shields her with an arm, and guides her out into the January cold, having to pry her off the dais. As he leaves, Alex casts a glance back to the casket. There's his father, the only one he'll ever have, the man who gave him the gift of words.

There are so many things he wants to say.

———

Michael 's final resting place is next to his biological mother, in a small and secluded Ukrainian cemetery near Willow Grove. Alex doesn't speak at the burial, but he remembers the hush of the onlookers watching him stand over the casket. Snow covers the ground. The silver is luminary.

He places a white rose down on the lid, leans in, and says, "Thank you Dad. I love you."

———

In an envelope, tucked in the folds of white cushioning, nestles a paper with these words:

Dear Dad,

You always told me how much you loved me, and now it is my turn to tell you how much I will always love and miss you. I cannot even begin to describe the sadness I feel at even having to think about, much less live in, a world without you here to guide me. Yet, here I am, only minutes before your funeral, imagining what life is going to be like without you in it.

You always said that you would look over me, and I sure hope you are right now. These next few months will be inconceivably hard for us, and only with the knowledge that you are still watching over us am I able to even begin to imagine the challenges of this world without you here to give me your never-ending love and support. All I can hope is that you will keep a close eye over all who come to cherish your memory today.

The one thing I know is that you are no longer in pain. That thought is a great help to us as we continue on in a seemingly darker world without your loving light. But in the end, you may have been a son, a brother, and a husband, but above all, you were my father. And I cannot find words to thank you enough for that.

I love you, and always will.

Alex Stephen McGregor

I'll never forget you.

30
February 17, 2011

It's over.

It's only him and his mother. Eve's back in California; Harlan's back in Willow Grove.

Everything is lost. All that stands before him now are the ruins of a beautiful dream: not of a marriage, not of a home burnt down, but of an intrinsic wound.

He sits in the same place he'd been when his mother told him of his father's final silence. It's the same hands on the keyboard, the same eyes looking at the black monitor displaying nonsense from the outside world. Approximately sixteen days after his father's death, he'd gone back to school. Some people know, some people don't.

He knows.

His father will never light up another cigarette in the kitchen, or give him words of encouragement sending him to bed happy after a horrible day.

He could've done something to save him, corrected the errors which befell them during the ordeal.

He's nothing but a failure, an ugly, beaten down, isolated disgrace. Why suffer in the daylight if he's only going to burn? Isolation is the answer, just as it had been for his mother and his father during their childhoods. He'll repeat a cycle, joining with Father Time in infinity.

Hammond's monitoring can be dodged, his mother's plastic worry brought on by obligation can be melted down like an emotionally detached recyclable. He's still writing lyrics, and they shelve his pain in menial concerns. Only a very observant eye can crack his masterpiece, his mask.

Around school, he smiles, makes jokes, laughs with people he barely knows. He's more social now than ever before in his life. He wants to scream at all of them.

His friends keep talking to him; they deserve his thanks. He's already been up to visit Harlan. Eve is back in California, but she's promised to return. If his father were alive, his funeral would've been a glorious event, filled with meeting old friends and the past joining with the future.

The tree in the front yard, planted by his parents, still stands. He walks under it occasionally, and it brings him back to the moment he asked "How Much" with the lyrics on his phone, only to collapse when shown the answer.

One day, his father will come home, and everything will be alright.

He doesn't believe in God anymore.

He thinks of the way his father's body was carried out of the bedroom and into the back of a car to be prepped for a ritualistic final viewing after he'd already passed. Alex shudders, his appearance unkempt, his homework sitting incomplete. His father is dead; nothing else matters.

He's breathing, talking, giving out fake laughs and conversation.

Yet he isn't alive.

He opens his browser and sees who's online.

He might as well talk to somebody.

He clicks on Leigh Meyers' name. The window pops up.

— Today —

Alex: Hey, are you going to be on the

afternoon bus tomorrow?

Leigh: Nope, I will not.

Alex: After today, I don't blame you. I think
we may have finally found the too far line, to
be honest

Kenny has started going too far with his drugs. Alex doesn't
care. One day at a time. *Survive.*

Leigh: No, I just have something to do. Well,
it was getting out of hand.

Alex: You seemed kind of...annoyed at it? Or
something?

Emotions. What's their use? He can't rebuild himself on a
shifting base.

Leigh: Well yeah, it was annoying. I'm
staying out of it from now on.

Alex: I think you're right, actually. Is that
why you've been sitting up further, I mean
besides the iced tea?

Kenny slammed an iced tea bottle over the seat last week. It
splattered all over the windows; the residue still paints the glass.
Alex chuckles.

His dad's dead.

Leigh: Yeah, I'll probably move up farther as
well. I mean it was fun and all at first but now
it's just getting ridiculous.

Alex: Kenny too, right?

Leigh: Definitely!

Alex: I remember how you guys used to joke
around and all, but now all he talks about is
like drug stuff. It gets old to me.

Everything is old to him.

A shift happens he doesn't expect. He finds himself typing the words, and then he sends them.

> **Alex:** This is gonna seem kind of off-topic, but do you know why I was out for the three weeks I was?

It took him three weeks to be Fixed from his father's death. Why did he ask her? Of course she doesn't know.

> **Leigh:** No, I don't actually, now that you mention it, were you alright?

> **Alex:** I wasn't the problem.

> My Dad actually passed away on the 11th.

> So I was on leave.

Alex stops typing.

His friends have instructions to remain silent. He's just violated one of his own principal rules. Why did he just tell this girl, of all people, about everything he's supposed to bury?

> **Leigh:** Oh my gosh Alex, I'm so sorry! That's so sad! How are you and your Mom?

> **Alex:** As well as we possibly can be, considering.

> I told Kenny about it yesterday.

> I was hoping to tell you on the bus today, but well....

> **Leigh:** Well I send my condolences...through Facebook chat...but I'm truly sorry, I hope things are as best as they can be.

> **Alex:** I'm trying, you know.

But it was so weird, because it happened
right after I got off the bus that day.

He had been sick for over a year.

Leigh: Aw Alex. Had he been holding up
well?

Alex: For a while, he was. But then from
December to January things rapidly declined.

That's why I was distant sometimes on the
bus.

Leigh: Totally understandable! It's a blessing
though that he could hold up that well for so
long.

Some other confounding, extraneous variables were involved
in the course of events.

Alex: The doctors predicted two years, but
he only lasted one month.

Leigh: Goes to show how unpredictable
things can really be.

It must've been so hard.

Alex: Well yeah, and almost to add insult
to injury, my parents were in the process of
a divorce since the end of my eighth grade
year.

What the fuck, Alex?

Leigh: Wow.

I don't know what to say.

That's something no one should have to go
through, having so much happen in so little
time.

I don't know what to say either, but here I am.

Alex: But what the hardest part might have been was that my dad was considering to move me to Willow Grove with my grandpa at any time, end or beginning or middle of the school year or not.

I literally could have gone to Freedom one day, and then the next week have been in another district.

Isolation starts to break.

Leigh: That's basically changing your whole life around! Though I'm sure things have definitely changed.

No they haven't, everything's still the same! Dad will be home any minute..

Alex: Well yeah, you could say that. But going to school every day was getting to be a challenge in and of itself.

Leigh: I can imagine so. I've lost people in my family too.

I just know going to school the next day was rough, I remember sitting in my classes just staring at the wall feeling like I shouldn't be there. So I had to take a little leave.

Alex: My Dad passed from cancer.

Leigh: I'm sorry.

It's definitely a horrible illness.

Alex: But with my Dad, we didn't catch it until it was stage four.

We had no warning at all.

He wrote a lyric called "No Warnings" a couple days ago. It makes him cry.

> **Leigh:** It's tough. And it sucks. I wouldn't wish it upon anyone.

> **Alex:** But I believe the part that was the hardest, besides the last day, is that he had a heart attack in September.

> And I went to school after that, too.

The picture-perfect life is a frame.

> **Leigh:** You are one strong kid, Alex.

Strong?

> **Alex:** So if you were ever wondering why sometimes I didn't really talk on the way home and just shut everything off, well now you know.

> **Leigh:** Well if you ever need anything, just let me know!

> **Alex:** Thanks. It really means a lot.

> **Leigh:** Of course.

> We were starting to wonder, but Kenny and I both didn't want to make assumptions like that.

> **Alex:** I didn't want to really make the entire thing common knowledge, you know? That's not something you share with everyone. But at the same point in time, it was really hard to hide it.

> **Leigh:** Well yeah it's hard, you don't wanna bluntly tell everyone yet friends and people that care about you will know something's up.

Alex: I know you guys did, right?

Alex waits.

Leigh: Yeah we did. I'm sorry we asked you about anything...we just didn't know it was that serious.

They knew. He's even failing at hiding.

Alex: No one did. But it became a blessing I was able to go to school at any time in the past like year and a half at all. I kind of stopped caring a little bit, to be brutally honest.

Leigh: It's ok, I would've done the same thing! But you're strong. And things will get better, I promise!

I have to go but again, I'm so very sorry and I'm always here for you!

Bye Alex!

Alex: Bye.

Strong? He isn't strong. He's talking about the death, which makes it real, and burdensome.

For some reason, he's relieved.

He opens up a blank document and saves the chat log, simply calling it "Today."

A light flashes in the darkness.

He opens up another document, and writes.

———

"Today"
I'm not alright today. I haven't been in months.
I think that you could see it. I'm not hiding from anyone.

Today I look to you. I'm looking out for someone,
Who's looking out for me? What am I considering?
You could say I'm not holding up too well.

I've been looking to tell you. To find a moment in time,
To kick out all these thoughts, to find a day so sublime,
To stop a speeding bullet, down a rapid decline,
To take a picture of a mountain, I know I'll never climb.

Chorus:
I was holding up well, but then I got up and fell.
All the words I'll never speak, all the things I'll never tell,
For the people I'll never meet, all of them couldn't mean,
As much as what you just said to me.

Verse 2:
Yes it was so hard. I'm surprised now I've made it this far.
Unpredictable yes, but now you see I've been acting despicable.
I don't know what to say, except for the words filling up an empty
space.
With so little time, and so much going on—this life isn't for everyone.
Changing times, don't rearrange the midnight sky.
Stars burning so brightly, they make me want to purify,
All the lies, all the distance, all the pain, all my resistance,
What would it be like for us not to suffer anymore?

Chorus 2:
I was taking a walk, inside my own mind,
To go back to a better place, so I could go back in time,
When I knew what I wanted, and I knew what I'd need,
But right now nothing means as much as what you just said to me.

Verse 3:

If what you said to me means I am not alone,

Why is it you saying you're sorry to me?

If when you are telling me the only thing I've truly ever wondered,

Should I be the one making the apology?

You said you'd be there,

If there's anything I need.

You said I was strong,

But I've never felt quite this weak.

If I am this strong,

Why am I still sitting here?

Holding back and facing down,

Yet another single tear?

Chorus 3:

I try to hold all this deep,

Somewhere back inside.

Somewhere all by myself.

A place I like to hide.

You saw right through it.

It's not hard to believe,

None of it could mean,

As much as what you told me,

Today.

EPILOGUE:

TUESDAY AFTERNOON

Present Day

Harlan stands on his porch, alone. The scent of freshly cut grass flits on the breeze.

Michael's never going to walk across the yard to meet his father, giving him a famous hug with his puff of cigarette smoke and strength inherited from years of struggle.

Harlan walks down the stairs and past the apple tree. There's a tree outside the house on Gruversville, he knows. Both are still alive.

The steering wheel of the Impala fits into the grooves of his hands. The seat next to him is empty.

He drives using the main roads, with no music playing. The U2 albums collect dust in the glove compartment. Pulling up to a red light, Harlan opens the small hatch and takes out one of the familiar CDs. Opening the case, he takes the disk out, and turns on the radio. Inserting the disk, he hits the 'seek' button twice, and then returns his attention to the steering wheel.

———

The object is gray, like snow laced with the ash from an arsonist's masterpiece. Wind, rain, sun, and falling stars have been unable to mark its face, which runs from the top of the slab and traces the letters MCGREGOR down to the grass of the base. The air is filled with thousands of voices, all fleeting and unheard under the overcast sky. Memories, futures, pasts, presents, and lives infuse the surroundings with palpable electricity.

At the bottom, a part of the stone is lighter; the letters are smaller, carved by a skilled hand with a blade forged from the whispers of time.

MICHAEL MCGREGOR
SEPTEMBER 30, 1961 — JANUARY 11, 2011

Harlan kneels in front of the headstone, placing his hands upon the soft ground, his knees joining together. The moisture trapped in the dirt conjoins with the fabric of his jeans, his plaid shirt deflecting the last glances of sunlight that still peek through the clouds covering the sky. The line of gravestones stands open, with only Harlan in attendance today. Four years ago, people crowded this same path; there had been music, and tears, and laughter, and sadness; an entire life squeezed into the few hours of a day.

His glasses crest on the bridge of his nose, pointed downwards with his gaze. Harlan prays. He prays to God, to Michael, to anyone willing to receive a signal. He simply slings his hopes and wishes out into the boundless sky, attempting to send a message in a bottle to a man orbiting around Jupiter.

The ground crunches a few yards down the path, next to a tall tree that acts as a spot of shade.

Harlan looks in the direction of the noise; his eyes open.

Across the grass walks a man who has traveled great distances. He's seen everything a life can offer, and also everything this world can steal. His black sneakers, which he's worn for two years without replacement, tread respectfully over the ground as he nears Harlan's crouching form. His glasses bear clear lenses; his eyes are completely dry. His simple t-shirt is a couple years old, maximizing the value of every stitch. The Khaki shorts he wears probably have been recycled in their usage over the past few days, and he doesn't care for such a fact at all.

Harlan rises. The two figures close the distance quickly, and soon, Harlan is giving the man an enormous embrace.

Alex pats him on the back, his hand making a slight popping noise as it hits the flannel shirt twice.

"Thank you so much for coming." Harlan says, releasing the hug to examine his grandson an arm's length away.

"I wouldn't let you come here all alone." Alex smiles, the muscles on his face moving easily.

"I figured you'd have something better to do on a summer Tuesday than come back here."

Alex shakes his head.

"Nope, I didn't have anything going on, and I haven't been down here in a while. I was in the middle of writing when you called me earlier, but Lord knows that's a process which takes massive amounts of time."

Harlan takes out a handkerchief from his pocket, wrinkled with repeated use, which usually presses up against a small piece of folded, lined paper from 2010.

"Your father always liked to write." Harlan dabs his face.

"Yeah," Alex says, walking past his grandfather. He bends down in front of the tombstone, and reads the precisely carved name.

A minute passes. Alex bows his head, silent.

He looks up.

"You know, I wanted to say something." Alex says.

"What's that?" Harlan asks, putting his glasses back on his

face.

"That day. On that winter day back in 2011, I felt like I needed to speak." Alex looks back up at his grandfather while he crouches on the ground.

"We all had something we wanted to say, Alex, but what was there *to* say?" Harlan walks over next to him and places a hand on his shoulder.

"I got up to the casket," Alex says, his mind fluidly playing back a tape. "I stood over it with the rose, and I remember everybody looking at me. I felt as if I could've almost said a word, said *any* word, to honor him, to let it be known that he'd never be forgotten no matter how much time passes. I used to think people were waiting on me to give some eulogy, some amazing speech regarding a man who meant the world to me, a parent who I gladly would've traded the sanctity of my own life to save."

"Right, but those aren't our decisions to make. We're not supposed to save anybody, Alex. We aren't heroes. We can only help them save themselves."

Alex's fingers trace the name, the stone absent of heat.

"I didn't say goodbye, either. I just walked into that room when he was in that bed that morning, came home from school and got on my computer."

"Nobody could've predicted how he passed. It's not your fault."

Alex sighs.

Birds chirp in the distance. The clouds are dissipating slightly, becoming less dense as the moments pass.

"Do you still talk to Mr. Hammond?" Harlan asks, stepping back.

"Occasionally."

"You saw him for what, two years after?"

"Around. Went back to see him earlier this year for regular visits, then stopped again a couple weeks ago."

Alex's fingers knead the grass of the plot.

"How's Aunt Eve doing?" Alex asks.

"She's alright; she's going to be coming to visit me in the fall. Maybe she'll eventually drag me out there to California."

"You'll be the next goddamn beach boy."

Harlan chuckles, a guttural noise misplaced in the silence.

"At least I won't be what your Dad was!"

"What's that?"

"The white Stevie Wonder!"

Alex stands up to prevent from falling into the headstone in laughter.

"God," Harlan says, blinking the residue of humor from his eyes. "I miss him so much. I even miss the cigarettes."

"I don't miss the cigarettes." Alex wipes some wet blades from his shins.

The two gaze at the headstone for a few moments.

"He's still alive." Alex says.

"Is he?"

"Yeah. The love he so effortlessly gave, the struggles he experienced throughout his entire life, the 14 years he devoted - all of them made me into who I am today. I've been to so many dark places because of his death, but every time I fell into a period where it seemed like everything looked hopeless, and every touch of gray was going to rise up and block out the sun, I thought of him. And I'm blessed with the best friends I ever could've asked for. I've walked for him at Relays, I've crawled my way out of every oblivion all the past hatred and sorrow brought to me, and here I am next to you, Grandpa."

"He would be so, so proud of you, Alex."

Alex smiles. "I know he is."

"How's your mom?"

"She's doing fine."

"How's Garrett?"

"He's doing well. I'm pretty sure having him around has helped my mom a whole lot in coping. She's still so angry, though, Grandpa."

"Am I invited to the wedding?"

"Nobody's going to be invited if they don't pick a date."

"I think your father would approve of him."

"Yeah, I think so too."

Harlan pulls out a card from the inside pocket of his shirt. He lays it on the ground in front of the tombstone gently, careful not to disturb.

A few minutes pass in silence. Harlan turns to Alex.

"Well, I won't hold you. I know you've probably got a lot to write about."

"Like I said, I don't come here too often. I know he's with me."

"That's right." Harlan smiles, and puts his arms around Alex's shoulders. The two ends of the McGregor spectrum link, even though the middle piece has ascended past the need for any earthly connection; he remains grounded in the foundations of the two men's souls.

"What exactly are you writing?"

"The same thing I was working on last year."

"Oh, the same project you wrote at my house?"

"Yeah, the same fictionalized memoir."

"Well, more power to you, kid. I could never write about my life like that."

"It's all therapy, Grandpa. And besides, it's not a direct retelling of our story. It's a gift made for those who helped me, for those in need of help, and to honor him."

The two turn and walk down the path back to where Harlan's Impala and Alex's younger, more-fuel efficient, 2010 Corolla wait patiently.

"It's just like John Green says: 'make gifts for people, because my responsibility isn't to the people I'm making the gift for, but to the gift itself.'" Alex's voice carries throughout the cemetery.

"Brilliant! Your dad would've liked that one."

"I know he does."

Alex casts one more look in the direction of the tombstone. His memory of his father does not lie cold and lonely under the ground; instead, it soars high and vibrant in the words that are the songs of his heart.

As the two reach the end of the path, the sun breaks through the barrier of clouds above the cemetery. Grandson and grandfather walk closely together. Off in the distance, the words of the birds ring true, singing about a phenomenon known as a beautiful day.

Parting, Alex and Harlan leave the paved entrance of the cemetery travelling separate directions, but sharing a bond between them and the man they continue to treasure. It's a bond that time, space, disease, depression, maturation, and death cannot hope to break.

Pain has a shadow. Hope fears no shade.

AFTERWORD

On a frigid morning in January of 2011, my family and I
made the ride to the funeral home which sits only ten minutes
away from my house; snow lined the grass, the asphalt streaked
with moisture, the sun shining defiantly overhead. A few days
after the viewing, we travelled on another blustery day to a
small Ukrainian cemetery on the outskirts of Philadelphia. We
followed the hearse all the way from the funeral home, across
the expanses of the landscapes which fuse rural America with
the commercialism and technology of the current day, through
the hills my family called home back in the 1960's, to eventually
arrive at the place where part of me remains to this very day.

The paths between the headstones were a sparkling white;
the dress shoes bought years before to emulate professionalism
crunched under the weight of a stunned and broken child of 14
years. His face remained dry as the crowds cried around him, the
numbness radiating from his core absorbing the embraces and
blessings of the mourners. He walked up to the casket, adorned
by sheeted silver and roses of white, figures from decades and
dreams quieting in a hush around him. He laid a single flower
down with the few already gracing the coffin's lid. All he could
offer, in a tone aversive to the detection of the eyes upon his
back and the puffs of breath surrounding him, was a small,
sincere, "Thank you."

There was no cinematic speech about the magnitude of what
I lost that day, or on the Tuesday afternoon of January 11, 2011.

I did not give a grand statement about the feebleness of life, or of how the woman I knew as my mother taught me invaluable lessons regarding compassion and grace. Ever since that moment, standing in the middle of my mother's friends, family, co-workers, ex-lovers, and the curious ghosts of the respectful deceased, I have sought after words which deserve to honor the woman who gave me her life. In the middle of her marriage ending, her world collapsing, and cancer secretly ravaging her body, the support and care she showed towards my well being transcended death.

This novel started as an idea—what if I could tell my mother's story, our story, in a way which might be able to help others? What if I could create a work worthy of representing the friends and family who helped me raise myself from the depths of depression and tragedy? What a triumph it would be to write such a story in honor of my mother's memory, dedicated to her and to the friend who, among many, showed me the value in hoping again after losing everything. I've been through two major stints with depression; one in the fall of 2012 wherein I found myself asking the worth of living anymore, and another in the spring of 2014 which nearly prevented me from graduating with my high school class. I've failed so many times and passed by so many opportunities which have kept me awake at night, asking if I could have said something, done something, anything, to change the outcome of that harrowing freshman year of high school. There have been many times where I've wanted to give into my demons and resign my worth to being defined by what I lost.

But I didn't.

I wrote. I wrote lyrics, I wrote letters, stories, and finally a manuscript which encompassed the spirit of my family's story: how a kid in a small Pennsylvania town learned about the ways in which life can be tragic, horrifying, and wholly cruel, but that beauty can come from terrible events, and light shines brightest in the darkest times. The persons represented in this novel are not factual depictions of the people from my life—I never wanted to write a memoir. Genders of central characters are changed. Family dynamics are re-invented. The book is an inherent work of fiction based on a story as real as the hands writing these words. The defining events of my life assume an existence of their own in the writing, backed by the unstoppable dream ignited by my move to college to make the most of the time, support, and tireless love selflessly given to me by my friends and family. I wrote the rough draft of the novel the summer of my Junior year of high school, and ended up realizing my vision over a year later after manically revising the manuscript in my college dorm and in the lounges of the Loyola Writing Center. The finished product is a work of art greater than I could have ever imagined back in 2011, and the mere fact I am writing this afterword to be placed at the conclusion of the novel is enough to humble me to the bottom of my soul.

The people in my life—the characters with whom I've interacted, those who love me and who I cherish—are all represented in the work in their own ways. What started as a sort of grand therapeutic project, a personal quest to find the words I didn't say, has resulted in a novel which details a simple story: resilience in the face of tragedy. I hope to take the experiences which have shaped my life and use them as a vehicle to help others; we are never alone in our personal battles. My deepest wish is that the story of my family's experiences enables others to help themselves in some way; if even one person is able to gain such an experience from this novel, then my goal shall stand completed—the notion of which fills me with a purely inexplicable joy.

I am unsure where the path of life leads me, but I know, wherever I go, I have accomplished a feat which justly serves my mother's memory, a force which inspires me in all I do and has shaped the person I've become.

And, I daresay, I know I have made her proud.

Thank you so much for reading—it truly means the world to me.

Karl Dehmelt

December 26, 2014

ACKNOWLEDGEMENTS

First and foremost, I would like to thank my mother, Patti, and my father, Bernard, for raising me.

I would like to thank my Grandmother, Dorothy Kuhns, and my Grandfather, Richard Kuhns, along with my Grandfather, Bernard Sr., and Grandmother, Emily.

I would like to thank my Aunts: Kathy, Jean, Micky, and Linda, and also my Uncles: Bill, Mike, and Chris.

I would like to thank my cousins: Jason, Stephen, Paul, Julie, Ann, Natalie, Cyle, Kara, Kate, and Megan.

My deepest gratitude to my friends: Chris C, Brandon, Gary, Keith, Shelby, Justin, Luke, Jillian, Emily, Ben, Mason, Drew, Chris M, Lindsey, Jeff, Steven, Chad, Joe, Blake, and Nate, along with everyone else who spoke with me these past three years.

I would like to especially thank my (former) therapist and (current) friend, who shall remain anonymous.

I am forever happily stunned by the decision of the students at Apprentice House Publishing who accepted this novel for publication, and my eternal gratitude goes to Dr. Kevin Atticks, Ms. Erin Richardson, and all of Apprentice House's development team for giving me the ability to realize this dream. Thanks especially to Katie Krzaczek for the amazing cover, and Katherine Connolly for her marketing guidance and expertise!

I am humbly indebted to the precise expertise and invaluable generosity of all who reviewed any parts of this novel, first and foremost Dr. Matthew Hobson. I thank Mr. Bill Jones, and all my friends who read and discussed the novel, for your time, effort, and patience.

I would like to thank the 2014 Upper Bucks Relay for Life Committee, and the 2015 Loyola University Maryland Relay for Life Committee.

I would also like to thank the faculty and staff of Palisades High School, especially Mrs. Cathy Beck and Mrs. Morgan Flagg-Detwiler, and every member of the Cybersonics Technology Team and the Student Government, especially the 2013 Relay for Life Team.

Finally, I'd like to thank whoever reads this novel.

Thank you.

ABOUT THE AUTHOR

Karl Dehmelt is a passionate, young writer from Kintersville, Pennsylvania. He began writing recreationally at the age of eight. Karl currently studies writing at Loyola University Maryland.

The Hard Way Back to Heaven is his first novel, which he began writing in 2012.

Apprentice House is the country's only campus-based, student-staffed book publishing company. Directed by professors and industry professionals, it is a nonprofit activity of the Communication Department at Loyola University Maryland.

Using state-of-the-art technology and an experiential learning model of education, Apprentice House publishes books in untraditional ways. This dual responsibility as publishers and educators creates an unprecedented collaborative environment among faculty and students, while teaching tomorrow's editors, designers, and marketers.

Outside of class, progress on book projects is carried forth by the AH Book Publishing Club, a co-curricular campus organization supported by Loyola University Maryland's Office of Student Activities.

Eclectic and provocative, Apprentice House titles intend to entertain as well as spark dialogue on a variety of topics. Financial contributions to sustain the press's work are welcomed. Contributions are tax deductible to the fullest extent allowed by the IRS.

To learn more about Apprentice House books or to obtain submission guidelines, please visit www.apprenticehouse.com.

Apprentice House
Communication Department
Loyola University Maryland
4501 N. Charles Street
Baltimore, MD 21210
Ph: 410-617-5265 • Fax: 410-617-2198
info@apprenticehouse.com • www.apprenticehouse.com

CPSIA information can be obtained at www.ICGtesting.com
Printed in the USA
BVOW06s1158260815

415216BV00011B/57/P